# someone

# you

# loved

Also by Robin Constantine

*The Season of You & Me*
*The Secrets of Attraction*
*The Promise of Amazing*

# someone

# you

# loved

## ROBIN CONSTANTINE

BALZER + BRAY
*An Imprint of* HarperCollins*Publishers*

Balzer + Bray is an imprint of HarperCollins Publishers.

Someone You Loved

Library of Congress Control Number: 2022951856
ISBN 978-0-06-243886-7

Typography by Catherine Lee
23 24 25 26 27  LBC  5 4 3 2 1

First Edition

 *For Grace & Dylan*

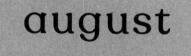

august

# sarah

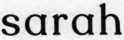

"EARTH TO SARAH."

I blinked as Marnie waved a hand in front of my face.

"Lunch rush, T minus ten minutes. Can you clear the tables by the window?"

I nodded, bit my lip. Marnie shot me a skeptical look, then gestured toward the gray busing bins as if I needed more direction. I grabbed a dish towel from the tub of bleach solution that was discreetly hidden behind the counter and headed toward the tables, bus bin propped on my hip. Marnie clucked her tongue behind me, which I interpreted to mean I wasn't hustling enough. Whatever.

The day started well enough. Mom had been pleasantly surprised when I appeared—showered and dressed without prodding—and joined her for some granola-topped yogurt. When she dropped me off, I felt something on the edge of cheerful.

Walking into Adele's always gave me a little lift. I loved working in my aunt's café. The decor was quirky and eclectic. Light fixtures made from kitchen utensils and colorful glass hung from the ceiling. Mismatched tables and chairs of various sizes were arrayed across the dining area. A modern interpretation of Renoir's *Luncheon of the Boating Party* encompassed the far wall, where people lined up for sandwiches and pastries. The overall effect was homey and made customers want to linger.

I swore today would be a good day. And it was, until Aunt Sophie asked me to write up the daily specials. As I set myself out front with the sandwich board, poised to write the date, my breath caught.

August seventeenth.

Mine and Alex's six-month anniversary.

How did I not know it was the seventeenth?

I scribbled the specials on the board, trying not to give in to the rush of thoughts and feelings the date brought up. It was futile. Even as I took breakfast orders from my place behind the counter, I couldn't help but think of Alex. Our first kiss at his house. Walking hand in hand in the halls of school. The dusty-blue prom dress I'd bookmarked online but never had the chance to buy.

My throat tightened as I approached the row of doubles by the long window that looked out onto the boulevard. I began with the table closest to the door, wiping the surface until I could practically see myself in it. Until I had no choice but to move on to the next table.

His table.

It was the only double with a large wingback chair the color of Kermit the Frog. Anywhere else in the world, the chair would have looked out of place, but it fit at Adele's. Alex loved that thing, sat in it while he tutored kids in science and math for community service hours.

I sat down, bus bin on my lap, and carefully cleared the dirty dishes. I closed my eyes and put my hand on the table, as if Alex could place his hand in mine. I tried hard to conjure the brush of his fingertips across my palm, the exact stormy greenish gray of his eyes, but it was hard to maintain focus. A flash of his face, and the image would dispel.

Once upon a time there was a boy named Alex McKenna. He was my best friend's brother, and that's how I saw him for most of our lives. Ash and I had been besties since second grade. Fate and classroom geography had put us together. Our mutual admiration for Rainbow Dash and One Direction further solidified our bond. Alex was always in the background: listening in on our secrets at sleepovers, bombing us with water balloons on the back deck, gloating over kicking our ass in *Mario Kart*.

At some point, he stopped being obnoxious and treated us more like friends. Like when he'd hang out with us as we binged *The Vampire Diaries* for the tenth time. Or when Ash convinced him to let us make up his eyes because we wanted to practice winged eyeliner techniques we'd seen on YouTube.

He was ours until high school, when his ability to sink a three-point shot catapulted him to hometown-celebrity status. Girls stalked him. He was dating a senior when he was a sophomore. He'd attended so many proms that he actually owned a tux. It easily could have gone to his head, but it didn't. Through it all, Alex remained Alex. Slightly goofy when you really knew him, but always able to charm the room.

Once Ash and I started high school, she relished the perks of being "Little McKenna"—invitations to parties, the inside gossip at Saint Aedan's, upperclassmen kissing her ass when we were lowly sophomores. As her best friend, I got perks by association. Not popularity exactly, but an occasional brush with it. We found our own circle of friends—an ever-changing cast of classmates from jazz band (Ash) mixed with drama club (me) with a dash of the occasional random hookup and their friends. Alex, while in a completely different social circle, never ignored us.

That was why I didn't think much of it when he started using Adele's as his tutoring home base. Lots of people did that.

Sometimes I'd take my break when Alex was between sessions. At first it was by accident. I dropped off the cinnamon streusel cake he'd just ordered and was about to head into the back for my break when he asked me a question.

"So, *Vampire Diaries* . . . were you really rooting for Klaus and Caroline to get together?"

"That's random," I said.

He smiled. "We were just doing a rewatch."

"You? A rewatch?" I said, sitting across from him and pinching off a small corner from the slice of cake. He laughed and pulled the plate closer to him. "Hey."

"It's my break, I'm hungry," I said, laughing.

"Fine, then." He teased me with the cake plate, pushing it forward, then pulling it back when I went to take another piece, a playful look in his eyes.

"That Klaus guy, he's pretty evil."

"Well, he's a hybrid vampire/werewolf, Alex, not an Eagle Scout," I said.

"Okay, but he's pretty much the worst. Just wondering, why is he your favorite?"

"Wait, did I ever say that?"

"Ash might have let that slip," he said.

I laughed, a little embarrassed. Why was she sharing our fangirl convos? And wait, Ash was rewatching *TVD* without me? Alex sat there, his eyes on me, twisted little smile on his face.

I shrugged.

"He's evil, but somewhere deep down there's good in him. I think Caroline brings that out."

"Right, even after he killed her boyfriend's mother," he said, as if we were having a rational conversation about people we knew.

"Okay, so that was awful, but he saves her. They have some sort of sexy, strange, love/hate chemistry; that's hard to deny."

"Sexy, strange, love/hate. You like the bad boys, then," he said, arching an eyebrow.

"Are you analyzing me using *Vampire Diaries*? Like a human BuzzFeed quiz?"

He laughed. "Maybe."

It was a silly conversation, but I couldn't deny it was the highlight of my shift. I convinced myself that our conversations were strictly friendly. That it didn't bother me the week he missed coming in to tutor because he was sick, or when he was out of town at a basketball tournament. And even if I was developing some sort of feeling for him, it was fondness—like big-brotherly admiration. It was nice being friends with him on our own terms. Something separate from my friendship with Ash, who would probably go ballistic if she thought I was thinking about Alex in that way.

The day we acknowledged our mutual feelings was the day I teased him about his choice of seating.

"Why do you always pick the ugliest chair in the place?"

He sat up straight, brows knit as if he was mildly affronted, and ran his hands down the arms of the chair, caressing the worn fabric.

"Ugly? I love this chair."

"Love? That's a little dramatic, don't you think?"

"Nah, makes me feel important, like I could be, I dunno, hosting a talk show or running a country." He stuck his chin out and mean-mugged for a moment before we both broke into a fit of laughter.

"Oooookay I apologize," I said. "Since you feel so strongly about it."

He leaned back, held my gaze.

"Besides it's the perfect place to sit and people-watch," he said.

I stood up and started clearing the table. He was expecting another student soon. I needed to get back to work.

"Sar . . . wait, didn't you hear what I said?" he asked.

"Um, yeah, perfect place to people-watch," I answered. I felt that way too. People watching was pretty much one of my favorite pastimes. Lots of character study.

He laughed, shook his head.

"Okay, more specific," he said. "One person."

"One person," I repeated.

He widened his eyes and pressed his lips together, holding back a grin.

It took a moment for my mind to catch up that he was talking about *me*. The room became instantly hot. Then I saw something in his eyes I never had before—uncertainty. He was serious, maybe even a little nervous.

"Anything, Sarah? I'm dying here."

I laughed. All those feelings that I'd convinced myself were platonic suddenly morphed into something else entirely. I liked him. *Liked* him, liked him. Maybe all of that was apparent in my eyes because his expression relaxed.

"Yeah?" he asked.

"Yeah," I said.

"What time do you finish work?"

Not soon enough.

"Hey, no time for a nap!" Marnie's shrill voice and nudge to my shoulder brought me hurtling back to the present.

I stood up. "Marnie, it's the seventeenth. I got lost for a moment. I'm sorry."

Her kohl-lined eyes softened.

Deceased boyfriend trumped lunch rush.

Marnie wasn't a friend exactly, but she was more than a coworker. She was taking classes at Cedar Hills Community College and had plans to eventually transfer to a four-year school. She used to roll her eyes at how swoony I became when Alex was around, but she was kind when it counted and had been patient with me in the weeks after his death. It had been almost four months. I knew her tolerance was wearing thin though.

I followed Marnie to the next table. She cleared the rest of the breakfast dishes and placed them into the bin I was holding as she spoke.

"Look, I get it, Sarah, I really do, but today is also the first day of the new semester at CHCC. Any minute there's going to be a hangry mob lined up out the door. I need you."

I nodded. "Okay."

Lunch rush was the perfect antidote to feeling sorry for myself. I pushed thoughts of Alex away for a moment and dealt with the ever-growing line of customers. I wrote checks, packed pastries to go, and turned tables over in seconds flat. Before I knew it, two hours had passed and the worst of the lunch rush was over. The work had been strangely exhilarating. I felt accomplished, at least momentarily.

Still, that bright and shiny Pandora's box of memories in my head beckoned. Adele's was the one place where Alex was solely mine. It was the place I could remember him best, maybe that's why I spent most of my summer picking up shifts. I knew once school started, things would change and my memories would fade even more.

I grabbed an iced coffee and retreated to the calm of the break room, phone in hand. The break room had the same charm as the front of the house. Mismatched and homey. I got lost in the cushy couch, propping my feet up on the coffee table as I sipped my drink and checked my messages.

There were ten from Ash. I scrolled through, stopping at a selfie on the beach.

**Wish you were here! Bored AF!** ☺

She looked tan and happy, even though I knew she was showing me her highlights reel. It was good to see her smiling.

The McKennas were in the Outer Banks the last two weeks of August for a family reunion, with lots of cousins and extended family in a ginormous house on the beach. Ash had invited me to go, but my mother thought two weeks was too long, and we couldn't work out the logistics for a shorter stay. Another time and place, I might have been more disappointed, but I was almost relieved. I'd always felt at home with Ash's family, but witnessing their grief and measuring my own against it had made me feel like an intruder. It was hard to know the right thing to say or do.

The next message was about missing the BF, Mike. Had I seen him around?

I thumbed in my reply.

**How can I see anyone when I have no life? Bored AF! For real!**

Which was better than saying, "Hiding out at work, going out of my way to avoid true human interaction!"

I heard a knock and looked up to see Aunt Sophie leaning against the doorjamb, signature baby-pink baker's jacket splotched with what looked like red velvet cake batter. I reflexively pulled my feet off the coffee table, even though she gestured to relax. She smiled.

"Are you busy?" She tilted her chin toward the phone.

Those three little dots told me Ash was still typing. I shook my head and put the phone facedown on the coffee table. Something about her expression made it seem like she wanted my full attention. My stomach clenched.

"Everything okay?" I asked.

She came over and sat down on the other side of the couch. She waved off my question. "Yes, yes," she said. "Just wanted to check in, see how you were doing."

"Oh, yeah . . . I'm, you know, good," I lied.

"You sure?"

I nibbled my straw a moment, winced. "Did Marnie tell you I completely flaked out?"

She laughed. "Not in those words, just that you were preoccupied."

I nodded. That was a nicer way of putting it. "I'm sorry. I know

CHCC is back in session and things are busy. I didn't realize what day it was. The date sort of blindsided me."

"The date?"

I nodded. "It's mine and Alex's six-month anniversary, or, you know, it would have been." The words left my lips and sounded so damn pathetic; my eyes pricked with tears. In reality we had been together two and a half months before he died. What claim did I have?

"I know it's stupid to count like that," I said, swiping my eyes.

Aunt Sophie moved closer, gave my knee a squeeze.

"Hey, I get it. Holding on to good memories is never stupid," she said. "But do you think maybe . . . well, your mom and I were talking—"

I sat upright. "Please don't fire me."

"What? No. Why would you think that?"

"Because I'm pretty sure I know what you're going to say. I'm working too much. I should be out living my life. Mom said as much this weekend when I pulled a double on Saturday."

She laughed. "You know I love having you here, Sar, but you are pushing the limit of child labor," she said, a little teasing, a little serious. "When school starts, I'm cutting your hours to two days a week."

"Wait, really? What about weekends?"

"How about every other weekend?"

I frowned. "I know I've been spacey. I promise I'll snap out of it."

"It's not a punishment, Sarah. Look, it can be a trial run, and of course if you really want to pick up a shift or I desperately need my macaron taste tester, then we can play it by ear. I get the feeling you've been hiding out here, with all the extra shifts. You're going to be a junior, you should, you know, get out more, experience life."

Before I could respond, Marnie poked her head in the room, looking between Aunt Sophie and me. "Am I interrupting?"

"Nope." Aunt Sophie replied.

"Sarah, there's—"

"I know, I know, I have to clear the lunch dishes," I said, standing up. Maybe if I ducked out of this conversation quickly, it would be like it never happened and Aunt Sophie would forget, and I could continue to push the limit of my work hours.

"Uh, yeah sure, but that's not what I'm here for. Some guy is asking for you."

"Me?"

"See," Aunt Sophie said, standing up. "It's like the universe is demanding you participate in life."

"Who is it?"

Marnie shook her head and pouted. "He's tall, sullen. By the register."

I grabbed my empty cup and dumped it in the bin as we walked out of the break room. I went through a mental checklist of all the "tall, sullen" guys I knew and came up empty.

"He's also kind of cute," Marnie said, raising her brows playfully, before pushing through the swinging doors.

My eyes met tall, sullen, and kind of cute.

I smiled.

Jake Hobbs.

What could he possibly want?

# jake

IT WAS A MISTAKE AMBUSHING SARAH AT WORK. MAYBE surprise would be the better word. That was a nice thing, right? I was sort of a friend, checking in on sort of a friend. Besides, I had news to share, and since I didn't have her number and school didn't start for a few weeks, casually dropping in at her workplace was the only way I could see her.

*"Dude, you could say something like 'I was just passing by.'"*

*Alex, for real? That's such a cliché. Why don't I just dazzle her with some dad jokes to break the ice? I don't need your advice on how to talk to girls.*

*"So you do want to talk to her?"*

*Only because I have something to tell her.*

*"No other reason? Yeah, right."*

I'd been consoling myself with these conversations with Alex since his death. I knew that sounded one jelly bean shy of being completely fucking bonkers, but my therapist, Dr. Hipster, had assured me it was a coping mechanism, and unless Alex was telling me to hurt someone or myself, then it was a way for my brain to come to terms with the fact that he was gone. In a small way, it made it seem like he was still around, like we could shoot the shit about life and stuff, the way we always had.

*Well, are you going to say something?*

"Hey, Sarah," I said.

"Hi, Jake," she said.

"Um, I was just, you know, passing by—and thought I'd check in to see how you were doing."

"Oh, wow, um, thanks, I'm okay, I guess. How are you?"

Shitty. Stressed. Hearing the voice of my dead best friend.

"I'm, you know, okay."

We stood there an awkward moment, then laughed.

"So, I'm here—" "Today's been—" We spoke at the same time.

"Sorry, what were you saying?" I asked.

"No, you go first," she said.

"I'm actually here about Alex's bench."

Her brow furrowed.

"You know, the one Coach Callard's family had dedicated to him, in the park? I got an email this morning that it's there. I wanted to see if maybe you wanted to check it out?" I was about to say *with me*, but that sounded too much like I was asking her on a date, which I wasn't, because who would ask a girl on a date to see a bench dedicated to the memory of her dead boyfriend?

*"Seems like you just did, Hobbs."*

*Not now, Alex.*

"Today?"

"Well, sure, I guess so?" I don't know why I made it sound like a question. It was the whole reason I ambushed—I mean, checked in on—Sarah at Adele's.

Her face brightened, like the sun came out from behind the

15

clouds in her eyes, and she flashed her knockout smile. There was the Sarah from the McKennas' house. The girl on the back deck in the black bikini. The one who'd occupied my thoughts a good portion of junior year, even before I realized it. Before she was Alex's girlfriend.

"I still have about an hour till my shift is over," she said.

"That's cool, I could, um, come back, or hang out," I said.

"Yeah, hang out. Want something to drink?"

"Ah, sure, water?"

"Boring," she teased. "No, really, get something. My treat."

I looked up at the menu. Three large chalkboards with small fancy writing. The words swam. Why was I so nervous? I'd been in championship games, six points behind with the clock running down, that had made me less jittery.

"Why don't I surprise you with something," she said. "Go find a seat."

"Cool," I said, even though I was anything but in that moment.

The place was packed. I spied an open table by the window with a large, green, velvety-looking chair and headed toward it. The chair was way more comfortable than it looked. I closed my eyes and sank into it, fatigue sneaking up on me. I must have dozed because when Sarah placed the dishes in front of me, I startled.

"Maybe I should have brought you an espresso instead of a lemonade," she joked, slipping into the seat across from me. "You really okay, Jake?"

There was something about the way she said it that made me believe she truly wanted to know the answer. Her eyes were sincere, or maybe it was the way her voice softened around my name. It felt like I could totally unpack my shit with her and she'd be okay with it, although I wasn't about to do that in the middle of her work shift. I leaned back, took a deep breath in.

"Yeah, just, you know, tired. This looks great, by the way, thanks," I said, suddenly starving. I broke off a piece of the cookie and scarfed it.

"You seem like a chocolate chip cookie person."

"That basic, huh?"

She laughed. "I was thinking more classic. Hey, Marnie said she wouldn't mind if I finished my shift early, so all I have to do is clear a few tables and we can go."

I finished chewing. "Great."

She smiled, tapped the table with both hands and started to get up, but sat down again, eyes wide. "Okay, I have to tell you something."

She caught me mid-sip, and I swallowed fast. "What?"

"This is going to sound . . . You know, just forget it," she said, waving her hand in the air as if she was batting the thought away.

"Well, now you have to tell me,"

She bit her lower lip, then spoke. "You're going to think I'm weird."

"What makes you think I don't already?" I joked.

"Ha, ha, thanks," she said. "Did you know you're sitting in Alex's favorite chair?"

Every muscle in my body tensed.

*"Did you hear that? My chair, dickweed."*

*Still flexin' in the afterlife? Geez, Al.*

"Oh, I, um, didn't know, sorry," I said, shifting to get up out of the seat.

"No, no," she said, motioning for me to sit. I sank back down in the chair; a coil dug into my back. How did I ever think this was comfortable?

"I felt awful today because I forgot it was . . . or, I mean, would have been mine and Alex's six-month anniversary. I feel like you stopping by, the bench, choosing this seat? It's a sign. Like Alex sending me an anniversary surprise."

I nodded, didn't have the heart to tell her that the ugly green chair had been one of the few seats open. If she wanted to believe Alex's hand was somehow involved, who was I to judge her coping strategies? I still heard the dude in my head.

"I know it sounds ridiculous," she said.

"It doesn't."

"I knew you'd get it," she said, looking back at me.

I couldn't take another second.

"You know, it's like, hot as balls out there. I better go start the car, crank the AC," I said, taking another long gulp of the lemonade.

"Oh, okay. I'll try to be quick," she said, getting up.

"No, no, take your time," I said. "I'm right out front. See you in a bit."

I scrambled out of there, exhaled when the door closed behind me.

My history with Sarah was complicated.

Only she didn't know it.

I don't remember the day I first noticed Sarah more than any other girl. My feelings for her weren't like a lightning bolt. I was aware of her mostly from being at the McKennas' house and seeing her around school. If anyone had ever asked me about her, I might

18

have said I didn't know her, but I *knew* who she was. She was Ash's friend. Cute blonde. Seemed sweet.

Although there were moments.

The black bikini on the back deck was definitely one of them, mostly because—I'd never seen her like that. Alex and I had been killing time playing H-O-R-S-E at his driveway hoop when Sarah and Ash came onto the deck to sit in the sun. I must have been staring because Alex thrust the basketball at me so hard my hands stung.

"Dude," I said, dribbling the ball. "What was that about?"

He grinned, came closer. "That's not happening; that's what that was about."

It didn't come across as jealous, more protective than anything. Whatever it was, I shook it off, but kept stealing glances when my vantage point gave me a clear view. After that, I couldn't help but notice Sarah any time she walked into a room.

Maybe that's why I began finding excuses to hang around McKennas' house. One-on-one pickup games. A new video game I couldn't wait to share. Sometimes I'd arrive early if we were going out, and I'd see Sarah and Ash, waiting for their own night to start. Wondering where she went off to, what it was she liked to do.

One Saturday night we all stayed in and watched *Train to Busan*. Ash and Sarah wanted to make popcorn old-school, on the stove, with coconut oil and loose kernels, and they forgot to put the lid on the pot, and when the popcorn started popping, it went everywhere. Pieces flying like projectiles all over the kitchen until I braved it, grabbed the lid as a shield and covered it up.

That night somehow stuck with me. One of those average nights where nothing much happened but was memorable all the same. Sarah's flushed face as I deflected a popped kernel coming her way. Laughing as we cleaned it all up and then made a fresh batch. The way Sarah hid her eyes when the scary or gory parts of the movie came on.

At some point, I realized I was having fun—and it didn't take a drink, or a winning game, or some girl's tongue in my ear. It was just chilling with friends, being around Sarah, and watching a movie. As it got later and Sarah had to leave, I asked her if she needed a ride home. It rolled off my lips without thought, a friend offering a friend a ride, but waiting for her response made me realize it mattered.

"My mom's on her way," she said, pulling on her sneakers.

"Maybe next time," I said.

"Sure, next time." She answered, smiling. She and Ash headed out the door to wait on the porch, and I bit back a laugh. Alex shook his head at me as I slumped down onto the couch. He tossed me the controller and started up a game of *NBA 2K*.

"You and Sarah?" he asked, keeping his eyes glued to the screen.

"Nah, I was just being nice," I said.

He turned to look at me, raised an eyebrow. "Sure."

"What? Would it be so wrong? She's cute, funny," I said.

"Would never work."

He sounded so certain; it pissed me off a little.

"Why?"

"C'mon, dude, this night was, like, an anomaly. You've got nothing in common. Different friends. Different lives."

"Sounds like you've thought about this," I said.

"Nah, just the truth. And what about Courtney?"

"That's not serious."

"Maybe not, but you think she'd sit back and watch you happily hook up with someone else?"

Even then, I hadn't suspected that Alex might have had feelings for Sarah. He'd been with Holly Matthews—one of Court's friends—since the end of sophomore year. I figured he was being protective again, offering some friendly advice. He probably wasn't wrong about Courtney either. We'd had an on-again, off-again, what-the-hell-are-we-doing-again hookupship for about a year at that point.

That night though, made me realize that maybe I wanted something more. I let it go—at least in the moment—holding on to those two words, *next time*, as if it were a vow for the future.

Next time never happened though.

Basketball happened. Exams happened. Christmas happened.

The ball came down in Times Square, and a monster snowstorm the likes of which no one had seen in decades hit the East Coast in late January, giving us a week of snow days.

Then, Alex and Sarah happened.

I know he didn't fall for Sarah on purpose. Maybe it took me showing interest in her for him to make his own move. I let the news roll off my back because it's not like I'd ever started anything with her. He must have remembered that October night though, because when he told me, the tone of his voice was apologetic. He resisted it, he said. Knew his sister wouldn't be happy, but in the end, he couldn't help it. *They* couldn't help it. Then he asked:

"We're cool, right, Hobbs?"

"Of course," I answered, and meant it, sort of. My first thought was *It won't last*—for all the same reasons he told me it wouldn't work. It's not like I would have gone for Sarah after that. There's some unspoken bro code about not lusting after your best friend's girlfriend, ex or otherwise, isn't there? I didn't like to think of that.

Now, as Sarah slid into the passenger seat of my car, those words came back.

*Next time.*

But it was nothing like I'd hoped it would be.


"What's in the bag?" I asked, as I pulled out of the spot.

"Oh, um, a piece of cake. Cinnamon streusel, Alex's favorite."

I nodded, hoping she would elaborate. She didn't though, just looked out the window and clutched the white paper bag on her lap as I drove. Damn, this was a mistake. I ignored that thought as I turned into the entrance of the park.

There were two sides to Cedar Hills park. One was the nice little family part with the playing fields, the basketball courts, and a man-made lake. There were benches and walking paths, a playground with a rock-climbing wall. Families picnicked on the weekend. People jogged, walked their dogs. Everyone converged there on prom night for pics by the lake, with the trees that blossomed white and pink in the spring in the background. It was a rite of passage.

Then there was the other side. The after-dark parking lot. The dense woods. The path to the cliffs.

The place people went to do, well, whatever it was they wanted without being seen.

Smoke.

Drink.

Screw.

A little bit of everything, or nothing at all.

It was a hangout. Our hangout.

Until last May, when Alex McKenna lost his footing and fell thirty feet.

Now, the very loose "no parking after dusk" rule was strictly enforced for the first time in thirty years. Not that I'd ever go back to that side again. I saw it enough in my nightmares.

The parking lot by the courts was empty, and I pulled into a spot close to the walking path. Sarah waited for me while I locked the car. I strode toward her, and we fell into step.

"Do you know which one it is?" Sarah asked, clutching the paper bag close.

"It's supposed to be near the courts," I answered. "We used to play pickup games here."

The wooden benches along the path were green, with ornate black armrests. We walked a bit before seeing a bench with a bunch of balloons in our school colors of purple and silver tied to it.

"This must be Alex's bench," Sarah said.

"Whatever gave you that idea?" I asked, chuckling.

She smiled at my attempt at humor, until we actually reached the bench and saw the note that accompanied the balloons. *I'll miss you forever.* ♥ *Holls.* Alex's ex-girlfriend. Aka the one he broke up with to date Sarah. Awkward.

The two of us stood in front of the bench, not saying anything for what might have been five seconds or five minutes. Time had slowed down to match the hazy August afternoon. There was a small silver plaque in the center of the top slat.

> *In Memory of*
> *Alex McKenna*
> *Gone too soon but not forgotten.*

I thought I would feel something more seeing the plaque. But it was odd, like it was still a big misunderstanding and Alex would show up and say, *Well, that was screwed up, wasn't it?*

"Should we sit?"

Sarah shrugged, still glaring at the balloons as if she could pop them with her eyes. I reached over, wrestled with the tangle of ribbon, and untied them from the arm of the bench.

"Jake, don't," she said, but it was too late. We watched as they sailed up above the trees.

*"Dude, won't that, like, strangle sea life or something?"*

*Please don't kill my moment of chivalry, Alex.*

"Better?"

"You didn't have to do that," she said.

"I know, but I did," I said, gesturing toward the bench. The corners of her mouth upturned ever so slightly.

"Thanks," she whispered.

We sat on either side of the plaque. Sarah tucked one leg under herself so she was facing me. She traced her finger over Alex's name.

"It's surreal," she said.

I nodded. "Perfect word."

Squeals of laughter from the kids at the playground sprinklers echoed across the water. Such happiness seemed out of place at the moment.

"I still can't say the d-word out loud," Sarah said, without taking her eyes off the plaque.

"The d-word?" I didn't want to confess the first thing that came to my mind.

*"Nice, perv."*

*Like you wouldn't think that, Alex.*

"You know, *D-E-A-D*," she said, spelling it out.

Okay, maybe she was a little weird.

I nodded.

"I don't like it much either," I said, and it was true.

"Too final," she whispered.

Sarah moved to face the lake, took out the slice of cake, and flattened the paper bag like a napkin on her lap. She offered me some.

"No, thanks," I said. I didn't want a piece of Alex's favorite cake. Or to sit in his favorite chair. Or have feelings for his girlfriend. Or take his place in any way, shape, or form.

*"Former girlfriend."*

*Whatever, Alex.*

I didn't want to hear his voice in my head. Or think about what the team was going to be like this year without him. All I wanted to do was fast-forward to a point in time when I could stop feeling so shitty about everything. That seemed impossible.

Sarah picked off a small piece of the streusel topping and ate it slowly, closing her eyes. The action was intimate, like she was getting lost in a memory. I looked away. I couldn't trust myself not to stare at her. I spilled out the contents of my brain instead.

"Sometimes I like to think of him on vacation or, you know, working at camp with those little kids at the basketball clinic who treated him like a rock star. It makes it easier somehow. Not looking forward to going back to school, but all I have to do is make it through this year, and I'm out of here. I can go somewhere where no one thinks of me as the guy who was with Alex McKenna the night he fell."

Sarah sniffled. When I turned toward her, I saw her cheeks were wet with tears. Why had I gone on like that? Especially after she told me she couldn't say the word *dead* out loud. What was wrong with me?

"Holy crap, Sarah, I'm such an idiot. I'm sorry."

She waved her hand. "No, it's nothing you said."

She crumbled the cake in her lap, mashed it between her fingers and scattered it on the grass where a few birds started to gather. Then she balled up the bag and tossed it into the garbage bin across from us.

"What's wrong?" I asked.

She ran a hand through her hair and took a breath. "I thought I would feel something more when I saw this, some connection, but I don't. I mean, why did I bring that stupid piece of cake? And 'gone too soon but not forgotten'—how generic is that? I keep looking for a sign that Alex existed, that he still exists somewhere, that he cared about me, but here I am, on a bench that his ex-girlfriend decorated with balloons and a note saying she'll miss him forever. She was here first."

"Sarah—"

"I'm never going to have more time with him. Here I am

pretending it's our six-month anniversary, and that's never going to happen. I'm so pathetic."

She crumbled again.

*"Help her, Hobbs. Don't just sit and gawk."*

"Hey, you're not pathetic," I said, putting my arm around her and sliding closer. She put her head against my shoulder, buried her face in my shirt.

"It's not fair."

"I know," I whispered.

I let her cry it out, wishing I could say something to make it better, but there was nothing to say. One thing I'd learned from my sessions with Dr. Hipster is sometimes you just have to feel it, which sucked, but reality sucked sometimes, didn't it? I took a deep breath, trying not to get dragged down into the feeling of dread too much myself. There were dark corners of my mind I didn't like to visit.

"Oh crap, I'm sorry." She pulled away, dabbed at my shirt. "I got mascara on you."

I looked down.

"Eh, it's fine, I've done worse with a slice of pizza," I said.

She laughed. She kept her eyes on mine as if she had something more to say, and a beat passed, where under different circumstances, I might have leaned in to kiss her. It was confusing, and I wondered if she felt something too, because she got flustered and slid back from me.

"Hey, I better go," she said, standing up and brushing crumbs off her lap.

"Sure, I can drop you off," I said.

"Nah, that's okay, I think I'm gonna walk," she said. "It'll clear my head."

I stood up. "Are you sure? It's so hot out."

"I won't melt," she said, smiling. "Thanks for letting me know about this, Jake. I don't think I would have come here on my own."

"You were the first person I thought of," I said.

She laughed, looked down at her feet, then waved as she walked off.

"Well, see ya."

I watched her leave; wanted so desperately to say something. She was slipping away again, along with any hope I'd harbored of . . . what? What did I think was going to happen bringing her here?

"Sarah," I called out. She stopped, turned.

"Take care."

# september

# sarah

THE FIRST DAY OF SCHOOL WAS ALWAYS A BIG DEAL TO me. With a few turns of the calendar page, all your mistakes from the previous year were wiped out and you had a fresh start. Anything was possible—at least that's what it felt like, until the excitement wore off and reality set in, and you were once again bogged down with homework, tests, and five-hundred-word essays on a book you had yet to read, due by Friday.

I'd laid out my uniform the night before, prepped my backpack with fresh pens and a three-ring binder, and tried to muster up some excitement. This year I was an upperclassman! Complete with a uniform change—from a basic green, black, and blue plaid skirt to one with a bold red stripe throughout—broadcasting to the world that I was older and wiser, at least in the halls of Saint Aedan's. College visits. Driving with friends. Prom. Junior year promised So Much Excitement. It also meant I was able to eat lunch outside in the quad in nice weather. Yay me!

Sophomore Sarah had naively looked forward to these perks, but now that they were right in front of me—I was more anxious than anything. How different would school be without the chance of seeing Alex roaming through the halls, that smile that could turn my day around? It had been hard at the end of last year, but that month and a half had flown by in a daze. I couldn't help but imagine how different the first day of school would have been if he were still here.

Ever since I'd lost my shit on that bench with Jake Hobbs, I vowed to stop ticking off time in relation to Alex and what might have been. Wishing for more time together was futile, and I knew that, but my heart had different ideas. I'd taken to wearing a seed bead bracelet, and any time I got too lost in thoughts of him, I snapped it against my wrist—the little pinch bringing me back to the present. It had been working for the most part, but sometimes I couldn't help it. My skin would probably be raw by the end of the day.

After arguing with my mom about not needing to eat breakfast, I headed off to see Ash at the same corner we'd been meeting on the first day of school since sixth grade. She was usually the one waiting for me, but as I approached the corner, I saw she wasn't there. I stopped and checked my phone. Nothing. Maybe I was a little early. I leaned against the utility box and mindlessly scrolled, trying but failing not to think of Alex.

Alex should have been driving us to school. Weirdly, it was this mundane thing I'd been excited about. Everyone knew arriving in a car with your friends was better than walking, or worse, taking the bus.

I snapped my bracelet against my wrist.

"Hey, you!"

Ash's voice brought me back to the present. She did a twirl in the middle of the street, the pleats in her plaid uniform skirt billowing slightly with the motion. A car full of Saint Aedan's guys waiting at the light honked in appreciation. I laughed.

"The red plaid suits you," I said.

"Yes, finally top of the food chain," she said. "Well, almost. I see you went with the side braid. Very Elsa-from-*Frozen*-goes-to-boarding-school vibe."

I tugged at the end of the braid and smiled. "Yeah, I thought something different would be good."

"I like it," she said, as we began the trek to school. "God, I can't wait until Mike gets his car and we don't have to walk anymore."

I took a breath, snapped the bracelet.

"Yeah, that will be great."

Mike Boyle and his friends were standing on the steps of school, waiting for us. I could already feel Ash's mood brighten. I should have been used to it, the way she lit up in Mike's presence. Over the eight months they'd been officially dating, Ash came to depend on me less and less. I hated him a little for it.

Maybe *hate* was the wrong word.

It was hard to hate Mike Boyle. He was like an overgrown greyhound puppy. Harmless, dopey, all limbs and angles. His uniform was always a mess, a random shirttail hanging out, his tie in a loose, uneven knot. Anyone else would have looked like a slob, but he somehow managed to make it work—his own brand of stoner chic, the Catholic school edition. I understood the attraction, but I'd never expected them to last more than a month or two; they barely had anything but lust in common. Mike had really stepped in and supported Ash through the horror of last spring though. For that alone, he earned my favor.

His friends Buzz and Kyle flanked him on either side, both only slightly more pulled together than Mike, which made them look like an indie power trio posing for the cover of their debut album, *Bored with Better Places to Be*. Mike's mouth curled in a half smile when he saw Ash. Within seconds she'd dropped her backpack at his feet, and they were in a lip-lock worthy of detention. Kyle, Buzz, and I averted our eyes until they finally pulled apart.

Mike grabbed Ash's backpack, and we continued into school.

"How was your summer? Didn't see you much after Fourth of July," Buzz said, falling into step with me.

"Boring. Hot. Spent a lot of time working," I answered.

"Bummer," he said.

"Yeah, pretty much." I was not great at small talk. That's why I loved drama club so much—there was always a script with the right thing to say at the right moment. Since Ash and Mike started dating, Buzz, Kyle, and I had been thrown together with the expectation that we'd get along. Sometimes it was okay, other times it was awkward. I suddenly realized I needed to reciprocate.

"How was your summer?"

"Too short, but otherwise pretty chill," he said, flipping his hair out of his eyes.

"How about yours, Kyle?"

He looked surprised I asked. "I'm more of an indoor person. Summer. Heat. The sun. Not my scene."

Thankfully the first bell rang, and we picked up our pace. Kyle disappeared down a side hallway with barely a chin tilt in our direction. Buzz mumbled "Later" and trotted faster down the hallway.

"This is me," Ash said.

Mike pulled her in for a quick kiss.

She waved at me. "See ya at lunch, Sar."

"Yep," I said, continuing down the hallway.

Mike caught up to me. "How was she this morning?"

"She seemed happy," I said. I felt like I'd been doing some version of the "Ash report" with Mike since last spring. When one of us had spent time with her, the other would check in. Kind of like a changing of the guard.

"Good. She was upset on the phone last night, didn't want to come to school. Not that I blame her. Who really wants to be here?" he said.

"I guess," I answered, wondering why I hadn't had that impression. Mike stopped in front of a classroom door. We let a few people walk past as he continued.

"I think I'm in the class next to hers, right before lunch. I'll meet up with her there. She wants to make sure we get a table in the quad. So, if you get there first, find a good one. Later, Sar," he said before ducking into his first-period class.

*Upset on the phone last night? Didn't want to come to school?*

I hated that Mike knew more about Ash's feelings than I did. Whose fault was that though? We hadn't spent much time together since she came home from the Outer Banks. Only a quick trip to Target for back-to-school shopping. She had invited me to sleep over, but I bailed. I hadn't been sleeping that well, and I didn't want to find myself awake in the middle of the night at the McKennas' house. That was just an excuse though, like me hiding out at Adele's. I needed to be a better friend.

The warning bell rang just as I hit the bottom of the stairwell. My first-period class was probably the farthest from the front of the building, and I hit the stairs running, along with the rest of the stragglers. I swear the powers that be invented the warning bell just to watch us scatter like mice. As I reached the top of the landing, someone behind me sped up and knocked into my backpack, sending my water bottle rolling across the hall and into a classroom.

"Thanks!" I called out.

I walked over to the door where it disappeared. My purple CamelBak sat askew about three feet into the room. Great. The classroom belonged to Mr. Rutledge, lit teacher and drama club mod. He was busy writing something on the whiteboard as I skulked in, trying to make myself as small as possible. I knelt to grab the bottle.

"Hydration that important to you that you'll risk the second warning, Miss Walsh?" he joked as he continued to write. Not exactly a stellar start to my school year.

"Ah, yeah," I said, grabbing the water bottle by the loop. As I stood up, my eyes locked on Jake Hobbs, who was staring back at me with an amused expression from the front row.

I murmured a breathless *hey* as I scurried out of the classroom, trying to ignore the rush of warmth in my chest that bloomed when my eyes landed on his. The same rush from that day in the park on Alex's bench.

I hadn't mentioned visiting the bench to Ash, mostly because I didn't like bringing up Alex around her. Seeing Jake again made me realize my reluctance to tell her was about more than Alex. It was about this *feeling* I got when I thought about Jake. This unnerving *whoosh* that had come out of nowhere as he comforted me. He didn't tell me to move on or experience life. He let me cry, made me laugh, a split second of joy in a place I hadn't imagined experiencing it. I'd closed myself off so much that it was overwhelming to be seen.

That had to be the reason for that fleeting thought I'd had that day.

*What if I leaned in and kissed him?*

The thought filled my head again as I made it into my first class. The warmth of his arms surrounding me. The look in his eyes, concerned and caring. The cottony clean scent of his shirt that I'd completely ruined with snot and mascara. And he didn't seem to mind.

These were all displaced feelings. I missed Alex; that was all.

Jake was Alex's best friend. Nothing could ever happen.

And whatever the *whoosh* was, I'd learn to get over that too.

# jake

*"DUDE, YOU REALLY THINK I SENT MY GIRLFRIEND INTO your lit class as a sign you should call her?"*

That's not what I meant, Alex. I thought maybe Sarah saw it as sign, because it seems she's into that stuff. I mean, what are the odds of dropping your water bottle and having it roll into the classroom only to see someone you shared a moment with a few weeks ago?

*"You're calling it a moment now?"*

Well it *was* something, *wasn't it?*

*"You're reaching, Hobbs."*

Okay, so maybe I was reaching, but Sarah had been in my thoughts since the day we went to see Alex's bench. The more I told myself to stop thinking about her, the more my brain decided to run a montage of the ways I should have acted.

In my mind's cinematic version of *Jake and Sarah Visit Alex's Memorial*, I'm smoother and know what to say even before we get to the park. Sarah is won over by my charm, and when I console her, we share a kiss—quick at first, just to test the water, but then we really go for it. Sometimes my brain even took me as far back as last October for *The Night Jake Saved Sarah from Projectile Popcorn*. This time she accepts my ride home. I tell her she's cute and ask her out. She says yes. Maybe in that version I'm the one who slips and falls in Cedar Hills park and Alex ends up consoling her on my memorial bench.

*"And maybe you're losing your fucking grip on reality."*

"Shut up," I said.

"Who are you talking to?" Courtney asked.

*Shit, I answered Alex out loud?*

We were in the quad. Lunchtime.

"What?" I played dumb. I could only imagine how Courtney would react if I told her I heard Alex in my head.

Her brow furrowed, she pushed a red-and-white container of zucchini sticks my way. I waved it off.

"Why aren't you eating anything?" she asked. She was in a good mood. The first day of school this year was her jam. Mostly because it was *the last first day and it had to be epic!* She'd also spent Labor Day weekend saying goodbye to College Guy. Not that I wanted to think about that. The best part of our hookupship was that it was easy, familiar. No strings.

"Not hungry," I said.

"You? Not hungry? That's a first," she said, laughing, then waved at someone a few tables away from us.

I envied Court's ability to compartmentalize things and move on. She was good at putting people and events in boxes. Me. College Guy. Alex's death. *That was so last year,* I could almost hear her say. Okay, maybe that was harsh. When it happened, she was just as shocked and sad as anyone, but she didn't get hung up on it. She was ready to take senior year by the balls.

I looked around the quad at the smiling, excited faces of my classmates. First-day lunch was a party, everyone seemed so carefree. I was on the outside looking in. All I wanted to do was fast-forward through the year, so I could graduate and go to some college far away, like in Colorado or Arizona or anywhere no one thought of me as that guy who was with Alex McKenna the night he fell.

Then I saw her.

Sarah was eating something with a spoon and staring intently at the dude across from her. Her face broke into a grin. What was she reacting to? From what I could see she was with Pat Boyle's little brother and two of his stoner friends. And Ash McKenna, of course.

"You should talk to her," Court said.

I damn near pulled a trap turning her way. "What?"

She placed her hand over mine, looked into my eyes. "You should talk to Ash McKenna."

I breathed out. "Why?"

"To reconnect. See how she's doing."

"She looks like she's doing okay."

She clucked her tongue, shook her head. "Well, I think you should. It's obviously bothering you."

"What do you mean? What's obviously bothering me?" I asked. This got the attention of Pat and Taj, who'd been sitting at the end of the table, minding their own business and scarfing down their Italian subs.

Court gave them a glance, then turned back to me. "All I'm saying is that maybe if you ask how she's doing instead of avoiding her, it might help you to move on. You haven't exactly been fun to be around. You get sort of spacey. You're so—"

"So *what?*"

"Serious. Mopey. On edge," she said, low, for only me to hear. "Like, now, are you trying to pick a fight with me?"

Was I?

"I don't want to fight with you," I said, finally taking a zucchini stick.

She smiled. "Well, good, that's a start, then."

"Hey, guys."

We both looked up as Holly Matthews put down her lunch tray and sat on the bench seat across from us. She slid over farther than she needed to, which somehow emphasized the empty space next to her. She seemed to realize this and readjusted. The numbers always felt off when all of us were together. I'd find myself thinking that someone was missing. Then realized someone *was* missing. Although maybe Alex would have been sitting with Sarah this year, or she would have been sitting with us. That would have been strange.

"You're getting that spaced-out look again," Court said.

"Okay," I whispered, but what I really wanted to say was *Stop badgering me.* I smiled at Holly, although it felt more like baring my teeth. Mechanical. Fake it till you make it, or some shit like that, right?

Holly opened up a dressing packet and drizzled the contents over her salad. Before making a move to eat, she reached into her backpack, pulled out a piece of paper, and handed it to me.

"I was thinking of ways to honor Alex," she said, placing the lid back on her salad and shaking it up. "I know there's that shrine at the cliffs, and the bench that Coach's family dedicated to him, but

I think this would be a more impactful way to honor him and bring attention to a subject that, frankly, is a problem for all of us." She placed her salad down, popped open the lid, and grabbed a forkful of lettuce.

I read the paper and passed it to Courtney.

"The pledge," Courtney said. "Why not suck all the fun out of senior year?"

Holly swallowed what she was eating and pouted. "How can you say that?"

The pledge was a promise not to drink or do drugs, aka a way to suck all the fun out of senior year.

"It's a little after the fact, Holls, is all I'm saying," Courtney said, passing the paper over to Pat Boyle.

"We signed something like that for the basketball team last year," I said, and wanted to add, *and you see how that worked out*, but she was visibly ruffled that we weren't immediately ready to fall into line.

"Once I have a few signatures, I was going to bring it to Monsignor Dolan and see if we can make it school-wide, or at least have a few reps from each grade. I think it's important."

"Got a pen? I'll sign," Pat said. He had a thing for Holly, probably would have agreed to be celibate for forty days if she asked, so no surprise there. Holly slipped a pen out of the side pocket of her backpack and handed it to him with a smile. When he was finished, he passed it over to Taj, who signed and passed it back to Courtney.

"Fine, I'll sign, but I'm only pledging until October, not including Halloween," she said. She finished with a flourish and handed it to me. I returned it to Holly without signing. She slid it back across the table to me.

"Jake."

I had no desire to drink after that night. I didn't need to sign a paper to make it official. The fact that Holly was sitting there, concerned but with that condescending *I'm the class president and know better than you* look on her face, as if I were a five-year-old—made me want to sign it even less.

"No."

"Jake, really? It's to support a friend, just sign it," Courtney said.

"It's dumb. You even said you're going to break it, so why bother signing at all?"

"I thought you out of everyone would—" Holly didn't finish her sentence. The silence that came after her words was a ghost hanging over the table.

"Me out of everyone, why?" I asked. I wanted to hear her say it.

She picked a crouton out of her salad and munched on it. Head down, ignoring me.

"Jake," Pat said, with the undertone of *Stop being a douche.*

Of course I knew what Holly meant. Me out of everyone because they thought it was my fault that Alex died that night, wasn't it? I'm the one who tossed him the bottle instead of just handing it to him. The one who hesitated before calling help. I shot up, grabbed my backpack. Courtney reached for my hand, but I slipped away too fast.

"Later," I said to no one as I headed back inside.


The woods were dense and dark, and it was difficult to move, as if I were walking against a strong wind. Alex was there too. There was always a mix of relief and fear when I saw him in my dreams. For a split second, he was very much alive, walking next to me. His

43

death all a misunderstanding. Then, of course, I'd remember the truth, or there would be something about him that wasn't quite right. He'd be dull around the edges. This night, he kept his eyes straight ahead, not speaking or smiling, his face completely devoid of expression as we pawed our way through the thick brush.

*Where are we going?* I wanted to ask him, but the words were physically painful, locked in my throat. He moved ahead of me through the tangle of branches. Then suddenly Sarah was next to me, her eyes hidden by leaves, her name on the tip of my tongue. Again, I couldn't speak. I reached out to move the branches, but they were always out of my grasp. Then she disappeared.

I was alone.

That's when I felt the invisible hands. On my calves. Tickling my sides. Grasping my shoulders. Slipping around my neck. Holding me back. Pulling me down.

Panic.

*Wake up, Jake.*

*You can wake up.*

And then I was upright, heartbeat in my head, gasping for breath, under a canopy of stars in a deep-blue sky projected on my ceiling. The soft sound of ocean waves. My bed. My computer. My basketball hoop trash can that I'd had since I was ten. My room. I was safe.

Safe.

I reached for my phone, checked the time—12:30 a.m.

Fuck.

It had been a while since I had a nightmare. Dr. Hipster told me being back at school might cause some difficult feelings to arise.

44

There'd be an adjustment period, and then everything should settle again. I stood up, shook it off. Only a nightmare.

I grabbed some sweats and my running shoes. Whenever I woke up in the middle of the night over the summer, I'd jog a quick two-mile loop. Running was dull as shit, but it helped punch down intrusive thoughts. The bonus was it conditioned me for the court too, which was pretty much the only effort I'd been putting into the training regimen Coach had given us to keep in shape over the summer.

The house was dark. I slipped out the back door into the night, imagining that I could really disappear.

Holly's words from the lunch table played through my head as I trotted down the street.

*"I thought you out of everyone would—"*

Thinking about it now, I regretted acting like a prick. I didn't regret not signing that piece of paper though. No one at that table had been with Alex the night he died. They didn't get it. No shrine, or park bench, or signature on a fucking piece of paper was going to change any of that. He was gone.

Maybe time was supposed to heal everything, but it was taking too damn long.

*"Hobbs, toss me a brew."*

Alex and I had been with the graduating seniors. An upperclassmen tradition. A bro night sendoff to the guys on the team heading off to college. Pat and Taj had been on their way when it happened. They hadn't witnessed it. Hadn't seen Alex there one second, gone the next. I was the only one left on the team who'd been there.

I ran faster.

Images from that night kept trying to squeeze into my brain, but with each footfall, I held them at bay.

By the time I reached my back door, I was panting and dripping with sweat, mind blissfully blank, body pushed to fatigue. I took a moment to catch my breath before going in. Mom was at the kitchen table with a mug of tea and our cat, Maleficent, perched on her lap. Both of them looked pissed, Mom's face etched with worry, Mal's tail twitched.

The door hadn't even latched before she said, "Where were you?"

"Out for a run."

"It's almost one thirty in the morning. You have school in a few hours," she said, getting up from the table. I felt bad for screwing up her night off from her nursing shift at the hospital. Mal hopped down and strutted over to me, weaving through my ankles like a furry land shark as I checked the contents of the fridge.

"I had one of my dreams again," I said, reaching for a Gatorade. I shooed the cat away and closed the door.

"Are you okay?" she asked.

I nodded. Her face softened.

"You want some warm milk?"

"Nah, thanks. I'm gonna head up and take a shower."

"You could have used the treadmill," she said.

"That's so loud. I didn't want to wake you or Annie," I said, chugging half the bottle.

"Jake, seriously, next time use the treadmill. Or wake me up. It's okay. I'd rather be inconvenienced by a little noise and know you're here than out God knows where."

"How did you even know I was gone?"

"Dad called. Said he saw you pass the firehouse. Well, and nothing gets past this one," she said, motioning toward Mal, who meowed as if to say, *That's right, bitch.*

"Snitch."

After the shower, I sat down with my laptop. I'd been seriously checking into out-of-state colleges for the past two months. Each website a glimpse into some possible future. Far away from anything I knew. A blank slate. Maybe I'd study film, or finance, or become like Dr. Hipster and sit and listen to people spill their guts about the whack stuff that filled their heads.

It would be a relief not to eat, sleep, dream basketball anymore, but if I got the itch to play, I could find a pickup game or rec league, or maybe I'd try something different altogether. Like snowboarding. Or surfing. Or smoking weed and watching documentaries. Make a YouTube channel and analyze the shit out of the MCU. Or nothing at all. Just be.

I pulled up the website for University of Colorado Boulder. Over a thousand miles away. Blue skies. Mountains. Something completely different. I clicked on the admissions tab.

Plotted my future escape.

# sarah

TWO WEEKS INTO THE SCHOOL YEAR, AND IT WAS AS IF I'd never left, and yet, Saint Aedan's seemed like a completely different place without Alex McKenna. Everything went on as usual. Classes. Assignments. I was almost grateful to be tasked with a group project on *The Great Gatsby*, so I'd have something concrete to focus on instead of dwelling on what was missing. The world was a little dimmer without the prospect of seeing his face.

Memories would pop up randomly. A certain section of hallway jogged my brain so intensely that I almost tripped over the person in front of me as I got lost in thought. I used to see Alex between bio and geometry. His smile would start the moment our eyes met. I could almost feel the jolt that surged through me as our fingers brushed together when we passed each other in the hall. Once, I thought I heard his laugh, and another time when someone was dribbling a basketball down the hall, I turned, expecting to see him. I was surprised my seed bead bracelet hadn't fallen apart already.

Even lunch in the quad, which was an enviable perk every freshman and sophomore at Saint Aedan's looked forward to, had become thirty minutes when I had to battle thoughts of what might have been.

It wasn't all bad though. Being outside in the fresh air and sunshine broke up the monotony of the day. And halfway through the first week I realized I could catch a sneaky glimpse of Jake. Any time that *whoosh* feeling threatened, I looked away. Would I have been sitting at his table if Alex were still here?

Or would I be where I was now, settling in across from Buzz and wondering how to break the ice today. I popped open my bag of salt-and-vinegar chips and offered them up to the table.

"Those are so rank. How can you eat them?" Buzz asked, taking a sizable mouthful of the cafeteria's special of the day—a sloppy Tom. Sauce dripped from the corner of his mouth. Kyle and I shared a glance as he reached into the bag for a chip.

Mike knocked on the table. "Hey, we were thinking of hanging out after school. Me, Ash, Buzz—my house, you game?"

It took a moment to realize he was directing the question at me. I wasn't sure why I needed a formal invitation. Then I realized he hadn't said Kyle's name. I looked at Kyle, who had resumed reading a book titled *Explorer's Guide to Wildemount*. When I looked at Buzz, he looked away, took another bite of his sandwich.

"You need a chaperone?" I asked.

Mike laughed. "No, just, you know, something to do." He motioned subtly at Ash. She stared straight ahead, looking like she wanted to be anywhere else but here. "We could shoot a game of pool or something."

"I have drama club today," I said, relieved to have a legit excuse to miss the planned fun.

"Drama club, you?" Buzz asked.

"Yeah, me."

"You don't seem like the type."

"What does that even mean?"

"You're, you know, reserved. The theater kids seem so . . . extra."

Kyle looked up from his book, reached for another chip and said, "I think drama club is dope."

"Thanks," I said.

"Of course you would think its dope. You order latex elf ears from Amazon."

"They were satyr ears, man, get it right," he corrected, turning a page in his book.

"Yeah, well, keep that shit up and it's probably the only thing made of latex you'll ever buy."

Mike burst out laughing and fist-bumped Buzz. Kyle smiled and shook his head. This insensitive ribbing went on between the three of them often, but they laughed it off. Buzz played soccer for Saint Aedan's, Kyle was part of the Dungeons & Dragons club, and Mike? Aside from procuring edibles and taking excellent care of Ash, I wasn't sure what he did in his spare time. They'd apparently known each other since kindergarten.

"Why do you have to be so gross?" I asked.

He grinned at me. "Just trying to help out a friend."

"Can't you skip out of one?" Ash's voice stopped our conversation cold. She looked directly at me.

"They're announcing what play we're doing this year."

"Sure, okay," she whispered, and got up from the table, leaving us all bewildered. I looked at Mike.

"She seemed okay this morning," I said.

"I don't know what happened, but that's what it's like sometimes.

Just comes out of nowhere."

"I'll go talk to her," I said, cleaning up the remains of my lunch.

I found Ash in the bathroom, splashing water on her face. She looked up as I came in, our eyes met in the mirror. I had the urge to apologize, but I wasn't sure what for. In the days after Alex's death, Ash had told me it was hard to go anywhere without feeling as though people were staring at her, like she might explode at any moment. I thought she'd been exaggerating, but when I started really paying attention, I noticed she was right. Sometimes though, I worried I looked at her like she might explode too.

"You okay?"

She shook her head and reached down to splash more water on her face before turning off the faucet. I grabbed a paper towel and held it out for her.

"Ash, any other day, I'd be fine hanging out."

"I'm not upset about that," she said, taking the paper towel and dabbing her cheeks. "I get it's your thing."

"Don't you have band on Thursdays, too?"

She shook her head.

"What?"

She crumpled the towel and tossed it in the trash bin. "I quit."

I was confused. "But it's *your* thing."

"Not anymore, or at least not right now. I used to be able to get lost in the music, and I tried, but all I heard was white noise. Everyone was overly nice to me too. I can't take that. I don't know what's fake and what's real anymore. I just needed to step away. Ms. Wallace said to think of it as a sabbatical and come back whenever I felt ready, but for now, yeah, I quit."

"I had no idea, Ash," I said. Two girls entered the bathroom. When their eyes landed on Ash, their expressions changed. Ash gave me a *see-what-I-mean* look as they walked into adjacent stalls.

And I don't know why I did it, but I made this explosion sound. It wasn't that loud or anything—just enough so we could hear it, and I played it up big, waving my arms. Ash's brows drew together, but then we both burst out laughing. Her face turned red. It took a moment for us to compose ourselves.

"Thanks for that," she said.

"Anytime," I said.

She took a deep breath, her expression serious again.

"I miss you, Sar."

"I'm right here."

"Are you really?" she said.

"What do you mean?"

The lock clicked on one of the stalls; Ash rolled her eyes, grabbed my arm, and we left the bathroom. In the hallway, she continued.

"You never come over anymore. I barely see you. You totally bailed on my invite to Outer Banks," she said.

"Ash, I didn't bail—I couldn't go. The logistics were off," I answered, using my mother's words, but it felt like I was delivering a line. And a bad one at that.

She stepped back, crossed her arms. Her voice was soft.

"Logistics? So, if Alex had been there, you still wouldn't have been able to figure something out?"

That truth bomb was a direct hit. I leaned against the wall, looked out toward the quad, could feel a sting building up behind my eyes. I thought about when Alex and I broke the news about us dating to Ash. We'd wanted to do it together, to make sure she was okay with it. Ash was surprised to see me at her house, and when Alex came down the stairs and we shared a look, all she said was "Oh hell no."

She'd been angry, more at him than me, but it took her a good twenty-four hours to come around, and there were contingencies she had for us.

"If there's a popular movie I want to see, I get first dibs on Sarah."

"Okay, but, like, can I come with you?"

"That would be a game-time decision," she said, "but don't count on it, and absolutely no PDA in front of me."

"Not even this?" Alex asked, putting his hand over mine.

She waved her hands. "Cringe, but okay, don't push it."

Then she turned to me. "We're friends first. Whatever happens, remember that."

Friends first was never even a question for me.

And as I stood in front of her now, I realized, maybe I had let that slip.

"You don't have to answer, Sar. A lot of things would be different if he was still here."

"I know that," I said. "I'm sorry."

"Don't be, but don't avoid me either. You can talk about him. I actually won't explode. If I can't deal with it, I'll tell you."

"Okay," I said, nodding. Then the doors to the quad opened and Jake Hobbs was suddenly there, one hand gripping the strap of his backpack, the other hand holding a caf tray. He slid the trash off into the garbage bin and placed the tray on top. When he looked up, he saw us. There was an uncomfortable beat, where I could totally see the wheels turning in his brain. He stiffened momentarily, looking between Ash and me, but then approached us. What if he brought up the day at the bench? What would I say to Ash then?

"Is he really coming over here?" Ash whispered.

"It looks that way," I answered, ignoring my quickened pulse.

Jake hoisted his backpack a little higher on his shoulder as he walked over, stopping about two feet away from us. He cleared his throat.

"Hey, Ash, how, um, how've you been doing?"

"Oh, I'm fine, how about you?"

He shrugged. "Oh . . . you know, okay, I guess. How are your parents?"

A bead of sweat slowly rolled down his temple. I had the urge to reach out and touch it. He ran a hand through his hair and wiped it away.

Ash blinked a few times fast, maybe a little unprepared for the question.

"Oh, they're okay. You know, dealing with it. Some days are better than others," she said, rattling off the generic catchphrases I'd heard her say before.

Jake nodded in response. "Well, tell them I was asking about them. I miss coming over there."

"Yeah," Ash said.

Then nothing.

A very

long

pause

as the conversation died.

"Welp," Jake said, nodding again. Then his dark eyes landed on me.

*Whoosh.*

I was glad I was leaning against the wall.

"Hi, Sarah."

"Hey."

"Guess I'll see you around," he said, looking back at Ash, then at me again, before turning away and heading off into the stairwell. Ash breathed out.

"Glad that's over with. It's not his fault, but he's just like a constant reminder, you know? Now he never has to say a thing to me, ever again," she said, as we walked back out to the quad.

I wanted to defend him but didn't think it would go over well.

"I'll skip out of drama club to hang with you guys," I said.

"You don't have to."

"I want to, Ash. You know how first meetings go anyway, contact sheet and dues money, blah, blah, blah, it'll be fine."

She smiled.

"Cool."

# jake

"HOBBS, HUSTLE!" COACH YELLED ACROSS THE COURT.

Handle drills were my least favorite. Or maybe they were my least favorite after a miserable night's sleep and a shitty school day. My body was running on pure adrenaline, and it showed. I dribbled the ball but couldn't make it do what I wanted. On my third time across the court, doing high-low crossovers, the ball got away from me and went rolling toward the baseline.

A quick chirp of Coach's whistle and I was against the retracted bleachers doing wall sits. That was more my speed, or lack of speed, at the moment anyway. I'd always been the champion of wall sits, could outlast anyone. For slacking on the boards, I had to endure a full five minutes. It was more of a mental exercise than anything. I took a deep breath, counted off the seconds in my head.

Thirty-nine, forty, forty-one.

Close to a minute in, my quads were on fire.

Maybe I should have paid more attention to strength training over the summer.

Focus. Push through the pain. Breathe.

My brain decided to torture me.

*Welp* . . . I'd actually said "welp" to Sarah and Ash in the hallway.

And the looks on their faces? I got douche chills just thinking about it. What had I expected to happen? For Ash to invite me over to see her parents? For Sarah to tell me it was good running into me again?

At least I'd done it though. That counted for something, but contrary to what Courtney might have thought—it didn't make me feel any different. I could have pretended not to see them, which had been my first impulse. Maybe if there'd been more people between us, it would have been easy to pull that shit off, but when I looked up it was like hitting a bull's-eye. Now or never, I thought.

*"You should have picked never, Hobbs."*

*Thanks for the advice, Alex.*

*"Still, you got to see Sarah. You should talk to her."*

*Right.*

*"No, you should."*

"Hobbs!"

Coach Callard waved us in for the usual end-of-practice pep talk. There were some new guys this year, and we had yet to really come together. Our first game wasn't until early December, but it was a huge adjustment not having our star player. Alex's absence not only left a hole in our lineup but it also messed with our confidence. It didn't help that some of the new guys were completely obnoxious.

Okay, one of the new guys.

Sebastian "Bash" Elliot was an asshole. He was new to Saint Aedan's, and Cedar Hills. As far as I could tell from practices, he was a greedy baller who was more interested in his own stats than being a team player. He was a sophomore, already bragging about making reels for recruiters. He was hungry to play, and I would have appreciated having such an aggressive teammate, if not for the fact that I wanted to punch him any time he opened his mouth.

Coach stood a few rows up in the bleachers while we fell in around him. I hung toward the back, wanting to make my exit that much easier. His arms were crossed, eyes sharp.

"I don't know what's going on with you guys, but if we don't start acting like a team, Union is going to wipe the court with us. Do you think they're dragging their asses across the court, not communicating with each other? Something's got to change. Hobbs, get up here."

Coach wasn't usually one to single us out, at least, not in this way. My heartbeat throbbed in my ears as I made my way over to him. When I stopped at the bottom of the bleachers, he waved for me to climb up next to him. It was only two or three steps, but my legs felt wobbly—nerves or wall sits, I couldn't tell. I mentally prepared to get reamed. He motioned for me to turn and face everyone.

"Crusaders, meet your new captain."

"What?"

Coach still faced forward, small smile on his face. My teammates clapped. My head was woozy; this felt like one of my nightmares. Captain? Me? I'm the one who stared down opponents, found the weak spot, picked fights. I was not leader material; I didn't know how to bring people together—he had to know that.

"Next practice I want to see that hustle." He gave two short chirps from his whistle to call practice to an end. Everyone dispersed, gathering up equipment and walking toward the locker room.

"You're kidding, right?" I asked him.

He shook his head as we climbed down the stairs.

"Your teammates voted for this," he said.

"When? Don't you think you should have asked me? Why not Taj or Pat?"

He turned to me. "They're the ones who suggested you; if you don't want it, why don't you take it up with them? I wouldn't have agreed if I didn't think you could handle it. Sleep on it at least."

"Thanks, Coach," I said. I jogged to catch up to Pat, who was on his way to the lockers. He smiled when he saw me.

"Congrats, man," he said.

"So, you knew about this?"

"Yeah, Coach spoke to me and Taj; we talked to everyone else," he said.

"Everyone but me," I said.

Pat stopped, looked at me squarely.

"Look, Jake, you're not here. I mean you are"—he gestured at me with an open palm—"but not really. I know what happened to Alex got to you. It got to all of us too. Sometimes I wonder if you realize that. We thought this might help you focus."

I wasn't expecting such an honest answer. I hadn't shared my "coasting till graduation" strategy with anyone, but I guess it was obvious. How could I be pissed when they thought this would help me? That's what it was like being on a team.

"Thanks, I guess," I said.

"Just don't be a power-crazy dick," Pat joked.

I took a quick shower and got dressed by my locker. I had about twenty minutes to get to my appointment with Dr. Hipster. As I stuffed my gear into my duffel, I wondered if anyone's opinion of me being captain would change if they knew I was seeing a thera-pist. That's when I heard Bash talking smack on the other side of the locker bay.

Normally I didn't pay attention. He ran his mouth a lot, but this was about me.

"Hobbs as captain? Bit of a mercy fuck, don't you think?"

A few guys laughed. A jolt of anger made it momentarily hard to breathe; I froze trying to talk myself out of punching a hole clear through the locker. See, this wasn't captain behavior. Alex had been a mediator. He was able to disarm anyone with some simple gesture or a few funny words. I didn't have that ability.

I don't know what bothered me more though, the fact that Bash said it or that I'd thought the same thing. This was definitely a mercy fuck. This was special treatment for Jake because his best friend died. I hated that, but I wasn't about to give him the satisfac-tion of getting to me.

"I know it's just a title, but the person should at least have some skills. His handles are shit."

Alex had always been there to talk me down.

*"Breathe, Jake. You're better than this."*

*He's not wrong though, my handles are shit, Alex.*

*"You had a bad day, hand his ass to him on the court, not here."*

*Not here.*

I took a breath. Closed my locker short of slamming it, just to make my presence known. Silence. I walked past, said "Later" to the shocked group of sophomores. Ignored the muffled whispers as I hightailed it out of there and off to therapy.

\* \* \*

Dr. Hipster wasn't a doctor, and the only thing hipster about him was the manicured beard that he stroked thoughtfully when listening, but that's the name that popped into my head when I met him, so it stuck. His office was low-key, more like a mix between a living room and a home office in the basement of a brownstone on the west side of town. My mother and I had trouble finding it the first time, the entrance tucked away under the stone stairs that lead up to the front door of the building. A tiny, laminated card on a plain, red door—*Gregory Hewitt, LCSW*—the only clue it was a place of business.

The way the door was tucked out of sight made it like a secret club. A private place where I could disappear for forty-five minutes. I began seeing Dr. Hipster because I'd had a panic attack at Alex's funeral. Heart racing. Head spinning. Couldn't breathe. Had-to-get-the-fuck-out-of-there dread that made it seem like the church was closing in on me.

A few days later, I started seeing Dr. Hipster once a week. I kept picturing each appointment like a vine I could cling to, and as long as I could see the next one, I'd be okay. I'd keep moving forward. In August, we'd decided to spread out my appointments to every two weeks, with the knowledge I could change back to weekly if I felt it was necessary.

"How has school gone so far?"

"It's been okay."

He nodded—waiting, neutral—like he knew that if he was silent long enough, I'd start talking.

"I mean, I hate it really. Wish I could just fast-forward to the start of next year, so I could be someplace else."

"Sounds like it's been tougher than you're letting on. What's been the part you hate the most?"

"I ran into Alex's sister today and I thought . . . I don't know what I thought. It's hard around her; I always feel like she's looking at me like, *Why are you here instead of Alex?*"

"Did she ever say that?"

I shook my head.

"Do you ever ask why Alex and not me?"

"Maybe, but I don't want to die. Or trade places with him. Sometimes it feels like I'm living his life but doing a shitty job of it. Like today, I was named captain of the basketball team."

"Congratulations," Dr. Hipster said, smiling.

"No, it's not . . . that's not me. It's Alex. Alex brought people together, I'm not like that."

"Do you think your teammates are expecting you to be like Alex?"

"Yeah, maybe," I said. "Sometimes I feel like I'm letting people down because I'm not more like him."

"That's a lot of pressure you're putting on yourself, Jake. You and he were best friends, your lives were similar before he died. Same school, same friends, same team."

*"Same taste in girls."*

*Not now, Alex.*

"One of the girls in my class asked us all to sign this pledge. A promise not to drink or do drugs as a way to honor Alex, and she got pissed when I wouldn't sign."

He shifted in his seat. "Why didn't you sign it?"

"Because . . ." I hesitated. It was a joke? So goody-fucking-goody

I could throw up? "If we wanted to really honor Alex, we'd throw a blowout kegger. And this pledge is just so hypocritical. Last year Holly served Jell-O shots with edible glitter for her New Year's Eve party and now she wants us to stop drinking like that's even going to matter. It won't bring him back. It won't change anything."

Dr. Hipster stroked his beard. Once, twice, then folded his hands in his lap.

"No, it can't change what happened, but it can change your perception. I wonder if she's trying to take some power back in a powerless situation."

I frowned. Of course Holly dealt with death better than me.

"Am I wrong for not honoring him this way?"

"No, there's no right way to honor someone. If you're not comfortable with it, that's okay. Maybe you could find your own way to honor him, if you'd like. Do you still hear him?"

"Sometimes," I said.

"At any specific moments?"

I shook my head. "I dunno, mostly seems random."

He nodded, took the notepad from his side table, and scribbled something.

"If you can, start paying attention to when you hear him."

"Why?"

"I think it might be interesting, maybe point to some unresolved issues or feelings. If it's too difficult to do that, that's okay too. Is it still a source of comfort for you?"

I nodded.

"Good. See you next time."

On my way back to my car, my phone buzzed.

Holly.

Call me when you can. Urgent.

With Holly, everything was urgent. Normally I would have ignored it, but after thinking about how I was living Alex's life but doing a shitty job of it . . . I decided to call her. I still wasn't signing the pledge though. She answered on the first ring.

"Wow, that was fast."

"That's pretty much the definition of urgent, right?" I said, chuckling. "What's up?"

"I need your help with something."

# sarah

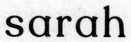

"WHAT'S THE PURPLE ONE AGAIN?" THE WOMAN IN the red hat asked, pointing toward the rows of macarons behind the glass display case.

"Earl Grey," I said with a smile. It was about the tenth time I'd gone through all twenty macaron flavors that morning. I prided myself on memorizing them; I considered it a dramatic exercise.

Saturday mornings at Adele's were somewhat predictable, which is why I liked them. I could count on the opening coffee and pastry rush, the midmorning slump, and the late-morning meeting of a group of older women who called themselves Red Hats. The rest of the early part of the day was filled with book clubbers and artsy laptop types, who loved the free Wi-Fi and in-house bottomless cup of coffee. It was my first Saturday shift since the beginning of school, and I was surprised to find how much I'd missed being there.

There was a lull in counter service, and I did a quick sweep of the dining area to see if anyone needed a coffee refill. When I got back to the counter, I was parched. A little iced coffee would hit the spot, get me through the rest of the morning. I grabbed a cup and filled it with ice, turned to Marnie. "Want one?"

"Yes, you read my mind! I have to hit the ladies'. Can you handle life without me for a few minutes?"

"I'll try," I said, grabbing another cup with ice. The counter bell chimed. I looked over my shoulder. Yikes.

"Trinity, hey," I said, my voice getting higher at the end because I knew I was about to face the consequences of bailing on drama club. I grabbed lids and covered the drinks before heading toward the counter to speak to her.

Trinity Suarez was president of the drama club—wait, let me rephrase that—was born to be president of the drama club, or maybe even the world. She was tall and willowy, with an extraordinary tangle of long dark curls that gave her a couple more inches of height. She planned on graduating from Juilliard, working only with A-list people, and eventually winning a Tony Award for direction. I learned all of that within two minutes of meeting her at freshman orientation. There are people who make those sorts of proclamations, and then there are people who can actually accomplish them. I had no doubt she could make things happen. She was formidable, and right now her focus was on me. I'd been ghosting her since I'd skipped the meeting on Thursday. I decided to play it cool.

"What can I get you?" I asked.

She placed a small yellow book on top of the counter and slid it over to me. My pulse quickened a little bit—it was the play. I reached over and picked it up, read the cover.

*ALMOST, MAINE* by John Cariani.

"We announced the play on Thursday, where were you?"

I ran my fingers across the title. I loved the feeling of a new play book in my hand. I couldn't wait to dive in and discover, and hopefully mark it up with notes if I was cast.

"I'm sorry I bailed—"

"You've never bailed, not once, in two years. What was so important on Thursday?"

Her directness made me squirm. What could I tell her? I bailed to play pool in a stoner's basement. Maybe emergency dentist appointment. I debated a hot second, then told her the truth.

"Ash had a bad day, wanted company. I couldn't say no."

Her red-lipped pout softened. "You could have told me. You know how Rutledge is a stickler for rules, you miss three meetings and you can't perform."

"I screwed up," I said.

And really it had hardly been worth it. Buzz was strangely intense about the rules of pool, which I was surprised to find out involved more than taking the white ball and hitting all the other balls with it. Ash thought he'd been trying to impress me and was just nervous. Mission not accomplished.

"Can I get you something, on me, truce?"

She laughed. I finally felt forgiven.

"Well, if you insist."

Once Marnie was back, I took my break and brought Trinity's café au lait and chocolate croissant to her. I found her along the row of doubles at the window in the Kermit chair, of course. When that chair was open, everyone gravitated toward it. She was running her hands down the arms as I placed her coffee in front of her. It was hard imagining anyone in it but Alex, but it sort of suited Trini too. I could totally see her running a country from it.

"I love this chair, it would make a great stage prop," she said.

I laughed. "It definitely has a personality," I said, sitting across from her with my iced coffee in hand. "So, what did I miss on Thursday, or are you still too annoyed to tell me?"

She ripped off a piece of her croissant before she divulged.

"Dylan Jacobs got an agent and is completely insufferable. He had a bit part in a CW pilot called *Doppelgängers* they shot in Manhattan, and all he can talk about is how he has a SAG card now."

She leaned closer and whispered. "Riley Summers's parents wrote a fifteen-hundred-dollar check to the theater department, so I'm guessing she's expecting a part this year."

"Really?"

She nodded, arched an eyebrow. "And Cullyn is desperate to find more people for crew because he lost so many from the graduating class. So if you know anyone who might want to join, let me know."

"I'm sorry I wasn't there, Trini."

"When you didn't show I was worried you might have quit. We always talked about how we'd run things when we were in charge, and now here's our chance. I need to know you're serious. No flaking out on me."

"I thought theater was supposed to be fun," I joked.

"Work hard, play hard, know your lines," she said. "You better read *Maine*, ASAP. I think you're really going to like it."

"Any juicy parts that are perfect for me?" I asked, knowing full well I was putting her on the spot.

"You know I can't talk about my directorial process," she said, playfully drumming her fingers against her chin. "But I may have imagined you in a certain part or two."

I couldn't tell if she was kidding or not. I hoped *not*.

"How do you feel about kissing scenes?" she asked.

I mock gasped, clutched my chest. "Kissing scenes? You know that's why I'm interested in theater in the first place."

We laughed.

"Really though, there's like a couple of kisses, obviously nothing too hot, the front office crowd—" Trinity continued, but her words became far away as I watched Jake walk through the front door of Adele's.

He was in black warm-ups and a plain white tee, looking sweaty and flushed. This was definitely not a part of a somewhat predictable Saturday at Adele's. Hands on his hips in a lazy, laid-back way, he looked toward the bakery display case, eyes scanning across the length of it. Trinity noticed I'd stopped listening and followed my gaze.

She turned back. "Isn't that Jake Hobbs?"

Trinity hadn't spoken that loudly, but at the mention of his name Jake turned toward us. He pressed his lips together, half smiled, then stepped back to let a few customers inside and go ahead of him. I tore my eyes away and focused on Trinity, my brain had completely blanked. What had she been saying?

"Is he here to see you?" Trinity asked.

"Who? Jake? No," I said, maybe too quickly. "At least I don't think so."

"Girl, you better practice your poker face because, wow."

"What?"

"You're blushing."

"No, I'm not," I protested, even though the temperature in the room had changed.

"Well, now you're in denial."

I looked back toward Jake, but he wasn't there. He'd gone up to the front. Maybe he was only here to buy something. I was surprised how that thought disappointed me.

"Why don't you go, you know, help him out," Trinity said.

I laughed. "Trinity."

"What?"

"I'm on break and sitting here with you having a very serious discussion about drama club."

She pushed back from the table, the Kermit chair screeching across the floor, and stood up. "Oh, us? We're done. Go up there and hook him up with one of those chocolate croissants. Or your number. You know you want to."

"Omigod, no," I said, picking up her empty plate.

She took a few steps backward toward the door. "Read that script. And answer your texts. Wait on that boy. Bye, Jake!"

She yelled the last part across the room before ducking out the front door with a huge-ass grin. I didn't even have to turn around to know that people were staring. I could feel it. I focused on the plate and cups I was holding as I walked back toward the counter, one foot in front of the other, willing my skin to become cooler, willing my heart to slow down.

Why was I so nervous?

I barely looked up until Jake's sneakers came into my line of view. He had the sort of grin on his face one would expect when realizing they'd been the topic of conversation.

"Hey," I said.

"Hi," he answered.

We looked at each other for a few long seconds, when Marnie interrupted.

"Here's your lemonade," she said, sliding the to-go cup toward Jake.

"I suppose you're going to want to extend your break," Marnie said, amused smile on her face. Was it that obvious? I mean, I really couldn't, I'd already spent most of my break with Trinity. Maybe Jake was just passing through. I put the dirty dishes in the bus bin before answering her.

"I think I have about five minutes left anyway," I said.

"No more than ten, starting now," she said, tapping her wrist, and winking.

I turned to Jake, who had that same wide grin on his face as before. Oh, damn, had he seen her wink? Why did she wink anyway?

"I don't want to put you out or anything, I'm just here for the lemonade," he said, lifting his cup.

"Oh, sure," I said.

"Just kidding, I do actually want to talk to you about something."

My heart dropped to my feet. What could he possibly want to talk to me about? I scanned the dining area. No vacant tables. Without thinking I motioned for him to come with me to the back. He widened his eyes, as if to ask *Is that really okay?* then followed through the double doors and into the break room.

"We can talk here," I said, gesturing for him to sit next to me on the couch. It took him a moment to settle down, he barely opened his mouth before I started in.

"Is this about the other day?"

"Ah . . . what do you mean?"

"The hallway, with me and Ash."

His brows pulled together in confusion. I continued.

"I'm sorry for not saying more to you. Right before you saw us, Ash and I had a fight. Not a fight really, more like a misunderstanding. So, if the vibe was off, that was why. I was worried you might bring up the day we went to Alex's bench."

"Oh, okay." he said. "Why?"

*Because I wondered what it would be like to kiss you*, I thought. And try as I might, my mind still went there when I looked at him. Maybe it was the white T-shirt, or the concerned look in his eyes.

"I don't really talk to Ash about Alex. When Ash is happy, or at least seems to be, I don't want to do or say anything to bring her down. Ash lost her brother. Her loss is bigger than mine."

He chewed on his straw, then put the lemonade down on the table. "Why do you do that? You were his girlfriend. You lost him too."

There he was. Seeing me again.

"Well, yeah, but . . . How do you do that?"

"Do what?"

"Say exactly what I need to hear in the moment."

He shrugged. "Maybe because I know what it's like."

"Sometimes I manage, even for a moment or two, not to think of Alex at all. Then I feel like shit. I can't sleep some nights, there's times I even think I see him or hear him in the hall at school. We only dated for two and a half months. I should be over this by now, right? What's wrong with me?"

"Oh God, Sarah, nothing. Dr. Hipster says—"

"Wait, Dr. Hipster?"

He hesitated, sat up a little straighter. "Yeah, he's my therapist."

"Is that really his name?"

He laughed. "No, he just has this beard, and wears skinny jeans, and, well, that's not important," he said. "Grief is sneaky and weird, and there's no right way to experience it. You just gotta go through it."

"So, you have trouble too?"

He nodded. "That's kind of why I'm here. I have a proposition for you."

"Proposition?"

"Holly Matthews is putting together an event to raise money for a scholarship, in Alex's name. She asked me if I wanted to help out, and now I'm asking you. I thought maybe it would help to be involved. A way to honor Alex."

"I don't know if I can be around her, Jake."

"You don't have to be, not that much anyway. I'm cochair, you'd be working with me."

Working with Jake? The idea both freaked me out and made me happy.

"Can I think about it?"

october

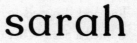

# sarah

THE FIRST WEEK IN OCTOBER, TRINITY SENT OUT TEXT
blasts with audition reminders almost daily.

Next Wednesday! Be there!

Hit us with your best!

Go hard or stay home!

Wednesday morning, I was ready. I'd gone over possible scenes
a few different times with Mom, by myself, and even with Marnie during my shift at Adele's over the weekend. Whenever I felt
unsure, I'd remember the talk I had with Trini—she'd said there
was a part or two she'd imagined me in—that had to be good,
right? Still, it didn't guarantee anything, and as the day wore on
and auditions loomed closer, the butterflies in my stomach decided
to dust off their wings and throw a rave. If I thought hard enough
about it, I could have thrown up.

This was all normal. Butterflies meant you cared. Butterflies
meant you could use that nervous energy and make it work for
your audition. At least that's what Mr. Rutledge always said. I took
a deep breath as I walked to auditions and had just about calmed
myself down with a little mental pep talk, until I turned the corner
in the hallway and saw the crowd.

There was a larger turnout than I'd ever seen, some familiar faces, but a lot of new ones too. I planted myself at the end of the line and dropped my backpack, suddenly realizing how much I wanted a part. What if I blew it?

The main stage was in the gym, but the auditions were being held in a neighboring classroom because of basketball practice. The thundering of feet on the boards resounded through the hallway and on instinct I walked over to take a peek through the window to catch a glimpse of Alex. My breath stopped, and I snapped my seed bead bracelet. These momentary flashes happened less lately, but it was always slightly jarring to remind myself I wouldn't see him. He was gone.

Trinity and Cullyn came out of the classroom. She had a wide grin on her face—this was her domain, and she owned it. She clapped to get everyone's attention. I hurried back to my place. Cullyn held a clipboard and began walking down the line.

"Welcome, everyone! Most of you know the drill. This could be a while. Cullyn's taking down cell numbers, so if you need to step out for anything, we'll be able to contact you. That's not an invite to get lost. Be forewarned you'll have five minutes to return. We'll be doing individual readings first, where myself or Mr. Rutledge will be reading with you. Then we're going to read in different groups. What you read and/or who you read with does not necessarily reflect the part you'll be cast in. Can't wait to see what you've got. Break a leg!" she said, walking back into the classroom.

I peered down the line, there were about thirty people ahead of me. Cullyn smiled as he handed me the clipboard. My palm was so sweaty, I worried the pen would slip out of my hand as I wrote my number on the contact sheet.

"How long do you think it'll be?" I asked.

"Hard to tell," he said, peering at the line. "You know Trini though. It could take twenty minutes or two hours, depending on her mood. Hang tight, this is only the first round. You're not nervous, are you?" he teased.

"No, not at all," I lied, handing him the clipboard.

The line moved quicker than I'd anticipated. When I was three away from the front, Cullyn handed me the sides for the audition. I read them through and smiled. It was a scene I was familiar with, and even though I heard what Trini said about not necessarily reading for the part you'd get, I secretly hoped that she was thinking of casting me in the role I was reading.

I took a deep breath before heading into the classroom. I'd known both Trinity and Mr. Rutledge since freshman year, but at the moment they were complete strangers. My heart raced. I'd imagined being able to make the gestures for the scene, but I clutched the pages like a security blanket. Why hadn't I taken a sip of water before I came in? Damn.

"Take a moment to get into character," Trini said.

I nodded, took in another breath, let it out slow.

*You got this!* I thought.

And as Mr. Rutledge fed me lines, I began to relax. The scene I was reading was about a woman who had come to Maine to see the northern lights and say goodbye to her dead husband. In her hand she carried a paper bag that contained the pieces of her broken heart. I'd rehearsed it about a dozen times at home. It was a lighthearted, hopeful part, but as I continued, I could feel my throat getting tight. Thoughts of Alex flooded my brain. I stopped, turned my back to Trinity and Mr. Rutledge.

There was nothing in the play or the classroom that reminded me of Alex. I'd never thought this much about him when I rehearsed the scene either. If anything, I thought I could bring some sort of wistfulness to the part. Instead, I was overwhelmed by a wave of sadness that came out of nowhere. I felt a hand on my back.

"Hey, you okay?" Trinity asked.

I swiped my face with the sleeve of my sweater.

"Yeah, I don't know what happened. I think I could go again," I said, even though I wasn't sure that was true. Trini shook her head.

"Nope, we got enough. Go take a breather. Have some water. It'll probably be about a half an hour till the next call."

"Half an hour," I repeated. I waved off the small bottle of water Mr. Rutledge held out.

"No, thanks, I have some," I said. Trini took the pages from my hand.

Both of them were all business. I forced a smile, trying to push down another wave of sadness, this time brought on by my completely botching the audition. I grabbed my backpack and headed out, not even looking at anyone else in line. I moved fast down the hallway, ignoring the call of my name. I needed to get outside before I burst into tears again.

I pushed through the front doors of school and walked over to the nearest bench to sit down. It was chilly but bearable, maybe the shock of cold helped snap me out of whatever I'd been feeling because after a few breaths, I began to relax. I searched my backpack for a tissue, ended up using the sleeve of my sweater again.

My phone buzzed.

A text from Cullyn.

**You're partnered with Dylan. He's looking for you.**

That gave me a slight boost of confidence. Dylan was always cast, so I doubted they'd pair me with him if I'd totally blown it. Still, I wasn't ready to be found, at least not for another five minutes. I fished my water bottle out of my backpack and took a few sips. The front doors of school were thrown open, and a group of boys spilled out.

Basketball practice was over.

The group was halfway through the parking lot before Jake came out of the building. Hoodie up, backpack slung over his shoulder. I wanted to call out but didn't. He looked my way, did a double take, and walked over. That wave of sadness threatened to take over again. What was wrong with me?

"Hey, what's—" He stopped, brows furrowed. "Are you okay?"

I nodded and looked up as if that would stop tears from spilling out. I hid my face with the sleeve of my sweater, dried my eyes. Jake's backpack hit the ground. He sat next to me; skin flushed from practice, dark hair slightly damp and curling up at the ends. Geez, for someone I barely knew, Jake saw a side of me I usually managed to keep hidden.

"I totally botched my audition," I said.

"Aw, shit, really? I bet it's not as bad as you think," he said.

"It was pretty bad," I said.

"Why, what happened?"

"I kind of burst into tears in the middle of my dialogue," I said.

He looked confused. "That sounds like it could be a good thing, unless you know, it's a comedy or something."

I chuckled. "It was definitely an unexpected thing."

"Why?"

"I was in the middle of the scene, things were going pretty well, and out of nowhere Alex just popped into my head, and I lost it. Has that ever happened to you? Like, you could be having a perfectly normal day and then this sadness just—"

"Drop-kicks you into next Wednesday?" he finished.

"Omigod, yes!"

"Nope, I have no idea what that feels like," he said, deadpan.

"So that's happened to you, then?"

He took a breath, looked at me squarely, a little solemn. "All the time."

Those eyes. *Whoosh.* I blinked.

"What would Dr. Hipster have to say about it?" I asked, trying to recover from that damn *whoosh.*

He crossed his arms, put a stern look on his face, and stroked an invisible beard. "Jake, the brain is mysterious. It protects you, only gives you as much as you can handle in any moment," he said in a deep voice.

I laughed. "Maybe you should audition for the play."

He scoffed. "Definitely not in my wheelhouse."

"So, what? My brain felt like being a jerk during auditions?"

"You must have let your guard down," he said, in his normal voice. "That's when it happens to me. Or maybe you're tired. Stressed."

"All of the above, I guess," I answered. "How are you doing?"

"Welp, I still see Dr. Hipster. Things have been okay though.

Some days are better than others. Today is a good day. Especially now."

My cheeks warmed. Whenever Jake looked at me, I felt so understood. I'd been on the fence about helping with the scholarship committee, but sitting there with him once again, as he helped me get out of my head, made me hop right off into yes.

"Hey, I never gave you an answer about the scholarship committee. I'll do it," I said. "Do you . . . do you need my number or anything?" I asked.

"That would probably be helpful," he said. "You know, in case of refreshment emergencies."

"Of course, refreshments are very serious business," I joked, as I shared my number. "So many things to consider."

"Cool. I'll keep you in the loop."

"Great," I said. I wanted to say more, like he could call or text me if he ever felt like talking, but what would that imply? We'd had these intense emotional moments, then went on with our own lives. All I knew is that I always felt lighter when I spent time with him. Maybe we could actually be friends.

"Sarah!"

We both looked toward the front doors of school. Dylan Jacobs was there waving at me.

"We're up in ten, feel like running lines?" he called.

"Sure, I'll be right there, gimme a minute," I said, shoving my water bottle into my backpack and zipping it up. Dylan kept standing there, watching. I turned back to Jake. "Sorry, I almost forgot I was in the middle of auditions."

"Well, good luck," he said.

I stood up, slung my backpack over my shoulder. "It's break a leg."

"I'm sorry?"

"Break a leg—it's better to say that—good luck is supposed to be bad luck for actors. A superstition," I said, realizing I was prolonging our goodbye. Not because I wanted to hit him up with some theater knowledge but because I wanted to stay there and talk with him longer.

"Didn't know that," he said.

"Um, okay, then," I took a few steps backward before heading toward the building. Dylan held the door open, eyebrows raised as if he'd just uncovered the juiciest bit of gossip. Right before I hit the stairs, I turned back toward Jake. He was still sitting on the bench, checking his phone as I walked back.

"Jake," I said.

He looked up, surprised.

"If you ever wanted . . . Would it be okay . . . You know, it was so nice . . ." I spluttered, losing my train of thought as his lips curled into a soft side-smile. Who did I even think I was? What was I doing? "Maybe we could talk sometime, you know, I could call you, or you could call me, if, you know, you wanted to. About more than refreshments."

He raised his eyebrows, laughed to himself.

Maybe I'd blown it worse than I did in the audition.

"All right, see ya," I said, turning fast, worried that I'd just messed up. I took the stairs two at a time and trotted toward Dylan.

"What was that about?" he asked, letting the door close behind us.

"What was *what* about?" I asked.

"You and Jake Hobbs." His tone was playful, suggestive.

"It's not like that. We're just friends. I've been meaning to ask you; do you know when the pilot of *Doppelgängers* is going to be on? We should have a watch party," I said, changing the conversation to Dylan's favorite subject—his career. It worked.

My phone buzzed.

I discreetly checked it before slipping it into my backpack. Smiled.

A message from Jake.

**Break a leg, Walsh.**

# jake

I'D BEEN IN THE DREAM FOREST AGAIN, THICK TREES
and invisible hands pulling at me, but I managed to fight them
off. Bolt from the scene. I kept telling myself to wake up. I became
vaguely aware that the panic from my dream had bled over into real
life, as I threw off my covers and ran out of my room. By the time I
was fully awake, I was already slamming the door to the bathroom,
as if the nightmare was following me. My heart thrummed in my
ears. My throat was sore. Had I yelled? I vaguely remembered yelling.

I flicked on the wall switch. My eyes stung from the sudden
plunge into the light as I sat on the rim of the bathtub to collect
my thoughts.

Creaking floorboards caught my attention.

A wrap on the door, two efficient knocks.

Dad.

"Yeah?"

"You okay?"

Trick question because physically? I was fine. Shaken, but fine.
But I wanted these nightmares to stop. They'd slowed down for
sure, but I couldn't wait until the whole episode was in my rearview

mirror. What if I did go clear across the country for college, only to wake up yelling, so I'd be *that* roommate. The weird one you tell your friends back home about.

"Jake?"

"Yeah, Dad, I'm good."

"Need anything? I'll be up for a bit, want some tea or something?"

I chuckled. What was with my parents and warm drinks?

"No, thanks. What time is it?"

"After midnight," he said. "Okay, then, you know where to find me if you need me."

I thought about going for a run, but it was legit cold out. NyQuil? I'd used that a few times out of desperation to knock me out and always woke up feeling groggy. Netflix? Meditation app?

*"You should call Sarah."*

*Yeah, right. She's probably not up now.*

*"She said to call her."*

*No, she implied I could call her if I wanted, and she never specified middle of the night. It's too late.*

*"Then text her, you know you want to."*

*You really want me to make a move on your girlfriend?*

*"Well, I can't. You should go for it."*

I picked up my phone from the charging dock. Twelve forty-five.

Maybe it was too late.

I opened my message app. Tapped in a word.

Hey.

Stared at it, almost went to delete it but didn't.

*"What are you waiting for?"*

I pressed Send before I could change my mind. A text was good, and if she didn't reply, or wasn't awake, I could tell her I'd texted her on accident.

One minute passed.

Two minutes passed.

Nada.

Nothing ventured, nothing gained.

My phone buzzed.

**Hey.**

I sat up.

**You awake?** I tapped into the phone, then deleted.

**Fancy a chat?** Delete, delete, delete. When had I become British?

**Wanna talk?**

*"Press Send already, idiot."*

I pressed Send.

My phone rang.

I picked up.

"Hey," I said.

"Hi, everything okay?"

I leaned back onto my pillows, smiled at the sound of her voice. "No, it's not. I'm really losing sleep over the refreshments situation. Can't decide if we should go for a classic like chocolate chip cookies or get those fancy ones that are all different colors, what are they called again?"

"Macarons?"

"Yeah, those, what do you think?"

"Hmmm, I don't know. Do you think Saint Aedan's is ready for something as sophisticated as a macaron?"

"Are you're implying I'm not sophisticated enough?"

"Of course not," she answered.

"But didn't you compare me to a chocolate chip cookie?"

She laughed. "No, I said you looked like someone who would *like* chocolate chip cookies. All the best people like chocolate chip cookies. But you can't really go wrong with either. Might be fun to have macarons in our school colors."

My flirtatious refreshment banter had run its course. I cut to the chase.

"It's about time you called, I've only been waiting all weekend to find out if you got that part."

"Really? No way."

"You didn't get the part?"

"Oh, yeah, I did get the part, the one I read for, but I thought I told you to call me if you wanted. Then when you didn't, I figured you didn't want to, and, well, you know, any time you want to chime in and save me, feel free."

"Is it okay to say congratulations for getting the part? Or is that bad luck too?"

"It's fine to say congrats. Thank you."

"Is it a big part?"

"It's an ensemble play. Lots of parts, but I guess it's a biggish part in the scene I'm in."

"So, you can get up onstage and everything and not be nervous?"

"Well, yeah, I'm nervous, but once I start, I don't know—I kind of forget where I am, and it's not like I'm on a stage at all.

That probably sounds strange."

"No, I get it, sometimes I feel that way on the court. When I'm focused in a game it doesn't matter what's going on. A UFO could land in the parking lot and it wouldn't even register."

She chuckled. "Right, well, there you go."

"You just seem so—"

"Oh God, no, don't say it."

"Shy?"

She groaned.

"I'm not. Not really. I just don't say anything unless I have something to say. Acting is easy. Someone else gives me the lines. I speak. When I have to make conversation myself, I kind of zone out sometimes. Worry about what I'm going to say next."

"You've never seemed that way with me."

"You're . . . different," she said, low.

I liked how she said it, with a pause. The word had weight. If I was flirting, I'd ask her different how, but this was our first call. Should just keep things friendly.

"What are you doing up so late anyway, it's a school night," I teased.

"This from the guy who texts me at quarter to one?" she said. "I had trouble falling asleep. I got sucked into a YouTube vortex of animal rescue videos, then felt too wired to settle down."

"Animal rescue videos?"

"Yes, seeing all those happily ever afters for puppies and kittens helps keep away the general existential dread. Why are you up?"

There was something about being on the phone in the dark, under my fake canopy of stars that felt almost confessional. I sunk deeper into my bed.

"I have nightmares sometimes. It's hard to get back to sleep. Existential dread is pretty much my vibe."

"What do you dream about?"

Could I really let her into my weird little world?

"Sorry, that was rude, you don't have to answer if it's too personal."

"It wasn't rude," I assured her. "I have nightmares about that night at the cliffs. It's not like I relive it or anything, but I know I'm there, only it looks different. It's good to see Alex for like a second, like it never happened, but then I remember and he . . . it's not like I talk to him or anything. Sometimes I just wake up with a feeling but can't remember why. Then I turn on Netflix. Or do a college search. Or, you know, text you."

She was silent. Oh shit. Well, it was nice while it lasted.

"I'm glad you texted me," she said finally. "You can do that, you know, if you wake up like that again. I don't mind. If I'm up, I'll text you back."

"Definitely," I said. I almost asked if I could call her at other times too but didn't.

"I never dream about Alex."

*"The conversation always comes back to me, doesn't it?"*

"Sorry," I said, because I really didn't know what to say to that. It had been nice, hearing her say I could text her whenever, but was it just because of Alex? Did it matter? He was the reason we were . . . well, whatever it was we were. Sort of friends?

"I don't even have many pictures of us together, a few random selfies here and there. I have one goofy Snapchat that I managed to save, but he wasn't really into that. And I read our texts, and I can almost imagine he'd text me at any moment."

*"Tell her you hear me in your head."*

*Not ready to divulge that gem, Alex.*

"I guess that sounds tragic," she said.

"No, I think it's normal," I said.

"I know I should move on, just don't know how to do that."

"Have you . . . Are you interested in anyone?" I asked.

Blatant dig for information alert.

"Oh, um . . . Sorry, Jake, I have to go, bye!"

"Sarah? Sarah?"

Did she really just hang up on me?

# sarah

THE FOOTSTEPS GOT CLOSER. I PUT MY HEAD ON THE pillow, jammed my eyes shut, but then tried to relax them, because who sleeps with their eyes screwed up like that? I slipped my phone under the pillow. I thought I'd been quiet, but I guess at one in the morning any noise in the apartment was worthy of investigation. The door to my room opened.

I considered myself a decent actress, sleeping should be easy, right? It wasn't. I tried not to flinch, focused on my breath, did not want to pull one of those fake wake-up, yawn, *What time is it?* moves. I'm sure my mother would have seen right through that. Then taken my phone to charge in the kitchen for the night.

The footsteps came over to my bed, paused.

*Focus, Sarah.*

My light snapped off. The footsteps retreated, the door snicked shut. I opened my eyes, listened as my mom got a glass of water from the kitchen and headed back to her room. When I heard her bedroom door close, I slid my phone out from under the pillow. Should I call Jake back? Maybe ending the "Are you interested in anyone?" conversation before it even got started was a good thing.

Was I interested in anyone?

Ash and Mike had been dropping subtle hints that Buzz was sort of into me. Not that they had to, I could feel it a little too, in the way he looked at me or how he teased me over lunch. And honest? It wouldn't be awful. Buzz was cute, we got along okay, maybe he was a little immature at times, but that could be charming, right? I guess creating a list of someone's good attributes to convince you that you're interested in them isn't a great sign.

Alex was the last person I'd kissed, and I held on to that like a talisman.

It was the one thing only I had claim to. I was the last person he kissed. And even thinking about kissing someone else—like the *whoosh* I felt when I saw Jake—made me feel like I was cheating. Could you really cheat on a memory though?

I would kiss someone sooner or later, I knew that. Hell, I *had* to kiss Dylan Jacobs more than once in our *Almost, Maine* scene. A fake kiss was still a kiss, and it would change that particular status, make it fade even more. And it wasn't even like the last kiss was monumental. It was a kiss that you gave someone when you thought you were going to see them again. A brush across the lips. A *See you later I have to get back to work* kiss.

Not like our first kiss.

After the night at Adele's, when we realized our feelings were mutual, Alex drove me home. I kept waiting for him to lean over, maybe at a light, maybe when he dropped me off. My heart was nearly beating out of my chest when he walked me to the door of my building, but it didn't happen then either. We stood there looking at each other for what felt like forever, and just when I thought he'd lean in, he said bye and left. Was he just screwing with me? I wasn't sure enough of myself to make the first move.

We texted and talked and flirted in the hallways at school, so I knew the conversation at Adele's had been real. Our first kiss didn't happen until the weekend after we told Ash. He invited me over. And it felt like any other night at the McKennas'. Well, at first. Gathering snacks, settling in, perusing Netflix trailers. Alex grabbed a fleece blanket and put it over the two of us, our legs stretched out and sharing the same ottoman.

I couldn't think of anything else but being next to him. Hip to hip, thigh to thigh, our socked feet playfully knocking into each other, his arm casually draped over my shoulder. I didn't want to move, for fear of breaking the spell. I was so hyperaware of my peripheral space that I could barely follow the sci-fi movie he had picked.

"There's something I need to do," he said, turning toward me. It happened so fast, but slow at the same time. I turned and his lips were on mine, I barely had time to think. Maybe we'd been right to wait, because when I felt his hands in my hair, his body pressed into mine, I just about melted. He pulled away, kissed the tip of my nose, and smiled.

"What took you so long?" I asked, catching my breath.

"I knew once I kissed you, I wouldn't want to stop," he whispered, planting his lips on mine again as we leaned back into the couch.

All these months later, I could still feel that heat. I wondered if I would ever, could ever, feel that way about anybody again.

I opened the photos app on my phone, went to the album I'd created with pictures of Alex. We'd taken a few goofy couple selfies, and I had one or two of him alone, and the snap he'd sent me when I complained he never sent me any. I let it play. He'd been coming over to my place so we could go for a walk.

*I'm on my way to see you, babe. Did I really just call you babe? Is that okay? Just sort of rolled off my tongue. Was that a good enough snap?*

The sound of his voice brought tears to my eyes, and I knew I had to stop doing this to myself. It wasn't comforting like it had been; it felt strange. And unhealthy. Oh God, and I'd shared the fact that I looked through these photos with Jake. *Cringey*. He probably thought I was a complete weirdo. Maybe I was a complete weirdo.

I texted Jake.

**Mom almost caught me. Talk soon?**

A moment later he texted.

**Sure. Nite.**

Hopefully he'd forget what we'd been talking about.

Early the next night I sat on my bed reading over *Almost, Maine*, wondering if I should even bother calling Jake. *Sure* didn't actually seem like that strong of a word. And I hadn't seen him all day, but maybe that was because I hadn't really looked for him. What if *sure* was snide? Maybe he didn't think I would call him back.

There was a knock at my door.

"Come in," I said.

The door creaked open. Mom leaned against the doorjamb. It was a work-from-home day for her, and she was casual in jeans and a tee.

"Got caught up in a spread sheet and totally flaked on dinner. Feel like heading over to Sophie's place?"

Adele's had been open for ten years and Mom still referred to it as Sophie's place when she talked to me.

"Yes, that would be great. A croque monsieur will cure all my problems," I said.

She laughed. "Homework that bad, huh?"

"Eh, you know, just drama club, homework, life," I said, grabbing my shoes.

"No need to rush, I have to finish something up. Be ready in fifteen minutes," Mom said.

Adele's was pretty busy for a weekday night; it felt nice being on the other side of the counter. After we ordered our food, I picked the table by the window with the Kermit chair.

Mom shook her head as I sat down. "Why would anyone willingly sit in that chair?"

"There's just something about it," I said, leaning into the high back. Alex was right, it did feel like I could host a talk show. I ran my hands along the arms, closed my eyes. I started falling into memories. No. *No.* I opened my eyes and snapped the seed bead bracelet. Mom noticed.

"So, what's going on with drama club, homework, life? It feels like we haven't talked in a while," she said, taking a sip of her iced tea.

"Mom, we hung out over the weekend," I said.

"I know, but bingeing *The Office* with pad thai is not the same as really talking. I've been so busy lately with work. Just wondering how you're *really* doing."

Mom had been great last spring after Alex died. That was when she started working at home two days a week, so she could be there when I got in from school. She knew loss herself. I was only a year old when my father died from an aneurysm on his morning jog. It was weird to think how much that one event effected the trajectory of our lives, but I have no memory of him, only pictures.

Sometimes when I looked at my mom's carefully curated scrapbooks, I could catch a glimpse of myself in my dad's pale eyes, the angle of his nose, the generous smile that dipped down slightly on the right side of his face. There were pictures from when Mom and Dad were in college, dating, and then their wedding. There were even some of me. Dad holding a squished-face baby me, wrapped in a striped blanket. Him holding my hands, arms stretched over my head as I attempted my first steps.

When I was younger, I liked to ask Mom questions about him. I felt something like nostalgia when I looked at those pictures, but for nothing I ever experienced, maybe for a life that might have been? It never upset me though. Mom, on occasion, could get teary-eyed and *that* is what made me sad, but I never understood it.

Not that I was comparing losing Alex to my mom losing a spouse, but I knew I never had to ignore my sadness with her. It was also why when she said things like "loss is a part of being human," I believed her. She wasn't just saying pretty words to make me feel better; I knew she lived them herself.

"Things are okay," I said. "I'm really looking forward to the play. It's nice to have something to occupy my mind, well, other than school."

"What's the play you're doing again? Something about Maine?"

"*Almost, Maine*," I said, smiling. We hadn't really started hard-core rehearsals yet, but it was fun losing myself in a completely fictitious life.

"That's right, Sophie looked it up on YouTube. I hear there's some kissing," she said, widening her eyes.

Why was everyone so obsessed with the kissing? I'd never done a stage kiss before, oddly it wasn't something I was actually looking forward to, even though I'd joked about it with Trinity. How was it not awkward?

"We didn't block out that part yet. I think I'm going to suggest we wait to kiss each other until opening night. Maybe the element of surprise will work better."

Mom smiled. "I don't know, maybe it's, you know, time to have a little fun again, Sarah."

Had she really just said that? "Mom!"

A new server I didn't recognize came to the table with our food. I was grateful for the interruption. He put Mom's soup down in front of me, my croque monsieur in front of her, and we switched as he walked away. Aunt Sophie came up to the table with a small plate of brightly colored macarons.

"Hey, this is a nice surprise," she said, giving Mom's shoulder a squeeze.

"We needed a little pick-me-up," Mom said, breaking through the crusted top of her French onion soup with her spoon. I took a bite of my sandwich. Perfection.

"Make sure you save some room for these, I need my taste tester," Aunt Sophie said, then pointed out each new autumn flavor. Caramel apple. Pumpkin cheesecake. Pomegranate goat cheese.

"Goat cheese? Soph, really?" my mom asked.

"The goat cheese ones are always popular," I said.

"Yes, big sis, get with the program," she said. "Speaking of popular, your friend came in asking for you today."

"Really, who?"

"The tall boy who comes in for lemonade," she said.

I laughed, I couldn't help it. Jake would probably laugh at her description too. My blood ran hot. I bit back a smile, but it was futile. I could feel the flush across the bridge of my nose.

"That would be Jake Hobbs," I said.

"Very tall, very cute. Someone I would have called a total hottie back in the day," my aunt said.

"A hottie, huh?" Mom asked.

"Ew, please stop being gross," I begged them. "We're working on something together. I've actually been meaning to talk to you, Aunt Sophie. There's going to be a fundraiser to create a scholarship in Alex's name. I'm on refreshments, so I was hoping, maybe, we could—"

"Get some free stuff?" she asked.

I nodded. She smiled.

"For my favorite niece, of course," she said. Someone in the kitchen beckoned my aunt, and Mom and I went back to dinner.

"I think that's great you are doing something to honor Alex," Mom said. "When did you decide to participate?"

"Oh, a week or so ago."

"Isn't Jake Hobbs the boy who was with him that night at the park?"

I stopped mid-chew. Sometimes I forgot that Alex's death was a huge local news story. Her question reminded me of what Jake had said when we went to see the memorial bench. How he wanted to go somewhere far away where no one knew him as the guy who was with Alex the night he fell. People really did link him with that. It must have sucked.

"Yes, but he's more than that. He was Alex's best friend."

"Of course," she said. "I think it's great that you are working on the scholarship, Sarah. It's good to see you getting involved again."

"Feels good too," I said, shutting down any further discussion involving Jake.

Our talk veered toward school, SATs, and maybe how we should make a list of colleges I wanted to visit. Although that big life stuff unsettled me even more than hearing Jake's name come out of my mother's mouth. A life beyond high school hardly seemed fathomable at the moment.

I had just taken a bite out of the caramel apple—*Omigod, so damn good*—macaron, when I noticed a youngish guy setting up a microphone near the corner of the room. He was in front of the large, old-fashioned breakfront, and the server who had given us our dinner was helping him move some of the tables around. Aunt Sophie trotted over to supervise.

"Bran Russo," I said, realizing that the youngish guy was from Saint Aedan's. He was in jazz band with Ash.

"Sorry?" Mom said, following my line of vision.

"I know that guy."

My aunt came back over to the table. "How'd you like the caramel apple?"

"Amazing," I said. "What's going on?"

I gestured toward Bran, who saw me and waved. I waved back.

"Oh, my friend from the music school around the corner convinced me to let a few of his advanced students get some experience playing live. Kind of low-key, background stuff. He's trying to talk me into having a showcase night for the holidays."

"Really?"

"You think it's a good idea? Anytime I've tried to do live stuff here, it didn't seem to go over too well."

"Sounds fun," Mom said.

I immediately thought of Ash. "Is it just open to his students?"

"Why? Know someone who would be interested?"

"Yeah, I think I do."

# jake

"CRUSADERS ASSEMBLE!" COACH YELLED.

We'd been practicing for almost two months, and we were finally going to have a scrimmage game against JV. I tossed the ball I'd been using for shooting drills into the bin and jogged over to the sidelines, where my teammates were in a loose huddle around Coach. I sidled next to Taj, who made space. Coach called out our starting positions.

"Elliot, point; Whittaker, shooting guard; Boyle, small forward; Jones, power; Hobbs, big."

"Big?" I asked, not sure if I'd heard him right. I hadn't played center since middle school, when I was head and shoulders above pretty much everyone. Sometimes Coach switched it up, but I'd found my groove in shooting guard, or at least I'd thought so.

"Trying something new, Hobbs, go with it," he said.

I walked to center court for the tip-off. Looked to see who'd be able to snatch it. Taj was my best bet, but Bash Elliot raised his brow and tapped his shoulder, which I think was supposed to mean something along the lines of *Bring it my way*. Eff that.

Maybe not team thinking or the thoughts of a captain, but hell, a little good-natured hazing on the court might set his ass straight.

I got into position, ready to spring. Tapped to Taj. Game on. We found our rhythm soon enough, it's not like JV was pressing that hard. Ten minutes in, we were up by eleven. At the end of the first quarter, we gathered in a loose huddle around Coach.

"You don't have to wipe the boards with 'em, but I like the hustle I'm seeing," Coach said. "Hobbs. Whittaker. Elliot's been open. He needs to see some action. Work on your screen this next round. I want to see teamwork. Okay, bring it in."

We all put our hands together. "One . . . Two . . . Three . . . Crusaders."

Walking back onto the court, Bash came up beside me.

"I know you saw I was open," he said.

"I don't know what you're talking about," I answered.

"Just pass it to me, I know what I'm doing," he said.

"Debatable."

"What?"

I looked at Bash. He was just so eager. Annoying.

"Your handles are shit," I said, tossing back the insult about me I'd overheard. "Watch yourself."

Before he could say anything, the quarter began. JV had the ball. We backed off a bit. They scored three buckets before we kicked it up again. When they missed their next lay-up, I caught the rebound and drove the ball toward our basket. They were on us hard. Jacked up from tightening the score. Taj set the screen. It should have been an easy pick and roll, but their defense was strong. I searched for a clear path out. My body knew what to do.

I pivoted to pass to Alex.

And for a split second, I expected to see him when I turned around.

Open.

Hungry.

Waiting for the pass to get us a three-point.

My mind thought Alex, my eyes landed on Bash.

Everything became sharp and unfamiliar. Like someone had snapped their fingers and I ended up in a completely different place. Bash was red in the face, and he was yelling something. My hand didn't feel like a part of my body. This one stutter cost us the ball. The JV center took possession, while my brain tried to make sense of what happened. My heartbeat in my ear, fast and hard. My feet planted to the ground. The air in the gym suddenly stagnant. I was aware, but couldn't move, just watched as my team raced down the court and the JV center scored an easy bucket.

I tried to take a breath but couldn't. My heart wouldn't slow down. I stood paralyzed as both teams thundered down toward me. I put my hands on my knees, tried to catch my breath. Jammed my eyes shut as the room began to spin.

No, no, no, no, no. This was not happening.

Not again.

I was vaguely aware of a whistle. A hand on my shoulder.

"Hobbs, dude, you okay?"

I opened my eyes. Took stock of what I saw.

Gym floor. Shoes. Scrimmage with JV.

*Basketball practice, Jake. You're not going to die.*

"Jake, can you stand up straight?"

I took a slow breath, let the air fill my lungs.

I nodded, stood up. Another wave of dizziness hit me.

Assistant coach McGuire looked me over, one eye, then the other.

"I'm cool. Just need to sit down," I said, shrugging off his help.

Once everyone was satisfied that I wasn't about to pass out, the game continued. I sat on the bench, nursing a Gatorade and trying to shake the foggy, spaced-out feeling in my brain. At least my heartrate had returned to normal.

The first time I had a panic attack was at Alex's funeral. Dr. Hipster told me what to do if I ever felt one coming on again. To focus. Take stock of where I was. Be present. It freaked me out that it could happen anywhere. What if it happened during a real game? I couldn't think of that.

I headed off to the locker room before the scrimmage was over. I told Coach I still felt sick, but in reality, I wanted to leave before I had to face anyone.

I was just zipping up my backpack when my teammates began filing in, hyped up from the win over JV. I hooked my backpack over my shoulder and acknowledged Pat and Taj with a nod. Without warning Bash was in my face.

"*My* handles are shit? What the hell was that out there?"

"Bash, don't," Taj said, shaking his head.

"Oh, so you two give me shit all you want, and I'm supposed to take it. I can run circles around both of you," he said, bumping past me to get to his locker.

A thread of insults filled my head, I picked the one that would hit him the hardest.

"You'll never handle the ball like McKenna."

Bash's jaw twitched, he shook his head and let out a derisive snort.

"Yeah, well, he's not handling much of anything anymore, is he?"

The locker room got quiet.

"What did you say?"

"You fucking heard me," he said.

I had fucking heard him but couldn't believe anyone could be that much of an asshole. The anger started in my feet, bolted right through me. I dropped my backpack and lunged at him. He was not prepared and almost toppled over. I grabbed his jersey with both fists, spun him around and slammed him into the locker. Taj and Pat were immediately at my side.

"Not worth it, not worth it, not worth it," they kept saying, trying to separate us.

"Show some fucking respect," I said through gritted teeth.

Bash said nothing, just stared at me blankly. He opened his mouth, but I shut him down. "You even say his name again, you won't be running circles around anyone."

I let go, Pat pulled me back. I kept glaring at Bash until he finally looked away. I had instant remorse for threatening him that way, but I wasn't about to apologize for any of it.

"We cool?" Taj said, looking between us.

I grabbed my backpack and stormed out.


I texted Sarah at eleven.

Hey.

She called right away, spoke before I even said hello.

"Sorry I didn't call back the other night. I didn't know if I should. Then I went out with my mom the next day, well, and . . . you know."

How quickly she called and the lightness in her voice brought a smile to my face. I felt my body relax for the first time since I'd come home that afternoon.

"No need to apologize, I get it, life and stuff. But you can call me back any time, I'll pick up," I said.

"Good to know."

"So, I completely lost my shit at practice today."

"Really? How?"

I regaled her with the sad story of my panic attack and nearly punching Bash in the face.

"He said *what*?"

"I know, I really wanted to hurt him."

"Well, it's understandable, he sounds like an asshole," she said. "And that name, ugh."

It felt good to have her back me up, even though I knew after cooling down, I'd played my part.

"Confession—I was a bit of a dick to him."

"Still, that was such a cold thing for him to say."

"I doubt he would have said it if he really knew Alex. I'm team captain, I'm supposed to know better than let some little shit get to me."

"Wait, you're captain?! You didn't tell me that," she said. "Congratulations."

*"Whoa, flex much, Hobbs? Subtle."*

*Shut it, Alex.*

"It's break a leg," I teased.

"Ha, ha," she said. "Seriously, that's great, Jake.

"Eh, I don't know, half the time I want to quit. I'm not captain material."

"I don't agree with that."

"Thanks, but you don't have to say that."

"I've seen you play."

"The McKennas' driveway doesn't count," I said.

"Hey, I've been to Saint Aedan's games. I was there when you guys played Holy Cross. You got kicked out of the game for picking a fight."

I do remember seeing Sarah with the McKennas, but I always thought she was one of those fans who was there more for the social aspect of being at a game than actually watching.

Not one of my prouder moments. "Wow, that's all? Nothing to say about my sick hoop skills?"

"You also make the sign of the cross before you take a foul shot."

"You noticed that?" I asked.

Blessing myself before a foul shot was a superstition I picked up in middle school during a playoff game. We needed the points and I was nervous for the first time ever. I signed, dribbled, took my shot, and the ball sailed in. We won.

Since then, it had been a part of my game routine. At least I hadn't worn the same pair of unwashed socks through the playoffs like Alex had one year. We won, but he had a raging case of athlete's foot for like, six months.

*"She must have been watching closely for her to pick up on that."*

*I guess so, Alex, pretty cool.*

"Yeah, I always thought it was sweet you did that."

*"Sweet, aww, isn't that cute, like a bunny."*

*Ha.*

"Sweet? I'm a Crusader. I'm supposed to be fierce," I said, deepening my voice.

She laughed. "You're fierce too, I just thought it was nice to see you do something so . . . I don't know, thoughtful. Seems like a captain should be thoughtful, as well as fierce."

"Well, thanks, I guess," I said.

Sarah yawned on the other end of the phone. "I better go."

"Can we stay on a bit?" I asked. "Please."

"Okay, but don't be surprised if I fall asleep."

"Hey, what do you prefer? A forest or the beach?"

"Did I miss a part of this conversation?"

"I have an idea, trust me," I said.

"The beach, then."

I reached over and turned on my galaxy light, set the white noise to ocean waves. I turned up the volume, so the sound filled the room, switched the phone to speaker, and set it next to me on the pillow.

"Do you hear that?" I asked.

"Yes."

"I use this to fall asleep lately," I said.

"Does it work?"

"Sometimes," I said. "What do you think?"

"I'm not sure it sounds like the ocean."

"Concentrate," I said.

"What time of day is it?"

"Uh, whatever time of the day you want," I said.

"Belmar or Seaside?"

I smiled. "Belmar."

"Are we on separate beach towels or one big blanket?"

"For someone who was falling asleep, you're getting pretty specific," I said.

110

"Just trying to set the scene in my head."

"Okay, then, one big blanket," I said.

"Can we get one of those smoothie bowls with Nutella? You know, at that place right across from the boardwalk?"

I smiled. "Um, sure?"

"Pass the sunscreen," she said.

This was not the scenario I usually imagined when drifting off. It was more along the lines of Tom Hanks in *Castaway*. Me. Alone. On a beach at night staring up at the stars and listening to the waves. Now that Sarah was there with a smoothie bowl and sunscreen, well it was different. She was in her black bikini, pushing her hair to the side, *Do my back?*

*"Thought this was supposed to help you fall asleep, Hobbs?"*

"Jake? Sleeping already?"

"No," I said, trying to get the image of her out of my head. "It's hard to sleep when I'm passing you the sunscreen."

She laughed, sleepy. "Okay, then, let's just listen to the waves."

"Now you're catching on, but it was nice being at the beach with you."

She was quiet. I closed my eyes.

"Good night, Jake."

"Night, Sarah," I whispered.

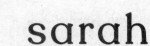

# sarah

THE FIVE OF US FOLLOWED THE NARROW PATH through the woods to the cliffs. Autumn had finally hit, the leaves all brilliant orange, red, and yellow. A chill was in the air too, I pulled my scarf up to my nose. Ash and Mike led the way, holding hands. I was behind them. Buzz right behind me, and then Kyle. We crunched through the fallen leaves, headed to see the shrine where Alex had fallen. I tried to ignore the heavy feeling in my gut. I didn't like to think about what happened there. Wasn't sure why Ash had suddenly felt inspired to visit, it wasn't a special anniversary or anything, but Mike informed me that she wanted to, so after school on Friday, off to the cliffs we went.

Cliffs made them sound dramatic, like the Grand Canyon or something. They were certainly high enough to fall from and get hurt. The unimpressive thirty-foot drop in Cedar Hills park was never more than a place to look out on the rest of the world. The cliff face marked with graffiti in places you never knew a human could get to, let alone deface. In the far distance, the Manhattan skyline beckoned like Oz.

I'd heard stories about the cliffs, everyone had. I'd never hung out there though, it had always been more of an upperclassman place. I was working the night Alex fell. Not that I would have gone—it was a basketball team thing he'd said, something about sending off the old guard, the seniors. He and Jake had stopped by on their way. We kissed. He told me we'd do something the next day. Later that night, when the ambulance and fire truck went by, when people in Adele's stopped and watched and wondered aloud what was going on—it never occurred to me they were on their way to Alex. That at that very moment, he was gone, while I was serving up fruit tarts and profiteroles and dreaming of spending the following day with him.

When we came to the clearing, we naturally fell into a semicircle around the shrine. In the months since Alex's death, it had become more like an unwieldy pile of crap. There were stuffed animals— teddy bears, puppies, a Pikachu. A red heart-shaped Mylar balloon. It was partially deflated but had enough helium to float, so it hung there, limp, a perfect 3D metaphor for how I was feeling. There were candles and photos and handwritten notes. My eyes landed on a small framed photo of Holly and Alex. A pinprick of jealousy pierced my heart. Really? Hadn't the bench been enough?

I wanted to look away but couldn't, and I couldn't control the rush of emotion, or the way it brought tears to my eyes. The gravity of the situation, the place we were standing, hit me all at once. Ash must have felt it because she grabbed my hand. Mike must have felt it too because he produced a small baggie of what looked like gummy bears from his jacket pocket. He fished one out, biting the head off and putting the rest up to Ash's lips.

"A red one, for you, just half, baby."

"Is it even going to do anything?" Ash asked, chewing.

"They're pretty potent," Mike said. He looked at me. "Want?"

I was about to shake my head, but something stopped me. I'm sure this wasn't what my aunt meant when she'd said experience life, but what the hell.

"Yeah, I do."

I swear there was a pause. A moment even the birds stopped singing. I'd never said yes before. It stunned them. Mike had even begun to roll up the pack as he asked. He fished one out, pinched it in half and handed it to me.

"There, Sar. Down the rabbit hole you go," Mike said. His tone made me chuckle. I put the half on my tongue, let it sit there for a bit before I chewed. Wondered if I'd feel anything.

"Shrines are odd," Kyle said, breaking the silence.

"He would have laughed at all this crap," Ash said, crouching down to get a better look.

"No one would do this for me," Buzz said.

Mike laughed. "What a whack thing to say."

"Just being honest, I mean, look, people loved the guy," he said.

*I loved the guy*, I thought.

Did I? I stared at the picture of Alex and Holly until it got blurry, and their faces were shapes and colors. I'd been with Alex for only two and a half months. We'd never said I love you. Of course, I did love Alex as someone who'd been in my life. As Ash's brother. As a fellow human being. That wasn't romantic love though, was it? I certainly had strong feelings for him, and kissing him made me dizzy. But that was lust, wasn't it? Just chemicals and hormones producing tingly-all-over good feelings.

Ash picked up a burned-out candle in a tall glass container that

114

had a very sad and solemn face of Jesus on it. Without warning she threw it. We watched as it arced high over the trees, then fell down, shattering on the forest floor below.

"Maybe you shouldn't have done that. Wasn't that, like, a religious candle?" Mike asked.

"Blessed by the clerk at Stop and Shop where you can find another one for five bucks in aisle ten," Buzz said.

Ash and I found his comment incredibly funny. The edges of everything softened. I glanced over at Buzz, who looked pretty pleased with himself for making us laugh. He ran a hand through his hair, pushing it out of his eyes. Maybe the edible was kicking in because I let my eyes linger on his a moment longer than normal. It didn't go unnoticed, the corner of his mouth upturning ever so slightly. I looked away.

"Doesn't seem right to toss something with Jesus on it, is all," Mike said.

"I think he'd be cool with it," Kyle said.

Ash looked at me. "Your turn."

"What?" I asked.

She leaned down and picked up the picture of Holly and Alex, held it toward me. I stepped back.

"You know you want to, c'mon," Ash said, placing it in my open palm.

"Ash, no," I said, poised to put it back on the shrine.

She grabbed my elbow. "Sarah, you can't tell me this doesn't piss you off. Holly has been acting like a grieving widow. You were Alex's girlfriend. He was with you."

Alex's girlfriend.

She was right. It did piss me off, but could I really get angry at Holly for being upset?

"Yeah, but," I said.

"If it makes you feel any better, all of this crap is getting thrown out anyway. The parks department emailed my dad. Told him if he wanted anything from here to come get it, that they would be cleaning it up every month from now on. That's why I wanted to check it out. All of this stuff is meaningless though."

I swallowed hard, studied the picture. It was overexposed—maybe from being out in the elements. Holly was on Alex's lap, her arms loosely around his neck, both were smiling. Holly's perfectly symmetrical face was washed out, her cherry-red lips, clownish. Or maybe I was being mean. I felt mean, the jealousy from before blooming in my chest, a real physical pressure that made it hard to breathe. They'd been together for seven months before they broke up. The fallout had been nasty. The gossip around school awful. I wasn't good enough for him. We were just temporary. Alex would be back with Holly by the end of the school year.

"You have every right to be furious," Ash whispered.

I closed my eyes, leaned into my anger. A yell that started deep in my gut escaped my mouth as I wound up and threw the frame. It sailed through tree branches and clattered once it hit the ground below. My fists clenched, chin tilted toward the sky, as the yell wound down. I took a deep breath.

It had felt good.

For a moment.

"Shit," I whispered.

"Sar, that was brilliant," Ash said.

"Brilliant? What are you two doing? I didn't come here to toss shit into the woods and scream," Mike said.

"Calm down, Mike," Ash said, wrapping her arm around him and leading him over to a grouping of small boulders people used as seating. Buzz pawed the ground with his foot, then followed them. Kyle knelt down to take a closer look at some of the notes people had left. I stood there, totally exposed. A freaking mess. Regretting I'd shown that much of myself.

I'd only been to the shrine once before. Mom had taken me, at my request. I'd never told anybody, didn't want to come off as ghoulish. I wasn't sure why I wanted to see it, as if it would make me understand what had happened. It had horrified me then, thinking about Alex falling. I didn't want that picture in my head. Now, I thought of Jake. How terrifying it must have been for him to actually witness it.

Alex was gone. And I didn't feel him around when I ate a piece of the cinnamon cake he loved. Or sat on a bench dedicated to his memory. Or looked at a shrine, where people left things to commemorate him. Why was there a Pikachu? Seeing the shrine made me feel like I hadn't known Alex at all. I wanted so desperately to feel him the way my mom said she felt my father sometimes—seeing a rainbow or hearing a song that they loved at just the right moment—like it was a hello. Standing there I felt nothing but sad. Empty.

I turned to join the others sitting down. Mike was behind Ash, arms wrapped around her. She leaned back into him. He nuzzled her hair, and she smiled, turned her head. They kissed. A deep ache stirred in me. As much as I rolled my eyes at their PDA, I wanted what they had, and it seemed impossibly out of my reach. I walked over toward where Buzz was sitting, ignored the squirminess in my gut when our eyes met. It wasn't the same as before, that lingering moment that held potential. The awkwardness was back.

"I'm sorry about that," I said, leaning against the boulder a few feet away from him.

"About what?"

I gestured toward the shrine where Kyle was still crouched down studying the collection of stuff. "You know, yelling like that."

"Don't apologize," he said, turning toward me. "It's nice to see you cut loose."

I laughed, soft, quiet, stared at the ground. "That's one way to put it."

"Wanna get out of here?" He stood up, held out his hand. I sucked in a breath; this was not what I expected.

"I don't feel like sitting here anymore," he said. "We can meet them out front by the parking lot."

While I didn't need help getting up, I took his hand. His fin-
~tips were strong but cold. He pulled me to standing, let go. I
~ed my hands in my pockets, nosed up my scarf so half my face
overed.

~eezing my cojones off over here; we'll meet you out front,"
~id to no one in particular.

~thers stared, as he gestured for me to go first. Dynamics
~he choice to leave, even if it was only to wait for Ash,
~Kyle to follow, had weight. I sheepishly looked over at
~e. Both smiling. Kyle turned away, looking toward the
~followed the path back out, hearing Buzz's footfalls
~ot looking back.

november

# sarah

WITH NOVEMBER CAME SHORTER DAYS, COLDER
weather, and lunch indoors. After our outing to the cliffs, dynamics
changed within our small group. Kyle didn't sit with us anymore.
He said it was because the indoor tables were more conducive for
groups of four, but since it was easy enough to pull up a chair,
I didn't buy that excuse. Buzz used less bro humor now, he was
thoughtful even, asking me questions about the play and how
rehearsals were going. And while it probably wouldn't completely
suck to date my best friend's boyfriend's best friend, I still wasn't
sure if I was ready for a relationship with him, or anyone else.

I also still hadn't told Ash that I was working with Jake on the
Alex McKenna scholarship fund. Mostly because I wasn't actually
doing anything yet, but I'd be lying if I said I wasn't worried how
she would react knowing I'd be working with Jake.

Last night on the phone though, Jake told me there was a meeting today, and it would be great if I could be there. I really didn't
want to go, my stomach was in knots just thinking about being
around Holly and her friends, but then I thought of Alex and how
it would be nice to be a part of something memorializing him in
a special way. I knew I had to tell Ash before she found out from

someone else. Halfway through my sandwich, I decided to just go for it.

"Hey, so I never told you, I'm working on that scholarship committee for Alex," I said.

"The one they announced today?"

I nodded. "Jake Hobbs approached me about it a few weeks ago. Wanted to see if Adele's could supply the refreshments."

"Really," she said, "and you said yes?"

"I told him I'd think about it. I like the idea of doing something tangible in Alex's memory. I think it could, I don't know, help." I said, glancing between Buzz, Mike, and Ash. "Maybe you guys want to join me?"

"I'm allergic to committees," Mike said. Ash gave him a playful pinch on the arm.

"Same," Buzz said.

"Isn't Holly Matthews in charge of that?"

I nodded.

"And you're okay being around her?" Ash asked.

I shrugged. Holly and her friends never tortured me or anything, but they were subtly unpleasant. I was accidentally on purpose knocked into a few times in the hallway, and once, at lunch, they made sure I overheard exactly what they thought of me dating Alex. He'd told me to ignore it, so I did. Tossing that photo at the cliffs changed something in me though. Being upset over past hurts seemed so stupid in the face of what happened.

"I don't know, but I want to try. Finally show her I don't care what she or her friends think of me," I said.

Ash surprised me by smiling.

"Wow, Sassy Sarah. Haven't seen her in, like, forever," Ash said. "I'd go, but I actually have a guitar lesson this afternoon."

"Oh, wow, do you think you might do that showcase?" I asked. When I'd told her about live music at Adele's, she didn't seem that into it. Mike suddenly became interested in the conversation. He and Ash shared a look.

"I'm considering it," she said, looking back at me.

"You should totally do it," I said. "We'd all be there to support you."

"You bet," Mike answered, but there was something strained in his voice.

"We'll see," Ash said.

After the day ended, I met up with Jake. He was sitting on the old church pew at the end of the hallway, right at the entrance to the school library. Head down, glancing at his phone. I smiled, warmth spreading through my chest at the sight of him. It was odd, we shared so much on the phone at night yet barely saw each other during the school day. We didn't talk every night, but we talked a lot, always ending with that virtual day at the beach to fall asleep.

Only, it was hard to fall asleep thinking about that.

I liked it, imagining hanging out with him. Maybe too much.

Seeing him now made me almost shy. He looked up. Smiled.

*Whoosh.*

This had to stop. As fun as it was, a harmless little nighttime fantasy, it would be all kinds of disastrous being interested in Alex's best friend. He stood up as I approached him.

"Ready?"

I tried to channel Sassy Sarah, as Ash had called me at lunch. "Yep, let's do this."

He opened the door to the library and gestured for me to go in.

"It'll mostly be Holly going on about stuff. No need to be nervous or anything."

"Why? Do I look nervous?"

He shook his head. "No, not at all."

Okay, so maybe I was a little.

We walked into the meeting room. There were quite a few people there, more than I'd expected actually. Jake and I sat in the second-to-last row of chairs. Holly was busy chatting with a girl up front. When she saw Jake, she excused herself and came over.

"Jake, what are you doing back here? You're my cochair, which means I need you up front," she said.

"I can cochair from here, can't I?" he said, not budging.

She crossed her arms. "You won't have to say much if that's what you're worried about."

"Fine, fine. Hey, you know Sarah, right? She's hooking us up with some stuff from her aunt's pastry shop," Jake said. Holly glanced at me, gave me the faintest smile.

"Yes, hi, Sarah, can't wait to hear all about it."

*Hear all about it?* I smiled. "Hi, Holly."

She tugged on Jake's arm. "C'mon, up front. We have to start."

Jake turned to me. "You okay?"

I nodded. "Yes. Go."

He started getting up, but sat back down, turned to me.

"Hey, can I give you a ride home after?" he asked.

I remembered that day at the park, at Alex's bench, when I refused a ride because I couldn't handle the confusing *whoosh*.

Maybe I was getting in deep here, toying with feelings I shouldn't even be entertaining, but . . . it was cold out, and I didn't feel like walking home by myself. And it was nice actually getting to know Jake, for himself. Not as Alex's best friend. The more I found out, the more I wanted to know.

"That would be great," I answered.

"Cool," he said. He left his backpack and jacket next to me, walked up to the front.

Holly began the meeting, talking about possible dates for a fundraising dance. It would be in February, but they were trying to decide if it should be semiformal or low-key. She was leaning toward low-key because who wanted to get dressed up to be in the school cafeteria but would put it to a vote.

Ten minutes into the meeting, when Holly was discussing color scheme and decor, the door opened, and Courtney Muldavy and two other girls barged in, laughing. Everything stopped, and the room turned its collective attention toward them.

"Oops, shit," Courtney said, putting her hand up to her mouth as people broke out into soft laughter. "Sorry, Holls."

"Glad you could make it, Court," she said, with a strained smile. She waited until they took a seat to continue speaking. Courtney and the two girls came down the aisle, her eyes darting around as she looked for a place. Her gaze landed on Jake's jacket and backpack, taking up the empty seat next to me. Then she looked at me before filing into the row behind me with the others. She leaned up, reaching over to grab Jake's jacket. Eyes almost daring me to say something.

"What did we miss?" she asked, smiling broad before pulling it back with her.

She didn't wait for an answer, and I felt my cheeks warm as the

125

girls giggled behind me. It shouldn't have bothered me, but it did. Jake sat up front, listening to Holly, oblivious to what just happened. And, well, what did just happen? Courtney grabbed Jake's jacket, that's all.

"So where are we on refreshments?" Holly asked Jake.

Jake smiled. Her question was so serious, official. I wondered how she would react to our joking about refreshment emergencies on the phone.

"We'll be working with Adele's for some sweet stuff. Still working on drinks, definitely some water bottles."

"There needs to be more than water bottles," Holly said.

"Of course, just tossing out ideas," Jake said.

"What kind of sweet stuff? Maybe Sarah could fill us in on that," she said, turning to me.

Oh, hot damn.

"Well," I began.

"You have to speak up, we can't hear you up here," Holly said.

"Can't hear you back here either," Courtney said.

So, this is how it was going to be.

Fine.

I took a breath, sat up straight, projected like I'd learned to do onstage.

"There's a lot of things to choose from at Adele's, but a few different small items might be best. My aunt is known for her macarons—they come in all sorts of colors and flavors. We could probably do them in school colors, that might be fun. She might even offer to create a special flavor for the event," I said.

"Macarons?" Holly asked, pronouncing the word in a perfect French accent with such force that I had to bite my lip to keep from laughing. "Is that all? What about cupcakes?"

"There's other types of cookies. Pastries. She doesn't really do cupcakes, but I guess I could ask her about that, I mean, if you want something that basic," I said, the word landing exactly the way I wanted.

"They have awesome chocolate chip cookies," Jake said, smiling. I appreciated his support.

"Yeah, I mean you should come in and check out what we have. Everyone should at some point, it's a great place," I said, stopping myself from saying that Alex loved it there. That would have been awkward in a way I wasn't ready to deal with.

Holly nodded, satisfied.

"We'll have to plan on that," she said, and moved to the next topic on her agenda.

Twenty minutes later, the meeting adjourned, Jake came back down the aisle. He barely opened his mouth before Courtney was in front of him, his jacket slung over her shoulders like a cape.

"Hey, so good to see you involved in this," she said.

Jake looked at me, then Courtney. "Yeah, well, Holly asked, and I guess she caught me in the right moment. Um, I was going to give Sarah a ride home," he said, reaching for his jacket.

"Oh, sure," Courtney said, pulling the jacket off her shoulders and handing it to him. "I don't mind." She looked at me. "We can drop you off."

I plastered on a smile. Whatever was going on with her, it had more to do with Jake than me. I wasn't about to get involved but I wasn't going to back down either. If she wanted to make it awkward, well, okay.

"Yeah, that would be great," I said, collecting my stuff, ignoring the stab of . . . what? Jealousy? No, I wasn't jealous, this was simply uncomfortable. I had nothing to be jealous over. Jake and I were friends. Who he hung out with when I wasn't with him was none of my business.

He had a bewildered look on his face, and when Court turned away to get her stuff and say goodbye to the others, he mouthed the word *sorry*. I smiled, dismissed it, letting him know there was nothing to be sorry about.

Once at Jake's car, there was no debate, Courtney sat in front. She slid into the passenger seat, I'm sure the way she'd done a thousand times before. Played with the heat controls. Plugged in her phone so we could listen to Taylor Swift's latest. I gave Jake my address and talked him through the turns once we got closer to my street, now regretting that I didn't back out of the ride at school.

It was good for me to experience this though. What Jake and I had during our phone calls was not real life. This was, and it was clear he and Courtney had some sort of relationship. Alex had explained it to me once; they were casual, although he used a crasser and more descriptive term for it that I didn't want to think about at the moment. When Jake finally got to my building, I couldn't wait to get out.

"Well, thanks," I said, grabbing my stuff.

My eyes met Jake's briefly in the rearview. I knew we'd talk at some point.

"Bye," I said, closing the door behind me.

# jake

I WAITED FOR SARAH TO GET INSIDE HER BUILDING before pulling away.

"Nice place," Court muttered.

"Stop," I said.

"What? My grams lives in an apartment like that. The hallways always smell like cabbage."

I bit my tongue; her comment was more to push my buttons than to diss Sarah. This is how it worked with Court, and for a while, I kind of dug it. I felt a little burst of satisfaction when she was jealous. That meant she wanted me. I'd convinced myself that our casual no-strings-attached hookupship was the best of both worlds. I could hang with my friends when she was out with dude-bro douchebag College Guy, and we could hook up and have a good time when the mood struck. In theory it was great, but the no-strings part only applied to her, not me. If I showed a hint of interest in anyone else, this was how she would get. Pissy. Possessive.

Not that I was interested in Sarah.

*"Dude, are you serious? You are such a liar!"*

*Well, what am I supposed to do, Alex? Ask Court what she thinks?*

"Let's get a latte or something; we haven't hung out in a while," Court said.

"I need to get home," I said.

"Oh, come on, just a quick drive-thru run, I'll buy," she said.

She pouted, which even after all this time, got to me. It was hard to say no to Court.

"Fine," I said.

One pumpkin spice latte and a mocha in hand, we pulled up to her house. I parked halfway in the driveway, kept the car running. She took a sip of her drink.

"So, why was *she* there?"

No need to clear up which *she* she'd been referring to.

"Why are you being so weird about this?"

She adjusted her position in the seat to face me, gestured using her to-go cup. "How am I being weird? You're the one who pulled Alex's girlfriend into it. You know it hurts Holly to think about that. It's like you're shoving it in her face."

I'd never thought of it that way. "That's not true."

"Have you talked to Holly about it?"

I hadn't talked to Holly before asking Sarah about helping out, but since she trusted me enough to be cochair, I got to make my own decisions, right? "No, she never told me to run anything by her. She seemed okay with it. Why wouldn't she? Adele's is a great place."

"So is Sweet Haven, or Double Batch, or any number of bakeries around town. You chose the one where Alex and drama chick used to . . . I don't know, flirt. It's where it all began apparently."

"She works there," I said.

"Exactly."

"Sarah knew Alex for years, before Holly even met him," I said.

"Are you going to be mad at Ash for introducing them in the first place? Maybe mad at Sarah's mother for choosing to live in Cedar Hills?"

She stared ahead, took a sip of her drink. "Why are you defending her so hard? You're Holly's friend."

"What, are we in second grade? This isn't about Holly, it's about Alex. And why should Sarah be excluded? She did nothing wrong."

"But why did you even reach out to her?"

I remained silent, more because I didn't know how to answer that. I couldn't imagine telling Court about my phone calls with Sarah. She wouldn't understand; she'd twist it somehow. I took a sip of my drink, waiting for the awkward to subside.

"God, Jake, I don't want to fight. I just thought you should be aware of how Holly feels, that's all."

"I'm not fighting, Court. Holly should have said something to me, if having Sarah involved bothered her."

"You say that like it's easy."

"What does that even mean?"

"It means this," she said, gesturing at me again. "It means you're touchy, and secretive, and moody as hell. Christ, Jake, you used to be fun, it's like . . . Forget it."

I had the urge to leave, but since it was my car, I had no choice except to sit there.

"Finish what you were going to say," I said.

"It's like you're not allowing yourself to have fun because of Alex. We've all noticed it."

"We?"

"Yes, we. Pat, Taj, the team, Holly, me—*your* friends. Do you think if roles were reversed Alex would be acting the way you are?"

None of them were there that night.

None of them saw or knew or had to live with the raw helplessness after Alex tumbled over the edge. Of course they could go on with their lives.

"That's a shitty thing to say to me."

She placed her hand on my leg. "Okay, I'm sorry, Jake. All I meant is . . . we miss you. I miss you."

It didn't suck to hear that.

I missed me too.

"I was really glad to hear you wanted to be part of the scholarship committee, and between you and me, I think Holly *is* going a little overboard, but that's how she is. She hasn't really changed. You have. It's like you're ignoring us. You didn't sign the pledge. You never came with us to the cliffs to add anything to the shrine. You don't hang out anymore. All I'm trying to point out is that Alex was a pretty chill guy, I don't think he'd want you to spend the rest of your life feeling bad that you're alive."

Was that what I was doing? I'd been avoiding my friends because it didn't feel like they understood, but then Court summed up my feelings in one sentence.

"I don't know how to stop feeling this way," I admitted.

"Let your friends help," she said. "Palmer is in school until Thanksgiving break. We should do something, go out this weekend. There's only thirty weekends left until graduation; we have to—"

"Go out with a bang," I finished, although I wasn't sure why she needed to bring College Guy into it. Any optimism I'd felt from finally being understood by her disappeared.

"Yes! Now you're getting it," she said. Courtney's porch light turned on. She gathered up her things, leaned toward me for a kiss. For a split second, I thought of Sarah. There was no need for me to feel guilty, but I did. Close-mouthed, I touched my lips to Court's. She pulled away.

"Later, Jake," she said, getting out of the car.

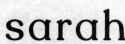

# sarah

THE FOLLOWING NIGHT I RACED THROUGH MY HOME-
work. After reading the same line from my physiology textbook
about four times, I picked up my phone. It was only seven. Too
early to call Jake? We'd never discussed the scholarship meeting,
and I imagined him picking up the phone and me saying "macarons" in an over-the-top French accent, and us sharing a good laugh
about it. Except for the bizarre ride home with Courtney, the meeting went well; I felt like I handled myself. At least I thought I did.
I hadn't seen Jake all day, which wasn't out of the ordinary but at
the moment seemed significant. My phone chirped with a text. I
startled, checked the screen.

Ash.

**Downstairs. Buzz me up?**

**K.**

I hopped off my bed and walked out to the living room. Mom
was on the couch, legs curled underneath her, book in hand. *Jeop-
ardy!* on for background noise. She looked up.

"Ash is here."

Mom took off her reading glasses. "Were you expecting her?
Everything okay?"

I shrugged as I pressed the entry buzzer and opened our door a crack.

It wasn't entirely out of the ordinary for Ash to pop over. Pre–Mike Boyle, it was a regular occurrence. I loved going to her house because she had a second floor and a fireplace and a yard with a deck. She loved coming over to my place because she thought it was cool she needed to be "buzzed up," that we had a breakfast counter with barstools and were on the fourth floor and could see over the tops of the houses. I guess it's normal to think what's different is more interesting. She hadn't been over since the beginning of last summer though.

Ash walked in, pulled off her woolen beanie hat and ran a hand through her hair. Her nose and cheeks were bright pink from the cold.

"Hey," I said, closing the door. Mom was already up. She embraced Ash.

"It's so good to see you, Ashley," Mom said. "You're like an ice cube. I was about to put on the kettle, you girls up for some tea? Hot chocolate, maybe?"

"Sounds good," I said at the same time Ash said, "No, thanks."

"I'll put it on anyway, so if you change your mind, the water will be hot."

"Thanks, Mrs. Walsh," Ash said as we left the kitchen and walked to my room. Once I closed the door, Ash stiffened, spun and fell backward onto my bed with a groan. She stared straight up at my ceiling while I plopped down by the headboard.

"What's up?" I asked.

Her brow bunched up; she glanced at me. "It's my parents. My house. It's everything."

I gathered up the books that had shifted with Ash's bounce on the bed and put them on my vanity, waiting for her to elaborate.

She rolled to her side and propped herself up on her elbow. "We're going away for Christmas break."

"Wow, really?" I said. For as long as I'd known Ash, the Mc-Kennas did Christmas up big. House full of lights, huge live tree, catered family open house that lasted from early afternoon until well after midnight the weekend before Christmas.

"I know, right? Mom pretty much can't handle anything without crying. Dad tries, but . . ." Her voice trailed off. "We're going on a freaking cruise for Christmas. Like it's going to be any better being stuck on a boat in the middle of the ocean. I think my parents decided to come up with the exact opposite of normal. At least some of my cousins are going too."

"Well, on the bright side, you'll be tan in January."

"But this is my and Mike's first Christmas together. I don't want to miss that."

"Ash, I think every day with you is like Christmas to Mike."

She laughed. "Stop trying to cheer me up. I want to be pissed."

"Okay, then. It sucks. Maybe I could stow away in some luggage," I said.

"We'd be killer on a boat," she said. A moment passed where I imagined being on a cruise with Ash and the McKennas. It was hard not to picture Alex there too. I ran my index finger along the seed bead bracelet, gave it a little pull. Ash's smile faded. Maybe she'd had the same thought.

"We haven't touched Alex's room. It's been months and my

mother still can't bring herself to change anything. They only just changed the sheets about a month ago. Until then the room looked like he'd just rolled on out of it. My father suggested we donate some of his bedroom furniture, and Mom freaked out. She keeps putting off going through his things. Not that I blame her. I went in there the other day; I couldn't bring myself to do anything except sit. You know he had about ten pairs of Sasquatch-sized basketball shoes in a big pile in his closet. I don't think he ever threw any out."

I managed a smile. My memories of Alex's room were limited. Once we started dating, everything changed. Not that I was ever in there alone with him before, but suddenly the door had to be left open. At least when Mr. and Mrs. McKenna were home.

"That must be really tough," I said.

"Maybe you can come over one of these days and help me go through stuff. I don't like being there by myself. It's too quiet."

"Of course," I said.

She sat up.

"Damn, I came over here to feel better, now I've brought you down too."

"Nah, it's okay. I'm glad you came here and not Mike's."

At Mike's name she rolled her eyes.

"Okay, you went from missing Christmas with him to this. What's with the eye roll?"

She took a breath. "Well . . . I'm ninety-eight percent certain that I'm going to do that holiday showcase at your aunt's place."

"Ash! Omigod, that's awesome! What's the two percent?"

"Mike."

"Oh no . . . why? He knows it's your thing, right?"

"I mean, yeah. It's not really about the guitar, it's more about Bran Russo."

"Bran Russo?"

At his name, Ash smiled, like *really* smiled.

"Oh shit, Ash," I said.

"Well, look there's nothing going on or anything. I wouldn't do that to Mike, but we've been texting since . . . well since September. Not like every day or anything. He checks in with me, tells me all the band gossip. He actually told me about the showcase before you did. I've been taking lessons with one of the teachers at that school around the corner from Adele's."

"The secret life of Ash McKenna! Wait, you've been taking lessons right around the corner? How come you never stop in?"

"It's on a day you don't work. And anyway, I kind of liked having something that was just for me, that didn't relate to anyone else in my life. Even Mike didn't know I was taking lessons again. I know that sounds selfish, don't hate me."

I thought about my calls with Jake. Our virtual beach dates. Not that it was the same, but I understood wanting something completely separate from your everyday life.

"No, I totally get it. I'm just really happy you're playing again."

She grinned and got up off the bed. "Me too. I have to get back. My parents don't even know I'm gone."

"Do you want me to walk you back?"

She tucked her long hair behind her ears and pulled her beanie over her head, smoothing it down as she looked in the mirror on my vanity. "Nah, it's too cold outside, if I had the choice I would stay here and drink hot chocolate."

I walked her downstairs to the front entrance of the building, folding my arms tight for warmth. I already regretted not insisting I walk her home. It hadn't been just the two of us for such a long time. It was nice.

"There's something else I have to tell you," she said when we got to the bottom landing.

Every muscle tensed. She sensed my unease. "No, no it's nothing bad, it's sort of good, I guess."

"Okay, please just spill it."

"Buzz is crazy about you."

I palmed my forehead. "Oh God. Stop, Ash."

"I know, I know, he's sooooo not your type. Mike has been bugging me for weeks to nudge you in his direction."

"Why?"

"He's sick of listening to him go on about you."

"Buzz goes on about me? I mean, about what?"

Ash widened her eyes. "Face it, Sar, you're a snack. What do you think he goes on about?"

"Omigod, stop, stop, stop," I said, laughing.

"I wouldn't have said anything, but there was that time at the cliffs, you sort of looked maybe a little interested?"

"I haven't kissed anyone since Alex," I said, tinkering with the seed bead bracelet again.

She nodded. "I get it, but maybe hooking up with someone for fun wouldn't be the worst thing. Just, you know, think about it."

"Okay," I said.

"Wait, really?"

"Well, don't tell Mike or anything. I don't want to be set up. If something is supposed to happen it should just, like, happen. Swear to me you won't tell him I said that."

She put two fingers up and a hand over her heart. "I swear. Okay, now I really have to get going."

"Text me when you get in. Don't forget," I said.

"I won't."

Back upstairs, I went to my room to finish my homework. It was futile, all I could think of was what Ash had said about Buzz. Could I hook up with him for fun? I wasn't sure I was a just-for-fun person. The phone chirped. My pulse quickened.

Ash. One word.

**Home.**

I sent her a heart emoji, then scrolled to Jake's contact info. It was still earlyish, but did I really have to wait until eleven to call him? What if he was avoiding me because he thought the committee meeting went shitty? I typed in the word *Hey*, which seemed to be our version of the Bat-Signal, and pressed Send. If he didn't want to talk, he wouldn't, and it would be fine. I would be fine.

Moments later a text bubble popped up, then disappeared.

The phone rang. I picked up.

"Macaron?" I said in an exaggerated French accent. "Iz dat all? Vat about cupcakes?"

Jake laughed.

# jake

"THAT WAS PRETTY OVER-THE-TOP," I SAID. "I CAN'T believe Holly did that."

She laughed. "Have to admit I was impressed by her French accent though."

"You handled it well," I replied. "Um, sorry about Courtney. That was more about me than you."

"Oh, yeah, sure," she said.

*"Tell her you imagined a much different ride home."*

*I don't know what I expected, Alex.*

*"Well, you at least expected to be alone with her and not in some awkward situation."*

"So, um, what was that about anyway?" she asked. Her tone was unsure. "Are you guys together?"

"Um, not really."

"I think that should be a yes or no answer," she said. "I know . . . well Alex told me you guys were . . . hookup pals."

*"You know I didn't put it that way."*

*Ah, yeah, that term is all Sarah, right there.*

I chuckled. "Hookup pals? Kind of sounds like a Christmas toy, doesn't it? Would probably involve cute puppies and Velcro."

"Jake, you know what I mean."

"Yeah, I do," I said. Would she think less of me? If she thought about me at all.

I'd liked Courtney since freshman year. It wasn't until I made varsity that she even looked at me. Maybe that should have been a flagrant red flag, but I didn't care—being with her was exciting. She was so pretty, outspoken, enjoyed going out, and didn't take crap from anybody. We were the basketball player and the cheerleader. Unstoppable.

Four months in, she told me about dude-bro, douchebag College Guy, but I was in too deep at that point.

"Um, yeah, guilty," I said. "We've been hookup pals, as you put it, since sophomore year."

"How does that work?"

I could not let that one go. "I'm assuming you've had health class, Sarah. You know the one where you have to get a parent's signature and all."

"*Jake.* I meant . . . how do you keep it . . . well, just for fun?"

I imagined her blushing, and smiled.

"I get to be with her, have some fun, we both have someone to go to school stuff with and when her college boyfriend is home, I get to hang with my friends. Kind of a win-win."

It certainly sounded good, and most of the time I'd talked myself into fully believing it, but somehow explaining it to Sarah didn't feel right. She was silent, and it was driving me crazy wondering what she thought of me.

"That's so . . ."

"Screwed up?" I said.

"I was going to say mature, I guess. You don't get jealous?"

"In the beginning, yeah. But now, not so much. We keep it casual."

"So, you can see other people, then?"

"I could, I guess, but I don't. I always figured when I found someone I wanted to be with more, I'd break it off with Court for good. We haven't hooked up since the beginning of the summer though," I added, just making sure she realized nothing had happened between Court and me yesterday.

"But you could, if you wanted to," she said.

"Why are you so interested in this?"

"Oh, um, I'm thinking it might be time for me to start dating again, but nothing serious. Just kind of . . ."

"Hooking up?"

"Well, no, maybe."

"That seems like it should be a yes or no answer."

She laughed. "Ha. Funny."

"Is there someone you're interested in?"

"Oh, um, sort of. One of Mike Boyle's friends. Buzz Leary."

"You want Buzz Leary to be your boy toy?" I joked, even though it felt like the words struggled to get out of my throat. Buzz Leary, for real?

"No, no, *no*," she said. "Just maybe thought I'd look at it as— what did you call it?—casual. Fun. But I'm not sure I'm wired for casual."

"No, you're not," I said, maybe a little too quickly.

"Why though? Can't I just do something without overanalyzing it?"

"You care about other people's feelings."

"I guess, yeah," she said.

"Sarah, you're acting like it's a character defect."

"You made it sound like one," she said.

"That's not what I meant. It's a good way to be," I said, realizing that it was one of the reasons I was so drawn to her. "It's why you came over to talk to me at Alex's wake."

I remembered thinking *Oh shit* when I saw her approach me. I'd left the wake to get some fresh air, and really, to be alone on the porch. Not realizing there was nowhere to be alone. I couldn't shake the feeling that people were staring at me, wishing I could give them answers about what happened, when I barely had a clue myself.

When she asked how I was doing, and I had absolutely no strength to bullshit anymore and say something like "hanging in there," I'd told her the truth. "Not good, not good at all." She didn't flinch. She didn't walk away or make it awkward. She said, "That sums everything up, doesn't it?" She turned it around, made me feel like maybe things could get better.

You remember when someone really listens to you.

*"Maybe you should tell her how that made you feel, Hobbs."*

*You think, Al?*

I cleared my throat.

"I appreciated that, in case you never realized it. So, consider this a very belated thank-you for talking to me. I know I didn't exactly make it easy."

"You were a little scary," she said with a smile in her voice.

"I think I was trying to be. It was hard to talk to anyone. It felt like everyone wanted something from me. Including you at first. Then you tried to make me feel better even when you must have felt shitty yourself. That's definitely not someone wired for casual."

144

"So then how do you do it?"

"Are we really back to this?" I laughed.

"All I mean is, you don't seem wired for casual either," she said.

What I wanted to say to her in that moment was *Fuck casual, be with me.* It was right there on the tip of my tongue, but I'd grown to love our nighttime conversations, our virtual beach dates, our looks in the hallway at school—like we shared a whole world no one knew about—when I happened to pass her. What if I confessed what I felt and she didn't feel the same? This would all go away. And *this*, above everything else was getting me through. I'd rather be friends with Sarah than nothing at all.

"Well, I don't recommend the casual thing. It can get intense and tricky pretty fast," I said.

"Okay, I'll take your word for it," she said, yawning. "Oops, sorry."

"I'm that boring, huh?"

"No, I'm just tired," she said.

"So, should we go to the beach tonight? Or do, like, a fireside camp?"

"I'm not into the crickets, let's stick with the beach."

"Okay, but how about we get pizza instead of a smoothie bowl."

"Sounds good. No onions though," she said.

"Pepperoni?"

"Sure."

I leaned over and turned on the galaxy light, let the ocean waves do their thing. Imagined the two of us on the big blanket.

"Night, Sarah," I said.

"Night, Jake."

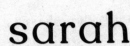

# sarah

SATURDAY NIGHT WE HUNG OUT IN MIKE'S BASEMENT.
The Boyles' basement was not one of those scary, musty places you
needed to stay out of like in a horror movie. It was carpeted and
had a large-screen television with three different gaming systems.
A large, comfy, cloudlike couch was on one side, and a few gaming chairs and bean bags littered the floor. A bar ran along the
side wall. There was a pool table, a dartboard, and an old arcade
machine that held about thirty classic games. Mike had told Ash
his parents finished the basement so he and his brother could get
into trouble under their own roof.

So, there we were—Mike, Buzz, Ash, and me—looking for
trouble with a twelve-pack of something that was supposed to
taste like lemonade but got you drunk. Kyle was not present. He
was Dungeon Master that night, running a D&D campaign he
couldn't miss but said he'd try to stop by after.

A Setup™?

Maybe.

Even though I trusted Ash not to say anything, I'm sure she
found a loophole because this felt different. It was conveniently the
four of us on a Saturday night. I'd changed my shift at work, wore a
new black sweater. If something was ever going to happen between

me and Buzz, the stage was most certainly set.

The lemonade stuff helped. Half a bottle in, I noticed small talk became a little easier. Buzz's jokes were a little funnier. He'd gotten a haircut since I'd last seen him, and he kept sweeping his hand across his forehead, a habit from when his sandy hair had been longer. He looked more vulnerable without his hair covering his eyes.

We were playing doubles in pool, and Ash and I were winning. I was trying to get Buzz to tell me his real name. He was even Buzz Leary in the Saint Aedan's yearbook.

"You're telling me Buzz is the name on your birth certificate?"

He lined up his shot. "Maybe."

"It can't be, who would name a baby Buzz?"

"My parents. Got a problem with that?" he joked, sinking his shot and grinning. He *had* to be messing with me.

Mike cheered. Ash glared at him, and he blew her a kiss.

I laughed. "It's a sound, not a name."

"This is getting to you, isn't it?"

"Are they, like, *Toy Story* fans or something?"

"How about: you win, I'll tell you; I win, we'll figure something else out," he said. His playful tone made *something* sound a little dangerous, suggestive. I credited the lemonade-warm-fuzzy feeling for not reacting with anything more than a smile. I traced my seed bead bracelet with my index finger. Were we actually flirting?

"Sure," I said.

Within five minutes, Buzz had singlehandedly won the game.

"Best two out of three?" I asked. He laughed.

A door slammed, followed by the pounding of footsteps down the stairs.

The four of us looked at each other, then over to the stairwell.

Mike's brother Pat walked in balancing a case of beer on his shoulder. He smiled, a more refined yet equally charming version of Mike's grin, put the case of beer down on the bar and looked us over.

"Hey, kids, what's up?"

The warm fuzzy feeling that had taken me out of myself suddenly morphed into painful self-awareness. Especially as the rest of Pat's friends filed in. There were a few guys from the basketball team, two senior girls whose faces looked familiar but whose names escaped me. Followed by Holly, then Courtney, and finally Jake. From the way they came in and took over, it was obvious they'd hung out in the Boyles' basement before.

Holly walked toward us. She acknowledged me with a nod and a small smile, then turned her attention to Ash.

"Ashley," she said, giving her a hug. Ash looked uncomfortable but hugged her back, making eye contact with me over Holly's shoulder like *WTF?*

They pulled apart and Holly took Ash's hand in hers.

"How are you?" she purred. Her voice sincere, warm.

I didn't wait to hear Ash's response. Buzz gathered the pool cues and put them back in the rack. I walked over to the bar to grab my drink, trying to ignore Jake. I knew if I looked over at him, I'd break out in a grin. I wouldn't be able to help it. Maybe it was good more people were here. Less likely for me to jump into something with Buzz that I wasn't sure about.

"Plot twist," Buzz said, under his breath as he reached across me and grabbed his drink. I chuckled at his comment, took a sip of mine. Ash and Mike joined us. Mike cracked open another spiked lemonade and handed it to her.

"You okay?" I asked.

She nodded, picking the label off the bottle. "Was just in the mood for a quieter night."

"Same," I said, and accidentally met Buzz's eyes. I looked away.

Some of the boys were already involved in a video game. Courtney sauntered over behind the bar and grabbed various bottles of liquor and began pouring them into a silver shaker.

"Hey, is that any good?" she asked me, motioning to the bottle in my hand. Strange to have her attention trained on me after the other day.

"Um, yeah, pretty good," I said.

"I can't stand beer, mind if I swipe one?"

"Sure," Buzz answered.

"I'm making blue lagoon shots, if you're interested," she said, grabbing ice out of the freezer.

"Very," Buzz said, his eyes locked on the sliver of pale skin showing between her dark jeans and emerald crop top. Maybe I should have been jealous, but I was staring as well, it was hard not to. She was one of those people who demanded attention. What was it like to have that sort of power?

She finished shaking the mixture and lined up shot glasses. She poured two and pushed them toward me and Buzz. Mike and Ash declined.

"Enjoy." She hooked a few of the shot glasses with her fingers, took the shaker, and went over to the others. Buzz clinked his shot glass to mine and we both drank them at the same time. I half expected fire to shoot out of my mouth. My eyes teared up.

"Your face," Buzz said, laughing.

"Is it supposed to taste like that?" I whispered, trying not to grimace.

"Gets the job done, I guess."

"If the job is to burn your larynx." I excused myself to find the bathroom, which was in the most basement-y part of the house—through a door and past the laundry room. I closed the door and leaned against it. Took a breath. I needed a moment away from the lights and the noise and the seniors. And okay, Jake.

It was hard to ignore him. I kept wanting to peek over, but for what? What if this was an "on" night for him and Courtney? They all looked so easy and relaxed. This was their hangout too.

I ran a hand through my hair, rinsed my mouth with water, watched as blue swirled down the drain. Blue? I stuck out my tongue and laughed at my reflection. Whatever concoction Courtney had given us had stained my tongue. Maybe it was a sign from the universe to lighten up, that everything was going to be okay, that I should stop taking life so seriously and try to have a good time.

As I left the bathroom, Buzz walked into the laundry room, shutting the door behind him. Our paths led right to each other. We tried to get by, but we kept stepping back and forth at the same time, like we were dancing or something. We stopped. I looked up at him.

Mistake.

In the dim lighting of the laundry room, Buzz looked so earnest. He took my hands in his. I didn't resist but looked down at our entwined fingers, maybe trying him on for size.

"My tongue is blue," I said. It cracked us both up.

"Really?"

I nodded, still looking down at our feet. His scuffed-up checkerboard Vans, my chunky heeled booties. He shifted to get my attention, trying to get me to look at him. Meeting his eyes would be making a choice I wasn't sure I was ready for.

"Sarah, you must know I like you," he said.

"Buzz."

He nuzzled my ear, whispered.

"It's Christian. My name is Christian."

I don't know what it was, him revealing his name—*which why would he want to be called Buzz with a name like Christian?*—the sound of his voice; the way his lips grazed my ear, sending an unexpected ripple of warmth down to my toes. I turned my face to his, met his eyes, and we went from zero to sixty in a hot second. Buzz made a low sound, and I wrapped my arms around his neck. We were kissing, moving, leaning, my back against either the washer or dryer. Something fell, but we didn't stop to pick it up.

He kissed my jaw, my neck, pulled back a moment.

"I really have to take a leak. Don't. Move," he said, kissing me before he went off. My fingers went to my lips.

*Shit.*

Christian of the sexy warm whispers had suddenly become lunch table Buzz circa first week of September in an instant.

I stood there, staring up a rustic sign that read "Laundry Stinks" and fought the urge to cry. Alex popped into my thoughts. That was it, I'd done it. He was no longer the last person I kissed.

*Shit. Shit. Shit,* I thought, snapping the seed bead bracelet each time.

I slunk toward the laundry room door, opened it quietly, and stepped out, closing it behind me. When I looked up, everyone was staring at me. Not my imagination. Heat crept up my neck. I searched for a friendly face and found Ash and Mike sitting by the bar. When I walked toward them, the other side of the room burst into laughter. I widened my eyes at Ash and mouthed, *What?* She shook her head but looked amused. Mike's brows were raised, he smiled.

"Guess someone forgot to put in the dryer sheets," a female voice called over.

More giggling.

"Please just tell me what's going on," I whispered to Ash.

"Well, we heard," she said, as she reached behind me and produced . . . a sock.

That had stuck to my back.

I wanted the floor to crack open and swallow me.

"I need air," I said to her.

I took the stairs two at a time. Heard someone say, "Christ, Leary, what did you do to the girl?" as I hit the top landing. I walked through the Boyles' living room to get to the front porch. Someone was watching television, but I kept my eyes to the floor until I was outside. I wasn't sure I could go back downstairs. I had nothing with me though. Not my phone, jacket, dignity. Why did this have to happen in front of everybody?

This was not how things were supposed to be.

If Alex hadn't died, would any of this be happening? Maybe I'd be with him, at his house, snuggling on the couch and watching a movie.

*I knew once I kissed you, I wouldn't want to stop.*

Far cry from *I really have to take a leak.*

I pulled on the seed bead bracelet with such force, it popped off my wrist and flew in a hundred different directions. I knelt down, seeing what I could salvage from it. The front door opened. Ash burst out. She knelt down next to me.

"Are you okay?"

"Yeah, my, um, bracelet broke."

"Oh, I'm sorry," Ash said, patting the ground to find beads.

"No, it's fine," I said, standing up. "I can't go back downstairs."

Ash gathered a few beads, stood up, and handed them back to me.

"You can absolutely go back down, no one was laughing at you."

"Yes, they were. I'm mortified. What did you mean by we *heard*?"

She bit her lip to tamp down her smile.

"It's not bad, Sar. We just heard some knocking around, someone made a comment. It's not the first time the laundry room has been used for a hookup. Think of it as a rite of passage at the Boyles' house."

"That doesn't make me feel better," I said, a tear spilling out despite my best efforts to conceal what was happening. Ash noticed; her smile faded.

"Was it that awful?"

I shook my head. "That's just it. No, it wasn't awful. It was kind of hot, actually."

"That's a good thing, right?"

"I guess."

"You know, we should get out of here, go get a slice of pizza or something. I'll text Mike to grab our stuff." She spoke as she texted.

"That sounds good," I said, looking at the beads in my open palm. I considered stuffing them in my pocket but then tossed them off the porch and onto the Boyles' lawn.

"I want to get out of here anyway. It's hard being around those guys, it's like I keep looking for Alex to be there. You know they all signed some pledge not to drink? Holly made a big deal of it, gave the list to my parents. I mean, whatever, I don't care if they drink or not, it's their business, but why do that if you're not going to follow through? And Holly is so intense, she acts like we're best friends. And then, well, Jake. I'd just as soon not be around any of them."

Jake.

"You know he didn't sign the pledge," Ash said.

"Jake?"

She nodded. "Again, what's the big deal, but, like, he can't even be bothered to do that? One little stupid thing to honor his best friend?"

"He's working on the scholarship," I offered.

She looked surprised I answered her and was about to say something when the door opened, and Mike and Buzz came onto the porch. Buzz held out my coat to me with a wary look, as if I might recoil. I smiled.

"Thanks," I said, shrugging it on.

"Palermo's?" Mike asked, looking between us.

"Perfect," I said, holding out my hand to Buzz. He took it, tentatively, as we followed Mike and Ash down the stairs.

"Thought you bailed on me," he said.

"Nope," I said, trying to sound cheerful about it. The way I felt was not his fault.

"What happened, then?"

I let him go before me and stopped on the last step, so when he turned back, we were eye to eye.

"This is the first time I've kissed anyone since Alex," I said.

"Oh, shit, wow . . . okay," he said. "Wish I'd known that."

I snaked my arms around his shoulders, leaned closer.

"It was nice," I said.

"Nice? I'd like to think I could do better than that," he said, low.

"Hmm, maybe we should try again, then," I said.

He wrapped his arms around me as I kissed him. There was a whoop and a catcall and Mike yelled, "It's about time."

We laughed but kept kissing until Buzz lifted me off the step and spun me to the ground.

As we walked down the street, my phone vibrated in my pocket. I reached in to check my texts. One message. From Jake.

R U OK?

I shut down the screen and shoved the phone into my pocket. Pushed down the absolute cringe. Jake had witnessed the entire episode, complete with the sock on my back.

I couldn't deal with that at the moment.

# jake

I STARED AT MY PHONE, WILLING SARAH TO TEXT ME back.

Nothing.

Not even those three little dots.

Maybe she hadn't read my text.

I put my phone facedown on the arm of the couch.

Just in case she texted back.

*"Maybe a little too eager there, Hobbs?"*

*Wouldn't you be, Al?*

Pat had thought it would be a good idea for us to break the ice with Bash and some of the new guys on the team. So he invited everyone over to hang in his basement. When Courtney heard, she wanted to hang out too.

"The Boyles' basement is so retro!" she'd said as if we hadn't hung out there in ten years. Playing video games and talking trash was less fun when you weren't having a drink or ten. Courtney had come over to me with one of her blue shots and rolled her eyes when I'd refused it.

She, Holly, and the other girls were busy picking songs off their personal playlists and playing them over the small Bluetooth speaker on the bar—squealing when a song came on that had been popular freshman year. Their arms were above their heads and their hips rocked back and forth. Bash and the new guys watched with greedy eyes. Pat and Taj played *Call of Duty*. I checked my phone again. Ignored the jab of . . . what? Jealousy? Anger? Whatever it was, it annoyed the shit out of me, and it made sitting there in the midst of people out for a good time agonizing.

Court came over again with an open long-neck bottle. She danced in front of the TV as Pat and Taj, half kidding, half not, yelled for her to get out of the way. I laughed. She sat down next to me and draped her legs across my knees.

"Jake Hobbs, is that a smile on your face?" she asked, holding out the bottle. I shook my head.

"Aw, come on, Jake. This is lightweight stuff, take the edge off," she said.

"Nah, I'm good, I like my edges," I said.

"Suit yourself," she said, taking a sip, then leaning her head on my shoulder. I looked at my phone.

"What do you keep checking for?" she asked.

"An email from Colorado. I sent in my application the other day, and they haven't confirmed it yet," I lied, but tried to sell it the best I could.

Court glanced at me as if to say, *Yeah, right*, but played along.

"You're really going through with that?" she asked.

"It's just an application," I said.

"Your parents are okay with you going that far? Out-of-state tuition must be insane."

"Yep, they're okay with it," I said, another lie. "I'll worry about that other stuff after I get accepted."

She didn't say anything, just snuggled closer to me.

It was not like Court to be a buzzkill. In my fantasies of getting the hell out of Cedar Hills I didn't entertain issues like tuition and moving and all those other things that went along with going so far away to school. I liked building the CU Buff Jake I saw in Colorado—outdoorsy, friendly, someone who might be vegan and own a hammock, like the students in the pictures on the website.

"I can't believe all of this is ending, you know?"

"Really? I feel like it already has and we're just waiting it out," I said.

She pulled back a little, went to say something but stopped.

"What?"

"Maybe you and I should hit the laundry room," she whispered.

Laundry room. Those two words a sharp, invisible jab to my gut. A sour taste at the back of my throat. The shuffling-around sounds that Bash had quieted the room about. *Shh, shh, what's that?* The slow realization of what was going on behind the closed door. Sarah coming out with the sock on her back. Court saying something about dryer sheets. That Leary guy. His smug grin that I wanted to sucker punch off his face. Him? That's who Sarah picks to move on with? She dated Alex fucking McKenna for crying out loud.

"I think we've graduated from that," I said, hoping it sounded more kidding than grumpy.

"Could be fun though, getting a sock on my back," she said, laughing, then taking another sip from the long neck. I laughed, but it came out more like a *hmmph* through my clenched jaw. I hated that she commented on Sarah as she left the laundry room and the laughter that followed. I should have said something then. Defended her.

*"Maybe she didn't need defending, Jake?"*

Maybe that's what bothered me most.

That she chose him.

I checked my phone.

Still no text.

A song came on, fast and upbeat, that made the girls shout again and call for Court to come over. She stood up and held out her hand. "C'mon, dance with me, Jake."

"Not happening," I said.

I wasn't the dancing-in-the-basement type, drunk or sober.

"Fine, I'm asking the new guys, then," she said.

She didn't ask Bash so much as placed her hand in his and pulled until he relented. He glanced over his shoulder at me before following Court. I wouldn't have pegged him as a dancing-in-the-basement type either, but there he was falling under Court's spell, just as I had three years ago.

Taj handed me a controller, "C'mon, Hobbs, play."

I took it reluctantly but found, once I started, it was easy to get lost in the game.

Better than checking my phone or thinking about what went on in the laundry room or watching my sort-of hookup pal dance with my sort-of nemesis.

I lasted like that for about an hour. Until I realized I was the only sober person in the room. I wasn't judging anyone. I envied them, if anything. A year ago I would have been right there, tossing back Court's awful shots and hooking up with her in the laundry room. I still wouldn't have been dancing in the basement.

Taking the edge off—which I'd always been down for—was deadly. I was afraid of feeling like that again—out of control, impaired judgment. That was something no one seemed to understand.

Court followed me up the stairs and onto the porch.

"You sure you have to leave?" she asked, folding her arms.

"Yeah," I said.

She sighed. Maybe it was my imagination, but it seemed as though she was tired of trying to coax out fun Jake.

"I want to stay," she said.

"Are you okay getting home?"

She smiled. "Don't worry about me."

"Okay, then," I said. She stood on tiptoe and planted a kiss on my cheek.

"Bye, Jake."

Once home, I went straight to my room, face-planted on my bed. Half an hour later, a text came through.

Hey.

Sarah.

Finally.

I didn't answer right away.

*"Are you really playing games, Hobbs? With Sarah?"*

*Self-preservation isn't a game, Alex. I can't be too in her face, like I was waiting for her to call.*

*"So, you're playing games."*

I ran downstairs to get a Coke and a bottle of water, took my time grazing in the pantry, fighting the urge to call. When I went back to my room, I called Sarah. She picked up on the first ring.

"Well, that was awkward, huh," I asked.

We laughed.

"I thought you'd still be in the Boyles' basement," she said.

"Nah, got home a little while ago. . . . You?"

"I've been home for a bit," she said. "Still recovering from that awful shot Courtney made."

"I should have warned you about her drink-mixing skills," I said. "It's pretty much everything on the bar plus blue curaçao to make it pretty."

"That explains it, then," she said, laughing softly.

There was an uncomfortable lull. A beat I heard her breathe. I wanted to ask about Leary, but I'm not sure I wanted to know. Sarah finally spoke.

"So, to answer your text from before—yes, I'm okay."

"Oh, good, it's just—"

"Please, do we have to talk about it?"

I could picture her blushing, biting the corner of her lip. "Talk about what? The sock in the room?"

"Omigodimhangingup."

"Sarah, wait, no. I'm just teasing you."

"Well, don't. Okay? That was . . . awful."

*"Awful, huh? Why does that make you happy, Hobbs?"*

*I don't know, Al.*

"What was awful? Being in the laundry room with what's his name? Buzz? Or the sock?"

"Why are you torturing me about this?"

I couldn't tell if she was really pissed or just joking, and I didn't want her to hang up.

"I'm sorry. No more sock."

"I had no idea about the sock. And then everyone laughing, that's why I needed to get out of there."

"It's not a big deal, Sarah. If that laundry room could talk."

"Ash mentioned that. I guess you . . . Forget it."

"What?"

"I suppose you have your own laundry room story," she said.

"Well, yeah, everyone does."

She let out a little huff and got quiet again.

I was trying to play it cool, like I didn't feel like clocking Leary for no other reason than being the guy Sarah kissed tonight. If friends were supposed to be able to talk about hookups, why did it feel so uncomfortable sharing this stuff? The question I'd been avoiding, the question I wanted to ask her the moment she'd picked up the phone, sat in my mouth like a stone. I couldn't wait anymore.

"Are you and Leary, like, a thing now?"

She took a breath.

I held mine.

"I don't know. Maybe?"

I'd been waiting for her to say *No way*, hoping that would make this tight feeling in my chest go away. *Maybe?* Well, shit. At least it wasn't *Yes*.

"Good luck with that."

She laughed. "What does that even mean?"

"I don't know. I guess if you're ready to move on that's a good thing."

"I don't think it's about being ready. It just sort of happened, we've been . . . I don't know how to put it, sort of aware of each other for a bit. Then at the cliffs—"

"Wait, did you just say the cliffs?" I asked. The mention of the cliffs knocked every thought of the evening out. Why would she be *there*?

*"Why haven't you been back there?"*

*Not such a great memory, Alex.*

"Oh, um, yeah," she said, softer. "I, well, Ash wanted to go. They were going to throw away some of the items at the shrine, clean it up so it didn't look so messy, I guess. We went to check it out."

"Oh," I said. "How was it?"

"Creepy. Sad. Strange being there."

"I haven't been back there," I said.

"I get that. There was so much stuff, some of it I didn't even understand the reference to, and it made me feel like I didn't know Alex at all. I can't imagine . . . or maybe it's because I *can* imagine what happened that night that made it unsettling. So, if I feel that way, you must—"

"My friends think I should go see it," I said. "Like it's a step in moving on. Maybe they're right; I don't know. I feel like I see it enough in my nightmares."

"Jake, Ash told me something tonight. About the pledge?"

"What?"

"Holly gave it to the McKennas. Something about—"

I cut her off.

"Not drinking or doing drugs, yeah, yeah, yeah. I know all about that." My sudden anger made her pause on the other end. I hadn't meant to get so harsh, but I couldn't help it. Of course Holly had given the pledge to the McKennas. She was into grand gestures. I wondered if she'd had the paper laminated.

"Well, they noticed you didn't sign it."

I sighed. "Christ."

"Why didn't you sign it?" she asked.

"Do you want to judge me too?"

"No, Jake," she said. "I want to understand."

If I'd known that this moment was going to happen, that Holly was going to give the McKennas that piece of paper with my name noticeably missing, I would have signed it. Such an easy thing to do, I'd been such a prick that day.

"Holly sprung signing the pledge on me, on all of us, over lunch at the beginning of school. The fact that she just about demanded that I sign it made me want to do it even less. I know that sounds like I'm five. The whole thing ticked me off. She wasn't even at the cliffs that night. None of them were. Signing that paper isn't going to undo anything. It's not going to bring Alex back. That's where my head was at then. I don't need to sign anything to promise I won't drink. Being there that night was enough for me to stop."

Either my confession had made her mute or she was thinking about what to say. I'd never put it in those words to anyone, well, except Dr. Hipster. When Sarah remained silent, I continued.

"It didn't seem right to me at that point, but here I am, months later, doing nothing to really honor him. That makes me feel worse."

"Don't do that, Jake," she said. "You're working on the scholarship; that's something."

I didn't want to tell her that my ulterior motive for being a part of the scholarship thing had more to do with her than Alex.

"What about Ash, what does she think?"

Her silence said everything.

"She's upset I didn't sign it too?"

"No, that's not it."

"Then what is it? C'mon, Sarah, I'm not an idiot, I see the way she looks at me. She barely said anything to me that day in the hall. Didn't acknowledge me tonight at the Boyles'."

"She was uncomfortable around everyone. Said she felt like Alex should be there with all of you. That's how she feels when . . ." She hesitated.

"When what?"

"When she sees you. That you're a reminder of what happened."

That was a splash of ice water to the face. I'd suspected as much but hearing it from Sarah was entirely different. All my worst fears come true. How was I supposed to respond to that? The thought of being the source of someone's pain sucked. I closed my eyes. My head so heavy on my pillow. A single tear spilled out, and I focused on it as it slid down my temple, pooled in my ear, made me itch. The answer to my next question could change everything. Make our talks end forever. Was I ready for that?

"Is that what you think?" I asked.

"No. Not at all," she said. "I think you've been through something that most of us can't relate to. That must be lonely, Jake."

I rolled over on my side, wished she was really next to me. Not virtually, not at a beach, but here, in my room, in my arms. I'd stay here with her forever. I needed to make things right. Whatever that took. Whatever that meant even. One place I knew to start.

"Hey, I have a favor to ask."

# sarah

WHEN JAKE ASKED ME IF I'D GO BACK TO THE CLIFFS with him, my gut reaction was *No freaking way*. He sounded so solemn though that I would have done anything to make him feel better. The fact that he asked me instead of Courtney or one of his teammates made it seem important. We were friends. Friends supported each other.

Between basketball practice, play rehearsal, and my shifts at Adele's and his Dr. Hipster appointments, we came up with a miraculously free window of time on the Monday before Thanksgiving.

He picked me up about a block away from my building. I'd insisted on that, on the off chance that Ash was somehow walking past my place at the exact moment Jake was picking me up. The truth was Ash could see us anywhere, and the five square miles of Cedar Hills suddenly seemed so damn small. What if she and Mike were at the cliffs? Or walking through the park for that matter? My palms were damp by the time Jake arrived. I slid into the front seat. He laughed.

"You look like Kim Possible," he said.

"Blast from the past," I said, tightening my ponytail. "I guess I was going for inconspicuous, and I don't have camouflage."

"We *are* heading to a public place, people might be around," Jake said.

"So, if someone happened to see us together, and, say, it got back to Courtney, it would all be okay?"

"Yeah, why, are you worried about Buzz?"

"No," I said, but that was only because I knew that he was at an away soccer game. We'd hung out only a few times outside of school since the laundry room incident, and always with Ash and Mike. We texted a bit, but not that much. Not the way I spoke with Jake. Even though we never put a label on what we were doing, I didn't think he'd like the idea of me being alone with Jake.

"Can I ask you something?"

He nodded, made a turn toward the park.

"Why me? Why didn't you ask Courtney or Pat Boyle to come with you?"

He didn't say anything for a few moments, lips pursed in thought, he took a breath and spoke as he drove.

"You listen, Sarah. You don't try to get me out of a mood or tell me what I'm feeling is wrong. I can talk to you. I trust you with my stuff."

He glanced at me.

*Whoosh.*

I smiled and turned to look out the window, didn't want him to see me flush. His words warmed me. I only hoped I could live up to them.

We parked by the lake, not too far from where we'd been the time we came to see Alex's memorial bench, then walked toward the entrance of the hiking trails that led to the cliffs. The ground was soft, the air damp and earthy. It was chilly but warmer than normal for late November. The trees were bare, which somehow accentuated the somber mood. The wooded ground, a carpet of browns and faded yellow, except for the path that led to the cliffs. Jake gestured for me to go first.

"I've never been here during the day," he said. "Looks different."

"Maybe that'll help," I said as we continued toward the shrine.

When we reached the clearing, I walked to the shrine. The collection was smaller than I'd seen it before, with a few new items, more burnt-out candles, a withered rose. There was even a new small Pikachu to take the place of the other one. I stepped to the side so Jake could get a better look, then realized he was still standing at the end of the clearing, taking it in.

"What is all that?" he asked.

"Random things people left here to remember him. Although I don't really get the Pikachu."

"I do," he said, a small smile crossed his face.

"Really?"

"Yeah, those kids he used to coach. Every one of them had a nickname from Pokémon, he used it to get them pumped."

"Wow, I didn't know that," I said. Feeling brave, I held out my hand to him. "Want to take a closer look?"

He put his hand in mine, and we took a few steps closer.

"That's not where it happened," he said, motioning to the shrine. "It happened over there."

I let go of his hand, and walked to the place he'd pointed out, an unpleasant, hollow feeling in my gut.

"Sarah, don't go over there."

"I just want—"

"Sarah, please." Jake's voice echoed. It shook me. I walked back. He was shivering.

"I'm sorry," I said. I gestured toward the smooth boulders and we walked over. They were cool to the touch and slightly damp, but we sat down next to each other.

"I didn't mean to freak out," he said.

"I think if this is your first time back here, freaking out is expected."

"I have nightmares about this place. Only it's dark and everything is tangled. In my dream I reach out for Alex, but it's not really him. I try to run and I can't move. Sometimes I fall and jolt awake. Seeing you there—" He stopped, his eyes glassy. "Fuck."

"Hey, we're safe. Right here," I said, putting my hand over his.

We sat with our own thoughts for a bit, the silence of the park broken every so often by a birdcall or some creature rustling through the fallen leaves. Branches creaked in the wind. The light was fading; I tucked my chin down into my collar for warmth.

"He was right there, and then he was gone. And I keep thinking, *Can't we get a do-over? Can't I tell him to get his own beer?* He wouldn't have been near the edge. He wouldn't have tripped. It didn't seem real at first. I kept expecting him to climb back up, dust himself off; I mean, he was Alex fucking McKenna—he could do anything. I kept calling down to him, waiting for him to pop out and say, 'Just messin' with you.'"

I didn't like to think about Alex's actual fall. The mental picture was chilling, but it was my imagination. Jake had actually witnessed it. He was right, Alex was the sort of person you thought would get through anything. He was so strong, alive—how could something as simple as tripping take him away?

My mother had been the one who broke the news to me about Alex. She arrived to pick me up from my shift at Adele's with the most peculiar expression on her face. My aunt must have known, because she was by my side in an instant as the two of them sat me down. My gut reaction had been denial. It had to be someone else. We had plans the following day. We were going to prom at the end of the month. I had just seen him. Kissed him. How had I innocently worked the entire night, not knowing the horror of what had been happening only a mile away?

I'd texted Ash. Called. There was no answer. I checked Insta. Alex was never one for posting anyway, so even though his last photo was from Christmas, it didn't mean anything. Except when I read the comments underneath and saw *RIP* and *So sorry, man*, and it slowly sunk in that it was possibly the truth.

"It took the ambulance forever to get here," Jake whispered. "I've never felt more useless in my life."

Jake and I had leaned into each other. I didn't remember it happening, but our heads were together, touching.

"I never knew that," I whispered, not wanting to imagine what it must have been like for him, but a picture popped into my head anyway. I laced my fingers through his.

"It was unreal."

"Ash said he would have laughed at all that stuff," I said, motioning with my chin to the shrine. "I think she's right, you know, but I also think there was a part of him that would have liked knowing that people did this. He had a bit of an ego, didn't he?"

"A bit?" Jake laughed.

"I guess it's nice to come here to remember him, to make sense out of it, but this spot will never mean anything to me. It's not like he's here."

Jake pulled back but kept his hand around mine, running his thumb across the top of it. I knew I should have moved, but it felt so good sitting there with him.

"I know we're supposed to believe all that stuff they tell us in mass and religion class about an afterlife, but I don't know." He looked at me, or into me, because my heart swelled. I'd never felt closer to anyone. I blinked a few times, collecting my thoughts.

"My father died when I was a baby, and my mom says whenever she sees a rainbow it feels like he's saying hello. And not just in the sky—like if she sees a bumper sticker or hears a song, she says it always comes to her in a moment she needs it. Coincidence? Maybe. But it's nice to think about, isn't it? We're all just energy, right? And if energy isn't created or destroyed, something must happen to all that potential."

"Energy?"

I thought of something that might help explain what I meant.

"Okay," I said, pulling my hand away from his. "Do me a favor, close your eyes and hold up your hands, like you're surrendering." He did it, slight smile on his lips. He squinted one eye open.

"You're not gonna, like, tie my shoelaces together and leave me here, are you, Walsh?"

I laughed. "No way, Hobbs. Just listen."

"Walsh and Hobbs, we sound like two grizzled detectives on a case," he said, eyes closed.

"Are you going to be serious?"

"Okay, okay," he said.

"I learned this exercise in a drama workshop. It's about how even when you're standing still, you're still engaging with the space around you," I said, putting my hands up to his but leaving about an inch or two of space between them. I closed my eyes.

"Focus on the palms of your hands. Imagine light between my hands and yours. Can you feel heat building?"

He chuckled. "Um, kind of?"

"It helps me to think of the Scarlet Witch, you know, from *Age of Ultron*."

"Wow, you're a Marvel nerd," he said, laughter in his voice.

"Focus," I said.

I took a breath, imagined the connection between our hands. A small ball of light and heat. I pulled my hands back a bit, imagining the ball stretching out, more like a web now.

"Can you—"

"This part of the park is closing in ten minutes," a voice boomed, startling us. Eyes opened, we pulled apart.

There was a park ranger with a large flashlight in his hand, standing about three feet away.

"Mr. Sackner?" Jake said.

"Jake, hey, I didn't realize that was you."

Jake stood up, and I got up with him, brushed the grit off the back of my pants.

"This is my friend Sarah. We're here to, um . . ." Jake gestured toward the shrine.

172

Mr. Sackner nodded. I said hello and continued past them toward the shrine so they could talk. I picked up the Pikachu and dusted off a few leaves, placed it back down. Smiled. I learned something new about Alex today. Not quite a sign or anything, but maybe a bit of a miracle. I stood up as Jake was telling Mr. Sackner we'd be leaving in a minute. He waved and headed back toward the path out to the parking lot. Jake came over to me.

"He thought we were having a séance," he said.

I laughed. "Are you kidding? I'm sorry, I guess I'm not a very good teacher. I swear it made sense in the workshop."

"No, I felt something," he said, keeping his eyes on mine.

One second.

Two seconds.

He broke away and looked at the shrine. I waited while he looked it over.

"Do you really think he's *somewhere*?" he asked, pawing the ground with his foot.

That was *the* question, wasn't it? Who had it right? What they told us in mass? Or religion class? Or was it like my scene in *Almost, Maine*, where souls followed the northern lights to heaven? Was Alex somewhere not giving a second thought to us, or could he see us here, confused and stumbling along without him.

"I'd like to think that," I said.

"Me too," he said.

"Guess we better head out," I said, turning toward the path.

"Thanks for today, Walsh."

I looked over my shoulder at him. "Don't mention it, Hobbs."

# jake

SARAH NAVIGATED THE PATH, HOPPING OVER A branch, kicking acorns, and every so often she'd turn and smile, point out something so I wouldn't trip. Her ponytail swayed with each step. This was a good memory now in this awful place. I hoped that if I had the dreams again, it would somehow include this. I wanted to close the space between us so much I ached. I dug my hands deep into my pockets.

Walsh.

Think of her as *Walsh*.

That kept it friendly. Like someone whose hair you'd muss up or greet with a shoulder punch or toss a few beers back with.

Only . . .

I wanted to take her hand.

I wanted to keep listening to her.

Hear her theories on life and death and Marvel.

I wanted to feel the heat between our hands.

And okay, everywhere else too.

I wanted to take out her ponytail.

See her hair fall around her shoulders.

I wanted to kiss her.

I wanted her.

*"Whoa there, Hobbs, that escalated quickly."*

*I know, came here to honor you, Alex, not lust after Sarah.*

Although my feelings hadn't escalated quickly. They'd been building for weeks, with nights on the phone and secret glances and a virtual beach date that sometimes went beyond just sitting there looking at the stars, at least in my head. And while I knew I couldn't act on those feelings, they were undeniable. I wanted to believe, someday, there'd be a way.

Until then, friends.

# sarah

THE LAST PLAY REHEARSAL BEFORE THANKSGIVING break, we worked on blocking. Everything would amp up more in January and February when Trinity wanted us to be off book, but for now, there was downtime between acts. I was looking forward to break, if for nothing else than just to chill, eat turkey, and hang out with my mom and Aunt Sophie. My scene had been one of the first to be blocked, and I sat on the sidelines starting to commit my lines to memory, when Dylan Jacobs came over to me.

He had this look on his face, very cat that ate the canary, and I wondered if he was going to regale me with an audition story. Rumor was that he was up for a McDonald's commercial and if he got it, he would be insufferable, which was fine—I'd probably be insufferable too. I steeled myself for one of his flex sessions. He sat down next to me on the floor, leaned back on his hands, and stretched out his legs.

"So, now I get why you don't want to rehearse kissing," he said.

My brow furrowed. I hadn't revealed the real reason, but even though that was no longer an issue, I thought we'd both react better during the scene if we weren't used to it by opening night. Trinity thought that idea was a stroke of genius.

"I think it would be—"

"You and Jake Hobbs, huh?"

We were onstage in the gym, and the basketball team happened to be practicing as we started rehearsal. Had he caught me glancing over at Jake before Trinity told Cullyn to close the curtain? I played dumb.

"I already told you, there's nothing going on," I said.

"Then why did I see you walking out of the woods together near the cliffs?"

My mind blanked. I had no response except to look at him, wide-eyed, which I'm sure was the equivalent of me saying "Guilty!" His grin stretched across his face. My first impulse was to tell him nothing happened, but I knew that would make it sound like something definitely happened. I kept my cool.

"Not that I owe you any explanation, but we're just friends. What were you doing in the park?"

"On my run."

"You run?"

"Do you think it's easy to look like this?" he said, sort of joking, sort of not. "The bigger question is what were you doing in the park?"

"Jake had never been to the shrine for Alex McKenna. I was there for moral support," I said, hoping that dropping Alex's name into the conversation would make him shut up like it usually did everyone else. Instant gravitas. And it was the truth, it wasn't like we'd been on a leisurely hike.

"Oh," he said. "It didn't look like you were just friends."

I put down my script. Maybe if Dylan had somehow seen us

closer to the shrine—holding hands, leaning into each other, then I could see him getting the wrong idea. But when we'd left? I'd been about three feet in front of Jake, negotiating the path and trying not to fall on my ass.

"Why would you say that?"

He raised a skeptical eyebrow. "Oh, come on Sarah. I've known you since middle school. I'm your scene partner. You can trust me."

I turned to check the surrounding area. Everyone was in their own bubble, either working with their partners or blocking out their scene.

"Wow, this must be really juicy if you're checking to see if the coast is clear," he said.

"That's not . . . no, nothing that juicy," I said. Was I really going to do this? I figured I had to give him something, or he'd be even more relentless. "We're friends. We talk on the phone at night."

He waited for more. "That's it?"

I nodded. "Anything more than that is impossible."

"Why?"

"I'm sort of seeing someone," I said.

"Easily fixed."

"And so is he. I think, sort of," I said.

"Okay, lots of *sort of*s here. What else?"

"Well, and Ash. Ash said Jake is like a reminder of the night when Alex fell. She would just as soon not have to see him again."

His teasing demeanor became more subdued, as he considered what I said.

"Is that what *you* think?"

I shook my head.

"Then it doesn't matter, does it?"

It was a relief to get this off my chest; talk to a neutral party.

"You don't think it would be strange for me to hook up with Alex's best friend?"

Even saying the words *hook up* in relation to Jake made me blush.

Dylan shrugged. "You both lost someone you were close to. Makes sense you would turn to each other."

"What would people say though?"

"Who cares what other people think? For what it's worth, the word *impossible* is not in my vocabulary," he said.

"Of course you would say that," I said.

"When I walked into that *Doppelgängers* audition last May, there was a long line down the hallway of ridiculously good-looking people. I almost left. Here in Saint Aedan's? I'm star material. In Manhattan? I'm just another actor trying to get a gig. Then I stopped psyching myself out and went for it."

"I've really enjoyed your TED Talk, Mr. Jacobs," I said.

He laughed.

"All I'm saying is, if you want something, you can't let being afraid hold you back. You go for it like you have nothing to lose," he said.

I did have something to lose though. Or someone.

I couldn't imagine not having Ash in my life.

I changed the subject.

"Have you memorized your lines yet?" I asked.

"Of course," he said.

"Hey, I need my 'Her Heart' people now," Trinity said, calling us over to center stage. I was relieved to get back to make-believe.

Before rehearsal ended, Trinity gave us a characterization exercise to think about over break. We were to come up with a secret for our character. It wasn't anything we had to reveal, it was to add dimension to our performance. Something to help us get a better understanding of the person we were embodying. Dylan nudged me.

"Don't think you'll have a problem with that, eh, Sarah?"

"Dylan!"

"Have a nice break," he called over his shoulder.

"You two seem to be getting along," Trinity said, sidling up to me.

"I guess," I said. "Hey, I'm sorry I keep tearing up during the scene. I know it's supposed to be more lighthearted than morose."

"Don't be. You'll get it. You and Dylan are in my favorite scene . . . but, shh, don't tell anyone," she said. I smiled.

My phone buzzed. I excused myself and walked over to my backpack as I checked the message.

Jake.

Maybe he noticed me noticing him.

Raining. Need a ride home?

I looked around. Most of the cast had dispersed. Should I chance being seen with Jake? It was just a ride. And it was raining. Nothing to hide despite what it felt like. We were friends. Friends asked friends if they needed a ride. Especially in the rain.

Sure. Be right there.

I slipped on my jacket, collected my stuff.

"Enjoy Thanksgiving, Trini," I said.

"You too, Sar," she said. "And don't forget about that secret."

"Already on it," I answered.

As Dylan had said.

I'd have no problem with that.

# december

# sarah

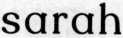

SAINT AEDAN'S GYM WAS UNCOMFORTABLY HOT AND deafeningly quiet.

The first game of basketball season began with a moment of silence for Alex.

In the gym, Alex belonged to everyone—the Crusader fans, the cheerleaders, his teammates. Holly. She sat behind the cheerleaders and, as usual, wore tragedy well. Appropriately tearful, tastefully dressed. Courtney kept turning to check on her.

I glanced over at Ash. Her head was down, curtain of hair shielding her face. We were all surprised that she'd insisted on coming to the game. Mike sat close and doted as usual. Buzz and I sat next to each other—this was our first official outing, something other than the Boyles' basement or the lunch table—and yet I felt worlds away from him.

My eyes wandered to Jake and the rest of the team, assembled in starting positions on the court. Jake's head was down—was that the rule for a moment of silence, to be somber and look at the floor? What could he be thinking about?

The moment of silence dragged on, and I realized I hadn't given it any thought except how uncomfortable it felt to be there. I said a quick Our Father, which was usually my default, but I wanted something more personal.

*You should be here, Alex. It's not the same without you.*

Would I have been sitting here wearing his varsity jacket and cheering? Or would we even have been together? If we had broken up, could I have been content sitting there with Buzz? Pressure built behind my eyes. Maybe the reason I didn't want to think about anything during the moment was because I knew it would lead to tears. Mercifully, Monsignor Dolan ended the silence, the buzzer sounded, and the game started.

By the end of the first quarter, Saint Aedan's was down by ten points. A situation that somehow seemed hopeless, even though the game was far from over. The team stood in a loose huddle on the sidelines, while Coach Callard made forceful hand gestures as he spoke. The cheerleaders were cheering about spirit, trying to get the crowd involved by doing a callback. There were quite a few people into it, but I didn't join in. Buzz leaned toward me.

"They want to get out of here," he said, motioning to Ash and Mike.

"We just got here," I said, making eye contact with Ash. She mouthed, "Let's go." I nodded. We stood up. For a split second, Jake glanced up from the huddle. Our eyes met, and I felt the slightest twinge of guilt that we were leaving. I knew he'd been nervous about tonight, how he didn't want to let anyone down. Was I letting him down by leaving? I looked away, focused on following Buzz as we made our way over to the stairway on the bleachers.

It's not like Jake needed me there. There was a whole stand

full of fans. He mentioned his parents and sister usually came to the games, or at least one of them attended, depending on their work schedules. Were they here now? Was I stepping over them as I exited the bleachers? And he had Courtney, his own personal cheerleader. She'd called his name several times during the first quarter. He'd been fouled, and during the free throw, I thought of our conversation when he blessed himself before shooting. The ball swished right through the net, and letting out a cheer of approval for him was natural. No one thought anything of it.

The biting cold outside was sweet relief from the hot gym, at least momentarily. Ash and Mike walked away arm in arm, as always. Buzz held out his hand, and I took it. We walked off school grounds.

"Where to?" Mike asked.

The four of us looked at each other.

"The basement?" Buzz asked, squeezing my hand. I wasn't sure if that was a signal or something, but the truth was I wasn't ready to hit the Boyles' basement yet. Too many hours left in the night. Ash spoke up.

"I'm in the mood for hot chocolate," she said. "How about the diner?"

"Awesome, let's go, it's freezing," Mike said. He and Ash started across the street. Buzz and I trailed behind.

"We should go to Mike's, we're gonna end up there anyway," Buzz said.

I didn't answer. The silence between us stretched out. My hand felt sweaty and unnatural in his all of a sudden. Nothing like when I'd taken Jake's hand at the park.

I had to stop obsessing over Jake.

Jake was impossible. This, being with Buzz. *This* was possible. And I got to hang with Ash. I focused on our surroundings, a few houses already had Christmas lights up, making the street look festive. I was about to comment on that when Ash yelled and broke apart from Mike. Buzz and I glanced at each other and picked up the pace to see what was going on.

"Why would you say that?" Ash said.

"Ashley, come on," Mike said.

"No, Michael, admit it, you don't think I can do it," she said.

"I never said that," he answered.

"But you think it," she said, and walked across the crosswalk in the opposite direction.

"Ashley," Mike said, following her.

"Shit, they're using full names, something must be up," Buzz said, which shouldn't have been funny, but made me stifle a giggle. If Ash and Mike weren't in a perpetual lip-lock, they were prone to dramatic disagreements.

She turned but continued walking backward toward the other side of the street. "Do. Not. Follow. Me. I don't want to talk to you right now," she said.

Mike looked stricken as he turned back to us.

"I'm going after her," I said, turning to Buzz.

"Sar, please tell her . . . tell her I didn't mean it. Not the way she thinks," Mike said.

"Um, okay," I said, wondering what in the world this was about. There hadn't seemed like enough time since leaving school to have that serious of a blowup.

Ash had already made it to the corner on the next street. I had to jog to catch up to her.

"Hey," I said, catching my breath. "It's me."

She barely slowed down. I finally caught up. Her cheeks were wet with tears.

"Ash, holy shit, what happened?"

She sniffled, shook her head violently, swatted away the tears on her face with her mitten.

"Let's go to my house," she said.

I turned to look behind us. Mike and Buzz were where we'd left them, under the streetlamp.

"Okay, sure."

Once at the McKennas', we made some hot chocolate, piled both mugs high with swirls of whipped cream, and climbed the stairs to Ash's room. She still hadn't told me what she and Mike had fought about, and I didn't press it, just followed her lead. The house was dark. Mrs. McKenna had always started decorating for Christmas the day after Halloween, but there wasn't even a speck of Christmas cheer around. No lighted garland on the banisters, no candles in the windows, no floor-to-ceiling Douglas fir in their living room.

It was still hard not to imagine Alex galloping down the stairs or lounging across the sofa in front of the television. I hadn't really hung out at Ash's house in months, not the way I used to. Before Mike. Before Alex. My heart beat faster as we walked up the stairs toward her room. Alex's door was across from hers, on the front was the fallout shelter sign he'd had there since middle school.

"You okay?" Ash said.

"Yeah, it's crazy, I haven't been up here since . . . well."

"I know. I guess I haven't been here much either. I like getting away from it. Mike's basement is my home away from home," she said.

Ash paused a minute, then turned toward Alex's door.

"You want to take a look?" Ash asked.

I nodded.

She turned the knob, leaned in, and flicked on the light switch. I stood at the threshold, holding my mug with both hands to stop from shaking. Most of my memories of Alex's room were from before we were even together. But somehow, when Ash opened the door, it opened up a flood of feeling I hadn't known was there. God, I missed him.

"Come in, I know it's strange. Looks like he'll be home any minute to tell us to stop snooping, right?"

Maybe that's what was unsettling about it. The bed had been made, so things had changed since the last time Ash had spoken to me about it. Everything was neat, but there were things here and there—the closet full of shoes spilling out, his phone on the end table, an unopened bottle of Gatorade, a half-finished roll of mint Mentos—that made it seem like he could be back any moment. His laptop sat on his desk, closed. His school backpack, slung over his desk chair, zipper undone. The fish tank hummed.

"My dad finally convinced my mom to change the sheets and make the bed, pick up the clothes from the floor. But she wanted to leave everything else as is. I kind of get it, kind of don't. It's like suspended in time this way."

"Yes," I said. I hadn't realized how much I'd been pushing down memories of Alex. I didn't know where to look, Alex was everywhere. Ash grabbed his phone.

"It took my dad forever to get into Alex's phone. Can you believe it was completely intact after he fell? Not even a scratch." She was so matter-of-fact, as if she were talking about a stranger. She placed it back down on the end table. I wanted to pick it up, but at the same time it felt wrong. It was his phone. Supposed to be private. My heart ached.

"Sometimes I go back over his texts, just to feel like I'm talking to him," I said. It was the first time I was admitting that to her. "I read them in his voice."

She gave me a small smile.

"Me too, although I'm sure yours are different," she said, nudging me.

"At some point, we're supposed to go through everything, box it up. He has so many T-shirts. I thought maybe you could help me; there might be something you'd like."

"Oh, um, yeah."

She fed the fish before we left the room and closed the door. We went into her room and sat on her shaggy carpet. She with her back against her bed, me against the beanbag chair.

"Ooh, wait, I have something for you," she said, getting up again and walking over to her dresser. She grabbed something from the top and walked over to me, smiling.

"I didn't wrap it or anything, so close your eyes."

"It's not Christmas yet," I said.

"Well, I'll be in the middle of the Caribbean for Christmas. I think you'll like this now, anyway. C'mon, close your eyes, hold out your hand."

I laughed. "Okay."

I was expecting her to place something in my open palm, but she took my hand and slipped something onto my wrist. "Okay, open."

When I opened my eyes, I saw a delicate turquoise braided rope bracelet around my wrist. There was a tragedy-comedy drama mask charm, and a little crystal bead, dangling from it.

"Ash, wow," I said, inspecting the charm. "Thank you!"

"I got one too. Mine has music notes, kind of like a reminder of our dream."

In middle school, Ash and I had this dream of sharing an apartment in the East Village. We'd move there right after college so she could pursue music and I could pursue acting, we'd both have jobs that would give us time to go to auditions, and we'd go out all night and have this crazy Manhattan life. It was a silly dream on so many levels, I mean, we'd probably have to start with about a billion dollars to live the lifestyle we'd imagined, but it had been fun to have that kind of dream together.

"I love it," I said.

"I thought it could be a replacement for that other one that broke."

"Oh, that one wasn't as special as this," I said, taking a sip of my hot chocolate. I didn't feel like getting into the meaning of the seed bead bracelet. It was gone; that was enough.

"I find it hard to believe your phone isn't blowing up," I said.

"Oh, it is, I'm ignoring it."

"Do you want to talk about it now?"

sighed, pulled her knees into her chest.

e thinks this holiday showcase is . . . well, stupid."

ed, immediately defensive, then remembered what he'd

said before I left him and Buzz at the corner.

"Okay, Mike wanted me to tell you that he didn't mean what he said, not the way it sounded, or something like that."

She shook her head and took a long slug of hot chocolate before getting up to retrieve her guitar from the corner. She sat down and strummed, tuning it before playing the opening notes to "Hotel California," a song she'd learned because it was her dad's favorite. She'd tried to teach me once, but I had no patience or tolerance for the pain in my fingertips. Ash got lost in some musical bliss when she played.

"I've never played for Mike," she said, not missing a note.

"He must have seen you last year at assemblies, you've played for the guitar mass."

She stopped. "That's different. I mean like this, songs I care about."

"Why not, then?"

"I don't know, maybe because I like that it's just for me. Something to get lost in. I stopped playing when we hooked up. Not on purpose or anything, and then everything with Alex . . . I didn't put any time in. Lately I've been fooling around with it. I want a challenge, something for me. Look, I got my calluses back." She smiled and held up her hand.

"You're going to be incredible," I said.

"Mike said, 'Are you sure you want to do that? In front of all those people? Are you really ready?'"

"So, he didn't literally say it was stupid?"

"No, but I can tell he feels that way by the way he acts whenever I bring it up."

"Break up with him," I joked.

"I can't," she said. "We've got that thing, you know?"

"What, chlamydia?"

She laughed, reached up, and grabbed the laughing face emoji pillow from her bed and tossed it at me.

"Hey, hot drink here," I said, holding my drink up and away as the pillow grazed my ear. Ash put her guitar aside and slid her phone out of her pocket. The screen lit up her face. She bit her lip as she scanned her messages.

"It's like there's this magnet pull with him. Even now, I'm so pissed, but I can't help it. I want his hands on me."

"I think that's called being horny. You know, I haven't always been Mike's biggest fan, but he's been there for you when you really needed it; that means something. He probably doesn't want to share you with the rest of the world. Or you know, Bran Russo."

"You think?"

I shrugged.

"How are things with you and Buzz going? I saw you holding hands," she said, waggling her eyebrows.

What could I say? I certainly didn't feel a magnet pull with him, not in the way she'd been talking about. And I wasn't ready just yet to have his hands on me. It wasn't awful having someone to hold hands with. Buzz was funny and cute, and hanging with Ash and Mike was the added bonus. Being with him didn't consume me. Maybe that's what a healthy relationship was supposed to feel like. It was certainly easier than being sick with desire 24-7 for someone.

"I don't know, it's okay. It's not like we've really hung out all that much or done anything besides play pool in Mike's basement."

"Omigod, *yes!*" she said pointing at me. "I've said that exact thing to Mike. We should go out, really do something. Take the train to the city or go to a movie. Mike's basement is fun and all, but we're in a rut, aren't we?"

There was a light *ping* at Ash's window. We both turned to look.

"What the hell?" she said getting up. I joined her. As we got to the window there was another *ping*. Someone was tossing something at the window to get her attention. Ash drew back the curtain, and sure enough, Mike and Buzz were down on the deck. They tripped the sensor, and the yard was flooded with light.

"I thought people only did this in movies," I said.

"My father will go ballistic if Mike breaks the window," she said, gesturing for him to stop. Mike held his hands out in a pleading gesture. I took the opportunity to check my phone. There was a text from Buzz.

How is Ashley? Michael is losing his shit. Help.

I laughed and texted back.

I predict a major makeup PDA in 3 . . . 2 . . . 1

Ash sighed, but the corners of her mouth turned up. "I guess I better go down there."

"End Mike's misery," I said.

"You're right though, Sar. We need a real night out, the four of us," she said, walking out of the room. I hadn't remembered insisting on the four of us going out, but if she wanted to give me the credit, I wasn't about to argue. My phone buzzed with another text.

Hey

Jake.

I shut down my phone and slid it into my pocket. It was ten thirty, was he home already? I collected our mugs and went downstairs. Mike, Ash, and Buzz were in the kitchen. Mike and Ash stood a few feet apart, staring at each other.

"I guess, um, I'm gonna get going, have to be home by eleven," I said, putting the mugs in the sink. "I'll grab my coat."

"I'll walk you home," Buzz said. Mike and Ash barely broke their gaze.

"I'll call you, Sar," Ash said.

"Yep, later."

Once outside, Buzz and I debriefed each other.

"Well, that was fun."

"Yeah, left a basketball game for a brawl. A Friday night for the books," he said.

"You weren't waiting out in the yard all that time, were you?"

We fell into step and clasped hands as we headed up the block.

"Nah, we went to the diner but didn't stay. Mike was texting Ash the whole time and got jumpy when she wouldn't answer."

"We went straight to Ash's. Did he tell you what the fight was about?"

"He asked her if she thought she was ready to play in front of people, and she flipped out. The dude would do anything for her, I don't know what the big deal was."

"Music is important to Ash. She didn't feel like he was behind her. That's pretty important, don't you think? To support the person you care about?"

"Yeah, sure. Like you know, coming to a soccer game?" He said, nudging my shoulder.

"Or a play?" I countered.

He smiled. "I'm game if you are."

We walked in silence after that, hurried our pace as if we could outrun the cold. I reached into my pocket for my keys as we arrived at the stoop of my apartment building.

"Thanks for walking me home," I said.

He pulled me toward him, and we wrapped our arms around each other. He lowered his face to mine, our noses touching.

"I really wanted to be alone with you tonight," he said.

"We're alone now."

"You know what I mean." He kissed the tip of my nose.

Laundry room alone but maybe more horizontal? I should want that, right? I should want his hands on me, the way Ash felt about Mike. Could you grow into that sort of heat?

We kissed. It was sweet. Slow. I pulled away.

"See ya," I said, heading into my building.

# jake

I HAD NO RIGHT TO BE ANNOYED THAT SARAH LEFT after the first quarter, and yet I couldn't shake it. I'd rarely noticed people in the bleachers before, the court had always been my focus, but I'd been so nervous about the game. The moment of silence hadn't helped. We were down in the first half, but by the second, we found our stride. We made it through and won; even Bash didn't get on my nerves, in spite of his cheering section and their "Bash Is Beast" T-shirts.

In the end they were cheering for all of us, and that helped psyche us up. Bash's family had invited the team back to his house to celebrate. I pulled the tired card, which wasn't that far from the truth. The win felt like it meant something, I should have wanted to celebrate.

Instead, all I could think about was Sarah leaving.

Staring up at my ceiling waiting for her to text me or not, I regretted not going to Bash's.

My phone buzzed.

Hey.

Sarah.

Finally.

I waited.

*"Playing games again, Hobbs? Just call her."*

*I can hold off a bit.*

*Make her wait.*

*"Mature, Hobbs."*

Why him though? I didn't know much about Buzz, except he was Mike Boyle's best friend, and Mike, while fairly harmless, was not exactly the brightest crayon in the box. How he'd hypnotized Ash McKenna into dating him was something Alex never understood either. Maybe Buzz and Sarah were together because it was convenient. He had the luck of proximity.

I didn't want to think about them together. Where had they gone? Boyle's basement? Somewhere on their own?

*"You could find that out with one simple phone call."*

*Fine.*

I called.

She picked up on the third ring.

"Hey," she said.

"Hey."

"How did it go?" she asked.

"We won," I said, in a way I hoped conveyed that it was her loss that she missed it.

"That's so great!" she said. "It wasn't looking good there in the first quarter."

"You missed the best part. We pulled it together in the second half. Felt good. I was on fire, but you know, you would have seen me in action if you'd stayed," I said.

*"You had to go there didn't you, Hobbs?"*

*Just flexin' a little, Alex, what can I say?*

"Jake, I'm sorry I didn't stay. It wasn't my choice," she said. "Ash wanted to leave. It was hard being there."

That made me feel like a complete idiot for being annoyed that she left.

"How is she doing?"

"Okay," she said. "You never know what might set her off, but being there, I even found myself looking for Alex. That probably sounds strange."

"No, I get it," I said.

"The part I did see, you were your usual fierce self," she said.

"Fierce, huh?" It was nice to know I looked objectively fierce—that first quarter had been rough. "So, what did you do the rest of the night?"

*"Subtle."*

"Ash had an argument with Mike. I played mediator. We went to her house and hung out awhile."

"The four of you?"

"No, just me and Ash, then Mike came by so they could make up," she answered.

Noticeably missing . . . Buzz. Yes.

"Sounds serious."

She laughed. "Nah, that's how it is with them. I think they fight so they can make up."

"You and what's his name looked pretty chummy tonight," I said. "How's that going?"

"It's going, I guess."

"Going where?"

"You really want to hear about this?"

"Yeah, we're friends, right? Not sure if I approve of this particular choice, but you know, it's your life."

"Why would you put it like that?"

Crap.

*"Tone down the feelings, Hobbs. Be supportive."*

"I'm just teasing, but I dunno, you go from Alex to this guy? He doesn't seem like a good fit for you. What do you have in common?"

She laughed. "I don't know. Ash and Mike. He makes me laugh. He's teaching me how to play pool."

He makes her laugh. Fucking great.

"Sounds like a perfect match."

She got quiet again. Our conversations were usually enjoyable. This one made me restless. Maybe I should have gone to Bash's house, hung out with the guys, celebrated our win. I wondered if Court was still there.

"I don't know what it is, Jake. Except, I know I won't get swept away by it. My feelings for Buzz are . . . manageable."

I was starting to feel a little sorry for the guy.

I didn't know what to say to that. As someone who had their own relationship compromises, it wasn't fair to judge her.

Still.

Is that what she wanted? Someone *manageable*?

"Hello, you still there?"

"Yeah, I'm here."

"You think that's asinine, don't you?" she asked.

Yes. I wanted to tell her that *manageable* sounded about as sexy as a 7:00 a.m. pop quiz in calculus. On a Monday. Instead, I took a breath.

"No, we all do what we have to do to get by," I said.

"Are you okay? You sound . . . odd."

"Just tired, the game took a lot out of me. I'm gonna go, you okay?"

"Oh, so no . . . no beach tonight?"

"Nah, gotta go. Night, Sarah," I said, hanging up before I could hear her reply.

It was a shitty thing to do, but I didn't feel like getting swept up in some fantasy of us on a beach blanket when there was no potential, was there? There were real people I could hang out with; people who wanted to hang with me. I didn't feel like spending another minute analyzing the reasons she was hooking up with Buzz Leary. The truth was, Sarah was moving on—maybe not in the way I'd hoped—but she was, and what was I doing? Sitting there staring at the ceiling. I checked the time: eleven forty-five. The night was beginning. I texted Court.

Still at Bash's?

It took a minute, but she finally replied.

Yes.

Should I stop by?

YES!! ♥

Maybe it wasn't moving on exactly, but it wasn't standing still either. I threw on some clothes and headed out.

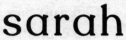

# sarah

ASH AND MIKE MUST HAVE HAD ONE SERIOUS CONVER-
sation when they made up because the following night, the four
of us had a genuine *date* date to the movies. Buzz even suggested
he come upstairs to meet my mom. I told him it was completely
unnecessary, but he'd insisted and even got there early. I was finishing applying my mascara when I heard the bell. To my complete
mortification, Mom buzzed Buzz up. She was loving this peek into
my life. It was torture.

I finished up and took a long last glimpse in the mirror. I'd
taken a shower after my double shift at Adele's, and I used a blow-
dryer to style my hair straight and smooth. Not half bad in dark
jeans, suede booties, and a white bell-sleeve sweater. I may have had
a random butterfly knocking around my insides, which I took as
a good sign. I walked into the living room and tried not to freak
at the improbable scene of Buzz and my mother in the same space.

Buzz had put in an effort too; he'd lost his usual denim and
hoodie look for a military jacket, dark jeans, and a gray sweater.
His hair was combed, neater than usual. He looked like he cared. I
was surprised at the pleasant rush of warmth that went through me
when I saw him, the immediate smile we both gave to each other.

Maybe this *could* become something more than manageable.

"I see you've met B—"

"Christian," Buzz said, grinning.

Mom crossed her arms, smiled. "Yes, you're going to see that Krampus movie?"

"Yes, what is it? *North Pole Massacre*? Something light for Christmas," I joked, grabbing my jacket. I checked my phone to see if Ash had texted.

Her dad was driving us to the movies; there was no way we were sitting in my living room with my mom, staring at each other until then.

"Okay, see you later," I said, opening the front door and motioning for Buzz to go ahead.

"Nice to meet you, Mrs. Walsh," he said. I swear his voice was deeper, like he'd matured five years since I last saw him. Did he find pointers on how to talk to parents on TikTok or something? My mom stood in the doorway as we walked down the stairwell.

"What time should I expect you home?" she called.

"Um, elevenish," I said. "I'll text you if I'm going to be later."

"Have fun."

As we reached the third-floor landing, I heard the door click shut. Buzz grabbed my hand and pulled me over to an alcove. His lips were on mine before I even knew what was happening. Unexpected but nice. We pulled apart.

"Ah, there you are," I said. "I wondered who this polite, parent suck-up guy in my living room was."

"Did pretty good, huh," he said, smiling.

We kissed again.

204

"C'mon, I don't need any neighbors complaining to my mom about hallway PDA," I said, starting back down the stairs to the front stoop. We piled into the McKennas' SUV, Ash's dad told corny jokes on the way. Mike sat up front with him and every so often turned toward the back and widened his eyes at Ash, who was loving every minute of putting him on the spot with her father.

We arrived just in time. The previews had already started by the time we sat down. Five minutes in and I regretted not getting popcorn. I leaned over to Buzz.

"I'm going for popcorn, want anything?"

"I'll go."

"No, no you bought the tickets, I'll pick this one up," I said.

"Um, okay, I'm good, popcorn is fine."

The line looked so long I almost turned around and went back to the theater but then realized I really didn't care about missing the first part of the movie. Horror wasn't my favorite. I'd been standing there less than a minute when I felt a tug on my hair. It was so light, I thought I might have imagined it, but then I felt it again and turned around.

Jake stood behind me in line, but he looked away as I turned around, pretending he hadn't deliberately tried to get my attention. I bit my lip to keep from smiling so hard. Seeing him was such a great surprise, especially after last night's phone call. He'd sounded almost annoyed when he hung up.

"Hey," I said.

"Sarah, hi, thought that was you," he said, keeping up his act until he finally cracked a smile. "What's up?"

"Oh, you know, getting some popcorn."

"Yeah, kind of figured that. I know how much you like popcorn."

He remembered that night too? Last year at the McKennas', *Train to Busan*, forgetting to put the lid on the popcorn pot, his asking me if I needed a ride home.

"Definitely better when it's not flying all over the room."

"That was sort of fun though," Jake said. "Here with Buzz?"

He dragged out the *z*'s a little bit, narrowed his eyes, making it sound annoying. Or maybe I was being sensitive.

"Yes, also with Ash and Mike. The four of us, seeing that Christmas massacre movie, whatever it is."

"So are we, but the only tickets they had left was for the 3D version."

"Lucky you. *We?*"

I was proud of myself for sneaking in that deliberate info dig.

"Yeah, I'm here with Courtney, Pat Boyle, and Holly."

I nodded. "And they sent you for popcorn?"

"They're getting cappuccinos. Can't see a 3D movie without cappuccinos, you know."

"So, you're the boy toy tonight, huh? Guess College Guy isn't home for winter break yet," I said. I'd meant it to sound funny, but it sounded more mean than playful.

Jake stepped back as if I'd physically pushed him away. A long minute passed before he spoke.

"What did you say?"

We moved up in line. My cheeks got warm. I knew he heard me the first time. I didn't want to repeat it, I wasn't good at sarcasm, apparently. "Forget it, I was kidding."

"Right, kidding," he said, looking over toward the coffee bar. When he turned back to me, his eyes were dark with anger. "What are *you* doing, Sarah?"

"Jake, I'm—"

"Don't kid yourself, you're just like Courtney."

"Don't compare me to her," I said, folding my arms across my chest.

"Why not? You don't care about Buzz—what did you say— your feelings for him are *manageable*? Does he know that's how you think of him? Because I doubt he feels the same way."

His words stung but also made me angry—was what I said really that awful?

"I actually feel bad for the guy, because at least I know what I'm dealing with."

"Right," I said. "That's such a *beneficial arrangement* you have going on there."

"It's my choice though. Buzz doesn't have a clue, does he?"

Courtney cozied up to him, large steaming to-go cup in her manicured hand. She slipped her arm through his. I wondered how much she heard of what we said, if she had even heard anything at all.

"Hey, it's Sock Girl," she said, grinning and nudging Jake.

His eyes remained sharp, and he smirked at her comment. She could have thrown her cappuccino across my sweater and it would have burned less. I hadn't realized the situation could get worse. I turned around as tears threatened. The moment the cashier called "Next," I bolted up and rattled off my order. I paid without turning around. Screw them both.

I stopped to collect myself before heading back into the theater. The image of Courtney laughing and calling me Sock Girl kept playing in a loop in my brain. Jake stood there. Smirking. Was he angry with me? I hadn't meant anything by calling him a boy toy. That's what he'd called Buzz. I'd tried to make a joke. I certainly hadn't intended to piss him off.

The door to the theater swung open, and the girl going out held it while I went back inside. It took a moment for my eyes to adjust to the darkness. I climbed the stairs to our seats and handed Buzz the popcorn bucket and placed the drink in the holder while I stepped over him to my seat. When I was situated, he handed the bucket back to me. The expression on his face—the soft smile— made me feel like such a jerk. Was what Jake said true? Was Buzz more into me than I was into him?

I leaned in to kiss him. Originally going in for a peck but lingering a little longer.

*I'm not like Courtney.*

I was trying to make something happen here. When I pulled away, Buzz opened his eyes and a slow smile spread across his face. Shit.

"Did I miss anything?" I whispered.

He shook his head. We both leaned back. I set the popcorn on the armrest between us and tried to focus on the movie. It was futile though. All the feelings I'd been stuffing down and rationalizing became a cyclone rushing through my head.

*Don't you get it, Sarah?*

*You're not like Courtney.*

*You want to be Courtney.*

*No.*

*Yes.*

*Shit.*

*Shit. Shit. Shit.*

*Yes. Yes. Yes, I do.*

Only, Jake would be more than a boy toy to me.

There'd be no College Guy, no one else.

Just Jake.

And me.

The thought of Jake and Courtney as a couple hadn't bothered me. Even when it was obvious she'd been in his car, that they'd had a history, the way she took his jacket at that committee meeting—it hadn't made me feel like this. Seeing them together tonight? I could still feel the burn of jealousy that gnawed at me when she hooked her arm through his. It was such a familiar gesture. Comfortable. They probably touched a million different ways without even thinking about it. It was second nature to them.

Whatever arrangement they had, Jake was still into it, no matter how much he dismissed it. How could I not have seen it? Did I really think I could just be friends with him? All those nights on the phone, spilling our guts about everything and nothing had made us close.

Closer in a way than I'd ever been to Alex.

We became friends by choice, not circumstance. Or maybe it was circumstance *and* choice. Alex's death had brought us together. Our late-night chats were by choice. He knew I snored when I was really tired. I knew he had a galaxy light. We shared our thoughts, stupid TikToks we liked, fell asleep together some nights. And then

there was our virtual beach date that played in my head any time we listened to the ocean waves setting on his white noise machine.

I'd been falling for him, despite trying not to.

It was beyond my control.

Later that night, when Mr. McKenna dropped me off at home, Buzz walked me to my door. I couldn't kiss him. Not with the way I felt. It wasn't fair. To him or me. I got out my keys and climbed up onto the stoop. Took a breath and turned.

His face was so open, sweet. He stepped toward me.

For a moment I almost lost my nerve. I took a breath.

"I can't do this," I said.

His brows pinched together. "Huh?"

"This. Us. You and me. It's been fun, Buzz, but I'm not ready, I guess." That was a gentle way to put it. Kind. True. Sort of.

"Not ready," he said.

We stood there looking at each other. I wasn't sure what more of an explanation to give him.

"Well, then, I guess that's it," he said, turning and heading to the SUV. His movements were jagged and swift, he didn't turn back.

"Good night," I said, fumbling with my keys to get in. Awkward but relieved. By the time I got to my apartment, there was a text from Ash.

WTF? Did you break up with Buzz?

Yes.

What happened?

I dunno. Not feeling it. Talk tomorrow, k?

She didn't text after that.

I gave my mother the briefest account of the evening.

Yes, the movie was good (although I had no clue).

Yes, I enjoyed myself (anything more would have required an explanation).

No, I didn't need any hot chocolate, but thanks, just needed sleep.

I left out the icky parts. My fight with Jake. Breaking up with Buzz. I hardly knew what had happened myself. I certainly didn't think that was how the night was going to unfold. After taking off my makeup and getting into my flannel lounge pants and tee, I sat on my bed and stared at my phone. Staring at the home screen as if it would give me answers.

I doubted Jake would call. He probably wasn't even home yet. Maybe they went back to the Boyles' house. Maybe he went over to Courtney's. I cringed thinking about what I'd said, how it had landed. Why would he think that was funny? I didn't want to think of him with Courtney, doing whatever it was they did together. Although hookup pal didn't suggest a rousing game of Cards Against Humanity and hot chocolate.

If he was happy though, who was I to judge that? I'd kept Jake at arm's length. He didn't only exist at night on the phone with me, even though those were the times I looked forward to the most. And it's not like I could really be with him, right? That would involve an unpleasant and unpredictable conversation with Ash, and we were finally getting close again.

I was about to text Jake that I'd broken up with Buzz but deleted it. I didn't want him to think it was about him, even though maybe a tiny part of it was. The bigger part of it was about me doing the right thing, not playing around with someone's feelings.

I typed, then deleted *I'm sorry* three times before finally deciding on a simple one-word text.

Sorry.

Concise. To the point. Only, what if he took it as insincere without *I'm* in front of it?

Ugh.

Overthink, much?

An hour later, when he still hadn't responded, I forced myself to go to sleep.

# jake

GHOSTING SARAH WAS BRUTAL.

It had been almost a week since she'd reached out. The longest we'd gone without talking or texting since we'd exchanged numbers. At first I'd been too upset to text her back. Only at this point, I wasn't sure who I'd been angry with in the first place. Her? Or me?

I was pissed at her for obvious reasons. What she said hurt. It was not like her to be mean, but was what she said so off base? She was just calling it like she saw it, right? Then I got pissed at myself for being so weak. For going back to Court out of boredom. Out of restlessness. Out of wanting something familiar, and hell, to feel wanted, even if that was bullshit too.

As I stood on the court, trying to perfect the offensive screen that helped us win our first game against Union Catholic, thoughts of Sarah filled my head. Avoiding her had been easy, but drama club was in the gym today using the stage behind the curtain. Any time the curtain billowed I was reminded that she was right there. The cheerleaders had ended practice early, so Courtney had already gone home. It would be so easy to wait for Sarah after practice, offer her a ride on my way to therapy and clear the air.

I still wasn't sure I wanted to.

Maybe it was better this way, to leave our friendship on bad terms.

Build up a wall.

Stop it all, cold turkey.

Except not talking to Sarah was also eating me up inside.

I missed her. Or at least being on good terms with her.

*"Seriously? Good terms with her?"*

*Okay, Alex, it's her I miss. Not the good terms.*

"Hobbs, look alive!"

Our first win had made Coach hyped too. Like maybe we weren't such a lost cause after all. I snapped out of it long enough to complete the play and watched as Bash landed a perfect lay-up. High fives all around. Being plugged in with the team again was awesome. The win had given us confidence, brought us together. Maybe this was the best way to honor Alex, to play the way I would have if he were here. I made an effort to focus on that the rest of practice.

After, Coach called me over.

"Hey, are you available over break? We're running a clinic for the elementary kids day after Christmas. I know we have the tourney, but it's during the day, and we could use the help. Thought you and Elliot could run the shooting drills."

"Me and Bash?"

Coach chuckled. "Yes. You two seem to be getting along better?"

Nothing got past Coach. Hanging out with the guys at Bash's house after the first game had been fun. Bash's mom had a lot of food and soda and snacks. His parents and two younger sibs hung out with us for a bit too, talking about the game, and what sort of season we could have. They were so into it. Bash sat back and took it all in, maybe trying to suss out what we were making of it.

I wouldn't call him a friend, more like I could tolerate him better. And seeing Bash's family in action explained *a lot*. He was their golden boy. They had a room dedicated to him, with every award he'd ever won, his jersey from middle school, framed newspaper clippings—they basically treated him like a star already. His mom even had a vinyl peel-off silhouette of Bash dunking a basketball on the back window of her Yukon, his name and jersey number above it. Douchey and over-the-top? Yeah, but kind of cool to have that sort of obnoxious support at the same time. They had a lot riding on him, it seemed—that sort of pressure and attention could probably turn you into an asshole.

"Maybe you could give him a pointer or two on perimeter shooting. He could use the help."

"I doubt he'd take pointers from me," I said. Even though Bash's father had pulled me aside and said pretty much the same thing over the deli spread they had put out. I wondered if he had spoken to Coach too.

"You're the best shooter on the team; even he knows that," he said, clapping me on the back.

"Sure, I'll do it, sounds good," I said, and headed off to the locker room.

Against my better judgment, I took a peek at the stage. The curtain was still. Maybe Sarah's rehearsal was over. Focusing on practice had been good for me. The pressure was off to talk to her, at least for the moment.

I sat on the edge of Dr. Hipster's couch, my leg bouncing up and down. Any time he noticed, I put my hand on my knee to stop.

"Why so edgy today?"

"Just came from practice, probably leftover adrenaline."

He sat silent, did his therapist mind-trick thing. I sunk back into the couch.

*"Tell him, Hobbs."*

"I'm in the middle of a . . . I don't know, sort of fight with a friend, and it's . . . well, I can't stop thinking about it. Or thinking about her."

His eyebrows raised slightly, he shifted in his seat. "What was the fight about?"

"She called me out on something, and I didn't like it, then I said some stuff to her, I guess calling her out on something too. I'm mostly pissed because she was right, but I think I was right too. And I don't know how to fix it. Don't even know if I should."

"Is there something about this friend that makes it harder to fix?"

I put my hands up to my face, massaged my temples, raked my fingers into my hair.

"It's Alex's girlfriend, and—"

*"Just say it."*

"Remember when you told me to pay attention to when I hear Alex's voice? It's always around her. Always around Sarah."

"What does he say?"

"Sometimes it's jokes, or encouragement. Like things he might have said to me if he were here, but then sometimes, I wonder if it's

216

just . . . wishful thinking on my part."

"Why do you think you hear his voice in relation to his girl-friend?"

*"Say it out loud."*

"I was kind of hoping you could tell me that," I said.

"You know," he said. "If you think about it, you know."

I didn't have to think too hard. The answer was a blinking neon sign in my head.

"Because I like her. God, I like her so much. I shouldn't feel this way, right? That's so shitty of me, isn't it?"

"Are you looking to me for approval? Or Alex?"

"I guess, Alex. But it's shitty, right?"

He gave me a small, serious smile. "That's the problem, isn't it? There won't be approval from Alex."

"I thought this was supposed to make me feel better," I said, ignoring the urge to bolt out of the room.

"What if you could talk to Alex? What would you say to him?"

My mind swam.

"I'd ask him why he didn't take his own advice about having nothing in common with Sarah."

"Don't tell me what you would say to him. Talk to him. Pretend I'm him."

"What?"

"Close your eyes if it helps. What would you say to Alex right now if he were standing in front of you? If you knew he could hear you."

"I'd say why did you stand so close to the fucking edge?" I said, half joking. "This feels wrong."

"Not to me, to him. Just go with it. No judgment, Jake."

I took a breath, closed my eyes. For a moment I was nervous the only version of Alex I'd see was from my nightmares, but that wasn't the case. We were in the McKennas' living room, shooting the shit, playing Nintendo.

"We're cool, right, Hobbs?"

In that original conversation I'd told him, "Of course," didn't want him to see that yes, it did bother me he and Sarah were together.

"No, we're not cool, Alex. You knew I liked her and you went and did your Alex thing anyway. I couldn't compete with that, never could. Were you interested in her when you told me I would have nothing in common with her? Did you know right then that you were falling for Sarah?"

The more I spilled, it's like I couldn't stop.

"And I'm still here, still like her, and I'm struggling to do the right thing out of some stupid loyalty to you. But you didn't think about loyalty or friendship, when you asked her out, did you? You wanted what you wanted, and you went for it. And it's not fucking fair that I can't feel this way just because you died."

I opened my eyes, waiting to see Dr. Hipster's scowl at what an absolute freak I'd been admitting all that. Instead, he was sitting there, as always, head slightly tilted, a neutral, almost pleased, expression on his face.

"You *can* feel this way, Jake."

"But how? Won't I always be thinking of Alex?"

"Was the fight you had with . . ."

"Sarah."

"Was the fight you had with Sarah about Alex?"

I shook my head.

"So you already have a relationship that doesn't involve him. Maybe mutual feelings of loss brought the two of you together, but that doesn't define your potential to be more. Unless you let it, of course."

"Will I always hear his voice in my head?"

"When it's okay to let his voice go—you will."

Outside of Dr. Hipster's office, I checked my phone, hoping I'd see a text from Sarah.

Nada.

Why would she reach out after I didn't answer her last text? Ghosting her weighed heavy on me. Sure, I'd been embarrassed by what she said, but she hadn't left our argument without getting hurt either. I'd said a few things, and I knew it had gotten under her skin when Courtney called her Sock Girl. Watching her storm off was hard, but it wasn't like I could run after her. Court grilled me on what happened.

"It looked like you were having an argument," she'd said.

"I hardly know her," I lied. "How could I argue with her?"

Thankfully, she dropped it.

*Stop being a stubborn ass, Hobbs. Call her, you know you want to.*

*What if she doesn't want to talk to me, Alex?*

*"You won't know until you call."*

I slid into the driver's seat, went to pull up Sarah's number, then decided to pass Adele's on the chance she'd picked up a shift. I wanted to see her. Needed to see her.

I had to circle the block before finally finding a spot. I noticed Sarah by the front of the shop, cleaning off the table where the ugly green chair was positioned. Her hair was in braids, she smiled and said something to the people at the other table across from her.

I called her, watched as she startled a bit and took her phone out of her back pocket. Her eyes widened as she looked at the screen, and in a frantic motion answered the call.

"Jake, hey," she said, breathless.

"Look to your left," I said, walking closer to the window. She turned.

Her.

Smile.

Made everything melt away.

"Wait a minute," she said, holding up her index finger and looking toward the counter. "Okay, Marnie's busy."

I walked toward the entrance as she maneuvered her way through the tables. We kept our eyes on each other. She hung up and opened the front door, coming out onto the street. She stopped two feet away from me. Both of us stood there, puffs of white air escaping from our mouths in the cold. She folded her arms.

"Jake, I'm sorry about the other night. I didn't mean to sound so bratty. I was trying to be funny. Total fail."

I don't think I realized until that moment how much it mattered what Sarah thought of me.

"I don't want you to think of me that way, Sarah."

Her eyes directly on mine, so welcoming and kind. "I don't, Jake."

"Look, I'm sorry too. I said some things too . . . and Court—"

She put up a hand. "You don't have to apologize about anything, what you said was true. I don't want you to see me that way either."

"I don't," I said.

"I broke up with Buzz."

I had to take a breath, plant my feet in the ground, to keep from celebrating. "Yeah?"

She nodded. "He deserves someone who's genuinely into him. Everybody does, right?"

"In a perfect world," I said.

"So, we're good?" she asked.

"Yeah, we're good," I said.

"What are you doing right now? Want to taste test some new macaron flavors? My aunt loves to get objective opinions on her combinations."

I smiled. "There's nothing else I'd rather do."

"C'mon, then."

I followed her inside.

# sarah

"ASH, YOU'VE GOT TO CALM DOWN. YOU'RE SWEAT-ing," I said, softly sweeping blush onto the apples of her cheeks. At the moment, it looked like two little pinkish blobs on either side of her face. I grabbed a makeup sponge out of her cosmetics bag and did damage control.

"Omigod, I know," she said, fanning her face, which made things a little worse.

We were in the break room, getting her glammed out for the winter showcase. I'd spent the day at Adele's, first with my morning shift, then a quick nap in the break room, before helping Aunt Sophie decorate for the evening. With some festive garland, evergreen branches, and fairy lights, the dining area looked, according to Marnie, positively hygge-delic.

"You would think I'm, like, prepping for Madison Square Garden. Why am I so nervous?"

"Because you care, and this is the first time you're playing in front of people in a long time. It's normal to have butterflies," I said, giving her a version of Trinity's drama club pep talk. I finally tamed her cheek color, added a little highlight for sparkle. I stepped back to admire my work.

"Flawless," I said.

She stood up and looked in the mirror, raking her fingers through her hair to add some volume.

"Thanks, Sarah. My hands wouldn't stop shaking at home. Okay, now the outfit, what do you think? Be honest."

She was in head-to-toe black. Faux leather leggings tucked into moto boots. Her top was sheer over a lacy cami; her hair long and loose.

"*Hot* is the word that comes to mind," I said.

"Actually, I would say *smoking hot*," Marnie said, joining us. "Hey, there's some dude out there asking for you, Ash."

Ash looked at me. "Mike's here already? Not sure if I can handle his energy right now."

I laughed, never heard her put it quite like that.

"No, not Mike . . . Bran?" Marnie said, then she looked at me. "You're working tonight, right?"

I nodded. I'd actually surprised myself at lunch on Friday by walking right up to Jake's lunch table and extending an invitation to him—and well, all of them—to stop by for the winter showcase, since it would be a good night to see what Adele's had to offer for the scholarship dance. I kept waiting for Courtney to call me Sock Girl or Holly to roll her eyes, but instead she said she'd "consider it," which Jake told me later was her way of saying yes. I didn't know if they would show up or not, but I wanted to be working so I could make sure they received the best we had to offer.

"Cool. So, should I send the moody guitar player back here?" she asked, looking back at Ash with a gleam in her eye.

Ash shook her head. "Um, no, I'll be heading out in a minute."

"Moody guitar player," I said, laughing when Marnie left. Ash gave me a puzzling look, somewhere between freaked and happy. "Okay, what's up?"

She took a breath. "Bran's playing tonight, but he's also accompanying me, kind of like for moral support."

"Does Mike know?" I asked, wondering why she hadn't told me either.

"Oh, yeah, I mean, he wasn't thrilled, but whatever. The bigger thing is—this is sort of an audition. Bran asked me if I was interested in joining his band, the other members are coming to see us tonight."

I shrieked. "Omigod, Ash, that is so cool."

"I know, right?"

"You'll crush it," I said.

"Sarah, Mike doesn't know that it's an audition. I didn't want to say anything because, well, you know, he hasn't exactly been supportive. He says he wants to make sure I'm ready to perform, but I think it's more than that. I get the feeling he's a bit jealous. If you see him getting, I don't know . . . antsy or sulky or anything, can you—"

"Give him a cookie?" I teased.

She laughed. "Yeah, thanks."

"Hey, what song are you guys doing?" I asked.

"Nope, you'll be surprised like everyone else. We're the last to go in the first set," she said. "I can't believe I'm really doing this. Thanks for the nudge, Sarah."


At six thirty, Adele's began filling up. First with people who looked vaguely familiar, like regulars mixed in with some new faces. Then friends began streaming in. Trinity came with Dylan and Cullyn, and a few other drama kids. Some of Ash and Bran's fellow musicians from jazz band and the music school arrived. Marnie and I were so busy that one of Aunt Sophie's pastry interns had to come out and help with serving.

About ten minutes to showtime, the front door opened and Mike entered, with his brother Pat, Holly, Courtney, and then Jake. They sat at one of the last available tables. Jake came up to the counter, Marnie was available to help him, but she stepped in and took over the customer I'd been with without even asking. I smiled as he strolled up to the counter, it was so nice to see him. So great to be friends again.

"Hey," he said.

"Hi, was wondering if you guys would make it," I said.

"Wouldn't miss it," he said.

"Did they send you up to fetch their order?" I joked, as he eyed up the pastry case. He smiled.

"Nope, I volunteered, seeing as I'm committee chair and all that," he said, looking at me.

*Whoosh.*

I smiled at him, blanked for a moment. "Well, what do you think would impress Holly?"

"Has anyone ever ordered one of everything?" he asked.

"Actually, yeah," I said.

"No way."

"Yep. My aunt can vouch for that. That was a fun order. Maybe we should start with the macarons and a few cookies, take it from there," I said.

"I trust you," he said. He waited and helped me to the table, which made me slightly less nervous in front of the others. After everyone got their hot drinks, we placed two separate large plates stacked with practically every kind of cookie from the display case. I shared which macaron flavors I thought were best and pointed out the individual cookies and tea cakes.

I noticed Mike looking toward the makeshift stage area, where Ash and Bran were off to the side, chatting while Bran tuned his guitar.

"Ash is going on last," I said, trying to distract him. "It's good you finally arrived; she's nervous, but I think seeing you will help."

"She doesn't look that nervous now," Mike said.

I took a napkin and put a chocolate chip cookie from the platter on it.

"She told me to give this to you," I said, sliding it over to him.

"Yeah?"

I nodded, smiled.

He finally relaxed. "Cool."

"If you want anything else, come up to the front," I said to the table but mostly to Jake. Just as I made it back behind the counter with Marnie, the lights dimmed and the showcase began.

The set started out slow, a young girl accompanied by someone on keyboard, while she sang a jazzy version of "White Christmas." The next few songs were up-tempo. Bran performed, first solo, then with two others to sing a song with different harmonies. Most everyone remained seated, riveted by the music, so Marnie and I were able to watch the majority of the set, undisturbed.

When it was Ash's turn to perform, she and Bran sat semi-facing each other but mostly toward the audience. She fumbled a bit with the mic and Bran helped her adjust it. She strummed her guitar, cleared her throat. Someone wolf-whistled. She looked up, laughed.

"Christmas was something I always looked forward to. My family celebrated big. This year is different. I think a lot of you know I lost my brother, Alex, last spring."

She paused. The silence became charged. My own breath locked. I had no clue she was doing anything related to Alex.

"He was the one who badgered my mom to put up the Christmas decorations right after Halloween. It was his favorite time of the year for obvious reasons. Presents, sleeping late, various built-in excuses to kiss someone."

A ripple of quiet laughter went through the audience. It was nice to hear her talk about Alex that way.

"We're supposed to play a holiday song, but I couldn't really find one for the way I've been feeling. My guitar teacher suggested this one, and when I heard it, I knew it was perfect. This is for Alex. 'River' by Joni Mitchell. Hope you like it."

From the first notes of the song, Ash transformed.

Her voice strong, clear, hitting every note.

I knew Ash was good, but this goddess at the mic was a far cry from the girl in denim cutoffs fumbling through songs on her back deck.

Her voice transported me, turned Adele's into the most important place on earth in that moment. She commanded the room. I wasn't sure why she felt like she needed Bran Russo for moral support—he strummed along, but Ash was the star. It was by far the bravest thing I'd ever seen her do. Her final note filled the space, and once again, there was an expectant heavy silence as if we were all trying to process what we'd witnessed.

Then the audience cheered for her. Louder than for any other act.

I clapped, swiped away an unexpected tear, remembering myself how pumped Alex had always been for Christmas.

"Wow, Ash was incredible," Marnie said,

"I know, right?" I said, as the room brightened again and someone announced a quick ten-minute break before the next set.

My first impulse was to congratulate Ash, but she got swallowed up as she stepped away from the mic. Mike enveloped her in a bear hug. She buried her face in the crook of his neck. I was genuinely happy to see them embrace. My congrats for Ash could wait.

People began coming up to the counter. Aunt Sophie and her intern brought out a few more trays of macarons and pastries. I helped put a few in the case, and when I looked up to help the next customer, I saw Jake and Courtney staring back at me.

"We're getting out of here," she said. "I feel like I could fall asleep if I hear another slow song."

"Glad you could make it at all," I said, ignoring her derisive comment. "I'm sure Ash appreciated it."

I knew I shouldn't be upset over them being together, but it was still hard. Jake's eyes held mine for a moment. The performance had gotten to him too, I could tell. He had one of the plates from the table in his hand, and he slid it over the counter to me.

"Hey, thanks, let me wrap the rest of these up for you," I said, reaching for the plate, hoping neither of them noticed how shaky my hands were. I grabbed a box and began placing the uneaten cookies inside as he spoke.

"Ash was . . . wow, something else. I didn't know she could sing like that," he said.

"It was pretty special," I said, closing up the box and handing it to him. Courtney reached for the box instead, then handed it to Jake herself. Something about her swift motion made me wonder if I'd been looking at Jake a little too long. I forced myself to smile.

Jake did his chin tilt that encompassed hello and goodbye, and my heart ached a little. I wished he didn't have to leave. I focused on the next customer in line as they turned away.

Busy was good.

Busy meant a successful night.

Busy was bullshit.

I kept an eye on them as they left the café.

# jake

"WELL, THAT WAS EXCRUCIATING," COURTNEY SAID AS we walked outside.

My car was parked three blocks away. On the way in, it hadn't seemed so bad, but going to find it again in the freezing cold was a trek. Courtney burrowed into me for warmth as we walked. Pat and Holly had decided to stay, only Court wanted to bail.

"Ashley McKenna was amazing," I said.

My ears were still ringing from her performance and the applause. It was brave of her to stand up in front of everyone and talk about Alex like that. Court's dismissiveness annoyed me.

"I guess," she said. "It was depressing though. Nice that she ated it to Alex, but maybe she could have found something more upbeat. I knew Alex. I can't imagine he would have t song."

u even listen to what she said?"

. The song fit her mood. I get it," she said.

do the box of cookies as I opened the passenger side a Cl like arguing with her. Her parents were out at hom over in the city and they weren't going to be thing three. Normally, Courtney telling me some- have set me on a spree of a thousand dirty thoughts, but tonight I wasn't into it. She slid in, and I closed the door behind her, trying to work out what to tell her when I dropped her off.

As I pulled out of the parking spot, Court rolled down the window and flung the box on to the street.

"What the hell?" I asked, half laughing. "Why did you do that?"

"You know why."

"No, Court, I actually don't."

"It's that place," she said.

I sighed as we came to a stop. "If Holly is okay being there, why do you have a problem?"

"It's obvious that girl likes you," she said.

Her comment stunned me, and I sat at the stoplight as it turned green, long enough for the car behind me to lay on the horn.

"What girl?"

"Sock Girl."

I flinched inwardly, kept my face a mask. Eyes on the road. The crazy thing was part of me wanted to know why she thought that, but I didn't think me enthusiastically asking, *You really think Sarah likes me, Court?* would go over too well. I played it cool.

"Can't you give the sock girl thing a rest?"

"There you go defending her again."

"You know her name. She dated Alex, and you guys gave her hell for it, for a month."

"Well, come on. She's a little generic for Alex, don't you think?"

She was baiting me into a fight.

"Alex didn't think she was generic. That's the only thing that mattered."

"And what do you think?"

"I think you're trying to pick a fight with me because you're bored."

She laughed. "Not true. Okay, then, *Sarah* likes you."

"Please stop," I said. "We're working on the scholarship dance together. That's all."

"I can tell by the way she looked at you."

I bit the tip of my tongue. How did she look at me?

"Nah," I said. "She's nice to everyone."

"It's not only tonight, Jake. Last week at the movies, whatever happened was not nothing. I'm not an idiot. You look at her a certain way too. You don't have that kind of tension with someone you don't care about. I can understand why you might want to keep it under wraps. Kind of shitty if you started up with Alex's girlfriend."

I focused on the road, on the various turns to her house. Strange how you can feel like you have your own little secret world with a person, only to find out you don't. I knew Sarah in a way I'd never really known anyone else, of course it was going to trickle out when we saw each other in everyday life. How could it not?

I just hadn't realized that Court was watching. And judging. Like everyone else would be. I had the urge to confess it all to her—to tell her that she was right, I was crazy about Sarah, but I knew that would be a mistake. Besides, Sarah didn't even know how I felt about her, and I didn't think the best way for her to find out would be some rumor going through the halls of school on Monday.

"So you're not going to say anything about what I just said?"

"You seem to have it all figured out," I said.

She sighed. "I mean it's okay. I know what we have isn't really, like, a thing. I think it's an odd choice to be with Alex's girlfriend."

"I'm not *with* Sarah. We're friends; you can make up shit all you want, but there's nothing more than that between us," I said.

"Okay, right," she said, as we pulled into her driveway. I put the car in park, kept the engine running.

"Okay, right? Really?"

"Jake, I don't want to fight," she said, reaching over to open the door. When she noticed the car was still running, she sat back in the seat. "Are you coming in?"

"No," I said.

She turned her body toward me. "When you get over whatever it is you're going through, call me."

"This isn't the same as before, Court. I'm done with this. With us."

She laughed. "Sure, Jake."

"Does Palmer even know about me?"

"Why would you bring him into it?"

I laughed. "I'm not the one who brought him into it. That's all you."

"I never lied about him."

I was about to point out a lie by omission is still a lie, but I didn't care anymore. "You didn't answer my question."

"No. He doesn't," she said. "But I'm sure he's not a monk at Syracuse."

"Maybe you should expect more than that," I said.

"Don't worry about me, Jake," she said, opening the door. "I'll be fine."

Her words were calm, as always, but she slammed the door. I waited until she was in the house before pulling away.

I drove around aimlessly for a while, just thinking. Should I tell Sarah how I feel about her? We were both free, but was it even possible for us to be together? Court might have been trying to get under my skin with the *Alex's girlfriend* comment, but I'm sure she wouldn't be the only one who thought about us that way.

*"Hobbs, grow a pair and tell her how you feel already."*

When I walked into Adele's, the place had cleared out. There were still a few tables with people around them, but the setup for the music had been broken down. I scanned the room, looking for Sarah. She was busy clearing a table up front. Marnie said something to her, and she turned. Her face lit up when our eyes met. I couldn't help but smile.

"What are you doing here?" she asked, coming over to me.

"I, um, I broke up with Courtney," I said.

Her smile fell.

"Oh, wow, I'm so sorry," she said.

"Don't be," I said. "I mean, I'm not. It was time. I just, I don't feel like being alone right now. Wanna hang out?"

She bit her lip, looked around. "Well, I have to finish my shift, but then I was going to drive with Marnie to the homeless shelter to drop off the unsold pastries from the day."

"Do you need help? I could drive you, if that's cool with everyone," I said, hoping I didn't appear too eager. Maybe it had been wrong to come here right after breaking up with Courtney, but I didn't feel like pretending anymore. This had to start somewhere, right?

The corner of her mouth upturned; her eyes lit up again.

"You really want to help me?"

"Yeah."

# sarah

MONDAY AT SCHOOL THE HALLS WERE ABUZZ—OKAY, well maybe not literally the halls, but there was a lot of talk about Ash's performance. She was taking the compliments in stride, blushing, shooting back with self-deprecating remarks, even though if anyone deserved a night like that, it was Ash. It was so nice to see her smile.

I was in a more-smiley-than-your-average-Monday mood too, and it had everything to do with Jake. Nothing really happened, but that nothing was the highlight of my weekend. After we'd dropped the pastries off at the homeless shelter, Jake drove me home and we talked in his car for a while. There was a moment we were saying goodbye that I thought maybe we would kiss, but we didn't. Like the *whoosh* moment at the bench. Did he feel it too? It was probably for the best that nothing happened, since he'd just broken up with Courtney. It only sucked that I couldn't share my excitement with Ash. Would I ever be able to?

All of that was on my mind as I sat down to lunch. Buzz was out with the flu, and Kyle was busy taking a makeup exam, so it was just me, Ash, and Mike. I was surprised to find they weren't in their couple bubble. Mike barely acknowledged me as I sat down. I looked at Ash, and she rolled her eyes. I concentrated on taking out my lunch. I wasn't sure if this was an Ashley/Michael situation, but I knew better than to dig deeper. I was in too good a mood.

"So, Bran asked me to be in Crush," Ash said.

"Wait, what?" I squealed.

Mike rubbed his ear. "Christ."

"When did this happen?" I asked.

Ash lit up with my response.

"This morning in English. He said the others really liked me. We're meeting at his house after school today."

"He didn't actually say you're in; he asked you to stop by and see if you were a good fit," Mike said.

"Can't you be happy for me, Michael? It's kind of cool."

"Kind of? It's, like, the coolest thing ever," I said.

"Well, just a bit of advice—the way he was looking at you the other night? I think he might want a little more from you than your guitar skills."

No. He. Did. Not.

Ash's jaw dropped. Mike's eyes widened, and he reached for her hand. She pulled it away, fast, then gathered her lunch and books with stiff, quick motions.

"Ashley, please, I'm—"

She stopped abruptly and glared at him.

"Just once I wish you'd surprise me," she said before storming away.

Life in the caf went on around us. The cacophony of voices and laughter surrounded the very empty space that Ash left in her wake. Mike laced his fingers through his hair, head in his hands, and stared down at the table. I started packing up.

"Wait, Sar, don't go."

"Mike."

"Can you blame me? Did you see them on Saturday night?"

"Yes, Mike, I did. They were about three feet apart, playing guitars. You should be happy for her. This sounds like a great chance."

He groaned. "Don't you think I know that?"

"Then what's the deal?"

He looked around, as if he was checking to see who was within earshot, then leaned in. "I know I'm dating up here, Sarah. Ash is everything to me, but I know who I am. I'm the guy who gets good weed, has a basement to hang out in, and whose older, cooler brother plays varsity basketball."

Mike never struck me as the jealous type, more aloof, mysterious stoner, but maybe that was because he never had competition for Ash's attention. He had this sad-puppy expression that just about killed me.

"That's not the way Ash sees you," I said.

"You see me that way," he said.

"No, I don't," I said.

He raised an eyebrow.

Self-aware Mike was scary.

"Okay, maybe I wasn't your biggest fan in the beginning, but after Alex, well, you were there for her in a way that I couldn't be. That no one else could be. You helped her through that, Mike. It doesn't matter that you don't play basketball, or guitar, or do anything special. You stayed with her. That counts."

"I guess."

"And most important, Ash is crazy about you. You need to trust her."

"I know, but it's not her I don't trust. It's Russo."

There was nothing much I could say that could dissuade him from that, but I had to try. "Ignore Bran Russo, focus on Ash. Support her. Ask questions. Be interested. You already know what happens when you don't do that."

"I end up alone, at lunch."

"Gee, thanks," I joked.

He smiled. "Can you do me a favor?"

"What?"

"If things ever get bad, just, can you be in my corner? You're her best friend. She listens to you."

There were so many times I'd hoped he and Ash would break up, but, sitting there, I realized Mike had grown on me. He was good for Ash, at least when he wasn't being a jealous weenie.

"Okay, sure," I said.

# winter break

# jake

DRAGGING MYSELF OUT OF BED TO TEACH KIDS HOW to shoot a basketball was definitely not something I ever saw myself doing, but there I was at nine thirty in the morning in the slightly chilly gym, staring at ten bored kids who, let's face it, were probably sent by their parents so they could catch a break the day after Christmas.

The large group had been divided into four. Each group of ten was at a station for fifteen minutes. The other three groups had already started their activities.

I looked over at Bash, who seemed equally as perplexed as me.

"Have you ever done this before?" I whispered. All Coach had done was lower the hoops to eight feet and give us a large rolling basket full of kid-sized basketballs.

"Taught? No. Been in a clinic like this? Yeah. I think we're supposed to, you know, play games with them and stuff. Not teach them lay-ups."

"Huh, okay," I said, turning back to them. "Games."

One of the kids yawned. Another was busy picking his nose. Two girls on the end were clapping their hands together and singing. I had to do something to get them back. I spun the basketball on my finger, a total show-off crowd-pleaser that I'd taught myself one long, boring summer ago. It worked, little by little all their eyes were on me and the ball.

"Listen up—does everyone know what this is?" I said pointing to the ball. I walked past them, giving the ball a little more spin. I lifted it over my head and then back down low.

"A basketball," a few of them said.

"Really? A basketball . . . What do you do with it?"

One kid laughed, a few of them looked at each other like it was a trick question.

"Can you make a milkshake out of it?" I asked.

"Noooooooooooo."

"Can you ice-skate with it?"

Laughter. "Noooooooo."

"What do you do with it?"

"Play basketball!"

"Right! And in basketball, what's the best thing to do?"

Silence.

I stopped the ball, dribbled, then tossed it over my shoulder. I hadn't done a reverse free throw in forever, but I knew my mark and decided to try.

"Did I make that one?" I asked the kid in front of me. He shook his head.

Bash caught the rebound and passed the ball back to me. I lined myself up with the basket and tried the reverse again, this time the ball swished in. At that point, the rug rats were mine.

"Wow, are we gonna do that?"

I laughed. "Maybe not today, but with practice you can. We're going to learn how to shoot, but first Sebastian here is going to lead you through some warm-ups," I said.

"Sebastian! Like in *The Little Mermaid*," one of the girls said.

Bash smiled and shook his head, then started the kids off with some jumping jacks. After that, we lined them up on the side of the basket to teach them shooting skills.

A little torturous at times, it was obvious that some of the kids had played before and others didn't have a clue. The fifteen minutes flew by though, and soon we were on to our next group, and the next one. The last group was hyped by the time they hit us. We skipped the jumping jacks and went straight to shooting.

Bash was by the basket, and I stood by the line. One little kid was pretty wound up and kept running in wide circles around the court. I trotted over to him and tried to keep up.

"Hey, little man, come on over here and stand in line, your turn is coming," I said. He turned and ran straight at me. I braced myself for impact, but he stopped short and looked up at me.

"Pika, Pika, Pika," he said.

God, kids were weird.

"Pika—what's—"

"Pikachuuuuuuuuuu," he said.

Pikachu?

Wait.

Was this one of Alex's kids?

"Ah, like the Pokémon, cool."

"Do you know Alex?" he asked in a singsong voice.

I hesitated.

"Yes, I do," I said. Should I have said *did*? Was it possible this kid didn't know? I was not prepared to break that sort of news to a six-year-old.

"He used to teach me basketball. He died."

He was so blunt, I almost laughed, like, *Thanks, little morbid Captain Obvious.* Then I realized, he didn't know me or my relationship to Alex, and probably was so nonchalant about it because he wasn't in touch with his mortality yet.

He was a six-year-old pretending to be Pikachu on the basketball court.

I envied him.

"So did Alex teach you how to shoot the basketball?"

He nodded.

"Wanna show me?"

When it was his turn, he dribbled the ball, held it, closed his eyes, and started up with his Pikachu chant. He opened his eyes, took his shot. It hit the rim and went in.

"Perfect. High five," I said. He slapped my hand and beamed. When his turn came around again, he did the same thing. I grinned. Alex had made an impression on this little dude.

Maybe it wasn't the worst way to spend a morning.

At the end of the clinic, I had that same spent but satisfied feeling I got after a good game or run. Endorphins. Or maybe because I was that much closer to seeing Sarah at Adele's. I wanted to stop by and surprise her with something I picked up for her. A Christmas present, sort of. Nothing that special, more of a joke gift than anything, but I couldn't wait to see her face.

We stayed with our last group, waiting for parents to come pick up their kids. The Pikachu kid, whose name was Benson, stood next to me. He was one of those fidgety kids who either had to be moving or talking. He tugged the bottom of my jersey to get my attention.

"Dad lost his job," he said.

"Oh, wow, really? That stinks."

"Yep, Mom was crying about it today."

What was I supposed to say to that? I didn't want to know such personal information about strangers. How would Alex have handled it?

"How are *you* doing?" I asked.

"We'll be okay."

"That's, um, great. You will."

"Mom," he yelled, waving at a woman with dark hair. She smiled when she saw him, walked up to us.

"Benson," she said as he closed the space between them and hugged her hard. She laughed, gave him a squeeze, looked at me. She seemed pretty pulled together, no bloodshot eyes from crying or anything. I smiled.

"How was he?" she asked. "I know he's a bit of a handful."

A bit?

"Oh, he was great. He's got some skills," I said.

"Yeah, basketball is one of his favorites," she said.

I probably should have left it at that, but I was curious.

"He mentioned he knew Alex?"

Her face softened, took on that semi-sad and concerned look people got when talking about Alex's death. "Yes, Ben was here last year. Did you know Alex?"

Now it was my turn to impart personal information to a stranger. Only they didn't feel like strangers anymore.

"Alex was one of my best friends," I said.

"I'm so sorry. He was really great with him. Not everyone can handle Benson's energy."

I laughed. That was one way to put it.

"Will you be here over the summer?" she asked.

"Oh, um, I don't know," I said. I didn't want to say probably, not as Benson stared up at me wide-eyed. "Will Pikachu be here?"

He smiled as his mom mussed his hair; she looked at me. "Maybe, if we get some scholarship money again. Right, buddy? I'm sorry, I didn't get your name?"

"Oh, it's Jake," I said.

"Can you say thank you to Jake?"

"ThankyouJake," Benson said, quickly and buried his face in his mom's hip.

"Thank you, Jake," she said, and led him away.

"Thought you said you didn't know what you were doing," Bash said.

"I guess it's not rocket science, they're just little humans, right?"

"So, um, do you have some time to help me with my free throws?" Bash asked.

"Oh, right, I forgot about that," I said. I checked my phone for the time.

"Or, you know, we can skip it," he said. "You probably want to get out of here."

I did want to get out of there, but it was still early. Sarah was working until midafternoon. I could spare twenty minutes or so.

"C'mon, let's see what you got," I said.

# sarah

"JAKE, HEY, I'LL BE RIGHT WITH YOU," I SAID, FINISH-
ing up the order for the person I'd been waiting on.

My hand shook with the adrenaline rush of seeing him. A great
surprise in the middle of my day. I felt like such a dork, but truth
was I couldn't wait for vacation to be over. Not that I didn't have
fun, it was Christmas after all, but with Ash gone there was no one
to really hang out with. Trinity had given us a break from the play
since she wanted us off book by January. That left me with Mom
to hang with, but she had work during the day too.

Jake ordered a hot chocolate and a blueberry cream cheese muffin. Marnie rang up his items at the register. I sidled next to her,
pushing the plate with the muffin toward Jake.

"Do you mind if—"

"Ten minutes," she said, barely looking at me while she handed
Jake his change. "Okay, twenty, but only because it's the holidays."

We laughed.

"I'll bring your drink over," I said to him.

There was always a risk when Jake stopped by that Ash could
show up. Even though the odds of it were slim, I never felt fully
relaxed and usually kept an eye out. Today was different. Knowing

Ash was somewhere in the Caribbean made me totally drop my guard. It was nice, and I knew on some level this is the way it should be, if only I could tell Ash about our friendship.

Jake smiled as I approached. There was a wrapped Christmas present sitting on the table. Was he going somewhere after this? Did he have someone else to see? I placed his cup down and sat across from him.

"Hey, what happened to the ugly green chair?" he asked.

"You mean the iconic Kermit chair? My aunt sent it out to be cleaned right after that winter showcase," I said.

He nodded, placed his plate between us.

"Here, have some."

"Thanks," I said, picking off a piece of the muffin and popping it into my mouth. "This is a nice surprise, didn't think I'd see you."

He cleared his throat.

"Well, um, had to stop by to give you this," he said, sliding the gift over to me.

My face was instantly hot. I grinned.

"Jake, omigod, you didn't have to do that," I said, truly blown away.

"I know. Open it," he said.

I slipped a finger under the end fold, gently tugged at the tape so the paper wouldn't rip. Usually I tore into presents, but for some reason, I wanted the moment to last. Jake looked amused.

"I'm sorry, I didn't think to get you anything," I said, working on the other end.

"Don't be, Sarah, it's not that big a deal. And you know, you can tear the paper off."

I continued to take my time because I loved the look of

anticipation in his eyes.

"C'mon," he said, reaching over to help me.

We finally got it unwrapped. I turned the box over in my hands.

"Omigod, a galaxy light," I said, laughing.

"Yeah, it's the one I have. Now when we talk at night, we can be looking up at the same thing. Or you can choose something different. It has a few different settings. I know, kind of corny, but—"

"I love it," I said. "Thank you. You really didn't have to—"

"I wanted to," he said.

We kept our eyes on each other, a long second passed. Maybe it was the feeling of goodwill, or the magic of the holiday season, or the fact that the five minutes I'd spent with Jake were arguably the best of break so far—all I knew is I wanted this feeling to last.

"We should hang out," I blurted before I lost my nerve.

"We're kind of doing that now, aren't we?"

"I mean, like, on purpose. Friends do that, right?"

He stopped mid-chew and wiped his mouth with a napkin.

"Um, yeah, sure. I've got tournament games the next two nights. I mean, you can come if you want; we could do something after."

Sitting in the stands alone wasn't exactly what I'd imagined, maybe he realized that because then he said.

"Or, I have a family party on Saturday. Maybe that's too much?"

Family party sounded wholesome, fun. A thing friends would do without raising any eyebrows.

"Sure, that sounds great," I said.

"Cool, I'll text you the details," he said.

When Jake said family party, I'd thought he was talking about something casual at his house, but it was an actual *party* party—an anniversary celebration for his great-aunt and -uncle in Brooklyn. He told me that his plus-one had been approved and that he and his brother would pick me up at six on Saturday.

Ash was on a ship in the middle of the ocean, there was no way she would find out about me hanging out with Jake, but to be on the safe side, I decided to cover my tracks and bend the truth a bit with Mom.

As far as she knew, I was going out with Trinity. If I told her the truth, she'd want to meet Jake. It had been awkward enough with Buzz, and I wasn't ready for that sort of naked display of feelings. I'd also have to tell her that she needed to keep it a secret from Ash. Then there would be more questions, and ugh. It felt less complicated to tell a teeny, tiny fib this one time. I texted Trini to cover for me on the off chance that it ever came up with my mother and promised to explain after break. Then I ghosted the rest of her questions.

My outfit was Saturday night casual: black tights, black mini, baggy sweater, booties. I kept my hair loose and went for a bold lip. A little spritz of some floral perfume that Aunt Sophie had given me for Christmas, and I was good to go.

Thankfully, Mom had gone out to the movies with a friend, so she was gone while I paced, waiting for Jake's arrival. I checked my look in the mirror twenty times, second-guessing it about ten times, before I finally got Jake's text and dashed downstairs. He was standing by a sporty red SUV and smiled as he opened the door for me.

"Hey," he said.

"Hey."

"Hope you don't mind sitting in the back."

I peeked in and saw a young girl sitting on the opposite end of the seat. She grinned, braces gleaming in the overhead cabin light.

"This is my sister, Annie," Jake said. "Annie, this is Sarah."

"Hi," I said, smiling as Jake shut the door behind me and went back around to the passenger seat.

"What, I don't rate?" A voice came from the driver's seat.

"Can I at least get in the car?" Jake said, clipping his seat belt. He looked over his shoulder at me. "Sarah, this is my brother, Joe."

Joe turned around so his face was peeking over the edge of the seat.

"Hi," I said, a little less bold than I'd been with Annie.

"Hey, Sarah. Nice to meet you. I'm Jake's older, better-looking brother. He's told us absolutely nothing about you," he teased as he put the SUV in drive.

Jake shoved Joe's shoulder. "Dude, don't."

Joe reached over and mussed Jake's hair.

"Hands on the wheel, eyes on the road," Annie said.

"Yes, ma'am," Joe said. "Next stop, Brooklyn."

The radio was on, and the pressure to talk was off. Jake and Joe argued a lot—whether to take Route 3 or the turnpike, which tunnel would have less traffic, how the Giants were the superior team and rooting for the Jets was the definition of futility. Their banter, the easy way they disagreed without really being angry, reminded me a lot of Alex and Ash. I liked how they'd had their own way of talking to each other, sometimes seemingly on the verge of being upset, but then in the next moment laughing. It had always made me wonder what it would be like to have a sibling, a built-in friend, someone to have your back.

I turned to Annie.

"Are they always like this?" I asked.

She rolled her eyes. "Yep. Worse, sometimes," she said. "I like your boots."

"Thanks," I said, stretching my legs out so she could take a better look. "I like yours too. Red is a great color."

"Thanks."

"Are you warm enough back there? My brother likes to keep his car set to subzero," Jake said.

It was a little cold, but I was fine, kept my nervous sweats in check. "I'm good."

"Just prepping you for when you're in Colorado, little brother," Joe said. "You think this is cold, you've got no idea."

"Colorado?" I asked no one in particular.

Annie responded. "Jake was accepted to CU Boulder. We don't want him to go."

Colorado? As in clear across the country, Colorado? Why had he never told me he applied there?

"Oh, nice," I said, because what else was I supposed to say?

Jake furrowed his brow and shook his head as if the whole thing was preposterous.

Jersey gave way to Manhattan with its lightning-quick, darting taxicabs; bright blinking lights; and throngs of people bundled up and walking every which way with their own destinations to get to. The scene changed with each block we passed, the excitement of being somewhere new, and the anticipation of what the night held, bubbling inside me. I tried to take in every second as we drove across the Brooklyn Bridge, to forget Jake's news, but it was hard to put out of my mind.

Was Jake really going to Colorado next year? When was he planning on telling me?

When we finally reached the venue, it took a good twenty minutes of Joe cursing and circling—and apologizing to both me and Annie for each new colorful f-bomb—before we got lucky and found a car pulling out of a spot. He parallel parked in "one expert-level try" he boasted.

We got out of the car and stood on the sidewalk. All at once I felt shy and awkward. I hadn't been this way around Jake since the first time we really talked. This was unfamiliar ground. Joe playfully grabbed Annie's hand, and the two took off ahead of us. Jake started walking, and I followed at his side. Both of us had our hands stuffed in our jacket pockets. I looked down at the ground as we walked.

"So, Colorado, huh?"

"Oh, that. I mean it's not a definite or anything."

My shoulders relaxed. "It's so far away."

"That was kind of the point," he said. "You know how sometimes you want to imagine a different life? That's all it is, a possible choice. I'm also applying to Rutgers and Stockton."

"I get it," I said.

"So, listen, I'm warning you, my family thinks this is *something*," he said, gesturing between us. "They keep saying your name with this suggestive inflection. I don't know if you heard Joe before, like there's all this subtext. Sorry."

I laughed. "It's okay."

"Your mom say anything?"

"No, she thinks I'm here with Trinity," I said.

"Oh . . . Why? Would she have said you couldn't come if she knew it was me?"

"No, no, it's not that. I don't know, it seems stupid now. I thought she might want to meet you, and she already met Buzz, and it was so awkward, and then there'd be questions and saying your name with subtext, and I don't know if I can handle that yet."

He laughed and put a hand over his heart. "Wait, your mom met Buzz and you didn't want her to meet me? Damn, Sarah, you know how to hurt a guy."

My face flushed. "I didn't mean it like that. I'd love to introduce you. I didn't think tonight was the right time. She wasn't home when you picked me up anyway."

"I'm kidding. I get why it might be awkward."

I heard the words, but I wasn't sure I believed him. Was he annoyed I lied to my mom? I mean, why did I do it in the first place? I liked having this thing between us—whatever it was—just for me, without analyzing it away or keeping my feelings in check. I liked having no one to answer to about it because then I didn't have to think about the consequences. We reached the place, a smallish-looking establishment with a neon sign that read "Carmine's Bar and Banquet Hall."

Jake tugged on the elbow of my jacket, paused as his siblings went toward the door. "Sarah, I know we're just hanging out. Friends. I'm cool with that."

I looked up at him. His lips quirked in a shy side-smile. He was so startlingly cute in that moment.

"I don't know if I'm cool with that anymore," I said.

# jake

HAD I HEARD HER RIGHT? HAD SARAH JUST SAID SHE wasn't cool being friends? Did she want more than that? Her eyes brightened; she bit her lip. God, she looked so pretty, I wanted to bite her lip or *be* her lip or something.

*"That escalated quickly, Hobbs."*

Not now, Al.

*"No, seriously, that lip thing is a little fetishy."*

*I don't mean it literally! Piss off!*

Annie came running out of Carmine's and gestured for us to follow her.

"C'mon, Jake, Sarah. Are you just going to stand out there all night?"

Without thinking, I took Sarah's hand in mine, at the same time realizing this would only validate what my family had been teasing me about all day.

"Who is Sarah?"

"Sarah, huh? How did you meet her?"

"Is she your girlfriend?"

"If you're friends, why haven't we met her before?"

Her hand in mine didn't feel like we were just friends as we snaked through the crowded bar toward the banquet room. Especially when I looked back and caught her eye and she smiled, and there was that rising sun in my chest again. It felt like we were the only two in the room, and I wanted nothing more than to find a place where we could be alone, which wasn't the most convenient desire to have when you were about to enter a room with wall-to-wall family.

As we approached our table, my mother and father had matching goofy grins on their faces. Dad's might have been from his generous pour of stout, but Mom had that look, her eyes going from me to Sarah to me again, the slightest chin tilt of approval. Introductions weren't as awkward as I thought, and Sarah held up her end of the conversation.

After dinner, Annie dragged her to the dance floor as one of those songs with dance steps in the lyrics came on. At first Sarah begged off, but with some persuading (aka Annie's pout) she went up.

I stood to the side, watching her dance with my little sister, and maybe falling a little in love with her for that. Every so often, Sarah would look at me with eyes pleading for me to join them, and I'd just laugh.

Joe came up to me, leaned in, and whispered, "Friend, my ass."

I elbowed him.

He smirked. "Calling it like I see it."

Damn, I wish I saw what he saw. Why was I so uncertain? She'd asked to hang out, that meant something, right? If she hadn't, I would have been here alone. It would have been me who Annie dragged to the dance floor. Sarah was so hard to read. Or maybe I was nervous because I wanted this so much, I was afraid to make a wrong move.

The song finished to applause, and the dance floor cleared. Sarah came over, her breath quick, her face shiny from exertion.

"You should have danced with us," she said.

"It was more fun watching you," I said, which I hoped sounded the right amount of pervy.

She laughed. "I think I need some air."

# sarah

"THERE'S A COURTYARD, WANNA CHECK IT OUT?" JAKE asked.

I nodded, hoping he'd take my hand like before, but he shoved his hands into his pockets. I followed him through a narrow hallway, past the bathrooms, and to a back door.

"Ah, success," he said, pushing open the door. My breath caught as we walked into the courtyard. The space was surrounded by ivy-covered brick walls, with fairy lights woven through the thick vines. Strings of old-fashioned-looking bulbs with incandescent filaments were hung across the top of the space, creating a crisscross canopy of light. The effect was magical. Space heaters stood in various places. We were alone, at least for the moment, but a table with empty glasses told me it wasn't exactly private. We moved closer to one of the heaters.

"You okay?" he asked.

"Yes, why?"

"Just checking, my family can be overwhelming," he said.

"Oh, no. Your family is—"

"A little much?"

"No, I was going to say wonderful. Everything about this night is, Jake."

"So, you're having fun, then?"

I stepped closer to him. "I never want it to end."

He looked over my head, past me, fidgeting, rolling back on his heels a little.

"Sarah, when you said that thing before, about being friends. You're not cool with it because you're sick of being friends with me? Or not cool with it because you want more?"

My pulse raced. "Isn't that obvious?"

"Do me a favor, close your eyes," he said.

"What?"

He stepped closer. We were toe to toe.

"Close your eyes, hold up your hands, like you're surrendering."

"Oh, I know this trick, Hobbs," I said.

"Are you going to be serious, Walsh?"

"Okay," I whispered, closing my eyes.

"Focus on the palm of your hand," he said.

With my eyes closed everything was heightened. This was the exercise I'd tried to teach him at the cliffs. Except it wasn't. "You're not going to tie my shoelaces together and leave me here?"

He laughed.

"Trust me," he said. A touch, feather light, ran across my palms, causing me to suck in my breath, as he laced his fingers through mine. I could feel his body moving closer, the warmth of him surrounding me.

"Jake."

"Sarah."

"What are we doing?"

"Exploring a feeling," he said. He touched his forehead to mine. I opened my eyes. His mouth was so close. I could feel the heat between us, the desire to close the space. We were sharing breath.

"What are you feeling right now?" he whispered.

"Scared."

"Not exactly what I was hoping for," he said, sounding amused. "Why scared?"

"What if this is a huge mistake?" I asked.

"What if it's the best thing that's ever happened?"

"What are people going to say? What about Ash?"

"No one's here. Just us. In Brooklyn. We may as well be on the moon."

"I think—"

"Nope, don't think. Feel."

All I had to do was tilt my face toward his and we'd be kissing. The feelings that had been growing the past few months coursed through me. It would be so easy, like the strike of a match.

Just us in the courtyard.

I leaned toward him until our lips touched.

So, so gentle, barely there at first.

A tease of a kiss that left me craving more.

"See, the world didn't end, did it?" he asked, kissing the corner of my mouth, my chin, lingering a moment on my neck until I thought I'd melt.

"No zombie apocalypse," I said, touching my lips to his again, more insistent. This time we explored the feeling longer, mouths parted, savoring the warmth of each other.

"No meteor rushing toward Earth," he whispered breathless.

I laughed, buried my face in his sweater. His chin grazed the top of my head. Our arms wrapped around each other. We were in it now, no turning back. Things were complicated outside these ivy-covered, fairy-lit walls; I knew that, but that reality was far, far away. And at that moment, all I wanted was more of Jake.

"No earthquake, no blackouts, no Sharknado," he said.

I ran my fingers through his hair.

"Less talking, more kissing," I said.

He laughed. "I'm here for that."

january

# sarah

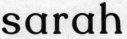

JANUARY WAS A HANGOVER. A THUD. A MONTH OF Mondays. Naked Christmas trees at the curb. Dark. Frozen. January was reality, and I didn't want to deal with it. I hunkered down in bed after hitting Snooze for the second time. Warm and cozy, head filled with thoughts of kissing Jake in the courtyard.

A few gentle knocks on my bedroom door brought me back to my end-of-break reality.

"Hey, Sar, if you want breakfast before school you have to get up," Mom said.

"Mmm-hmmm," I replied sleepily, wondering what it would be like to stay under my covers for a month. Or until spring thaw.

My night with Jake was a dream. And in the continuation of this dream—I imagined telling Ash about us and how happy she'd be for me. Then a dull ache would fill my stomach because I knew it wasn't going to be that simple. And honest, I didn't even know where to start. It's not like I could walk up to her and say, "Hey, I hooked up with Jake Hobbs over break! How was your cruise?"

Or could I?

Definitely not.

The way I felt about Jake should have been motivation enough to have that discussion, but I couldn't get past the thought of disappointing Ash. The next time my alarm went off, I got up, giving myself a pep talk as I dressed for school.

*Just tell her!* I said to my reflection.

What is the worst that could happen?

She could hate me and never talk to me again.

Major suckage.

I hated conflict.

Maybe she would come around, I thought as I walked out of my building and into the freezing morning. Now that she had so much going on with the band, things would get better, right? Ash seemed more upbeat. I could find a moment and just come out and tell her, and everything would be all right because it had to be. Our friendship could survive this.

The moment I saw Ash, who was all tan skin and smiles, standing out on the cold gray morning like the ghost of summer past, my resolve fizzled.

"Rocking a tan in January, I'm officially jealous," I said, walking toward her.

She grinned as we continued to school.

"Don't be, there was pretty much nothing else to do on a boat for seven days except eat pizza and lay in the sun. I'm so psyched to be back though," she said.

"Back from the Caribbean or back to school?"

"Both, I guess."

"I couldn't wait for break to be over, but I forgot how much I hated January. I wish it was spring already."

"No, don't say that! This winter is going to be epic. The band.

Making money—okay, maybe only enough for a latte and some disco fries—doing something I love. Mike is getting a car at the end of the month, so no more trekking to school. We'll be able to go anywhere. We won't be confined to the Boyles' basement and awkward rides with parents. I really can't wait. How was your break?"

"Oh, you know, boring as hell. Memorized my lines for *Almost, Maine*. Worked at Adele's for a lot of it." *Hooked up with Jake Hobbs and can't wait to do it again.*

Mike was at the entrance of school, his face lighting up when he saw Ash. She threw herself in his arms like she hadn't seen him in seven years, not seven days. I kept moving past them, figured I'd let them catch up without an audience.

"See ya at lunch," I called over my shoulder. Back in school only three minutes and it felt like I had never left. I climbed the stairs to my first class, remembering the first day of school when my water bottle went rolling into Mr. Rutledge's classroom and I saw Jake. I smiled at the thought of catching a glimpse of him and ended up practically running into him at the top of the stairwell, where he was waiting. We both grinned. I did a quick look behind me to see if anyone else was there, at least anyone I knew. Nope.

"Hey," I said.

"Hey," he said.

Two words with so much meaning behind them. A cold, star-filled night. A brick courtyard. We really couldn't risk being seen like this, our connection too obvious. Soon, I hoped. I'd tell Ash soon. I walked ahead, Jake followed.

"How was your break, Walsh?" he asked, all mock business.

"Oh, totally boring, I did nothing worth talking about," I teased. "How about yours?"

We stopped right before Mr. Rutledge's doorway. He leaned down, mouth by my ear.

"Hot," he whispered, discreetly brushing his lips across my cheek in the process.

I glanced around.

"Jake," I whispered, thankful no one had seen.

"Have a good one," he said, raising his eyebrows playfully, then disappearing into the classroom.

I didn't have a coherent thought all morning.

# jake

"YOU WANT TO MAKE SURE YOUR FEET ARE FACING THE basket. That's the same from anywhere on the court. That'll square your hips and core. Don't just think of your hands, it starts in your feet," I said, taking my shot and watching as the ball went through the hoop with a satisfying *swish*. I grabbed the ball and handed it to Bash.

Bash and I had stayed after practice to play a quick game of H-O-R-S-E, so we could work on his shooting skills some more. Bash missed the shot. I laughed.

"What is that, *S* for you?"

"Yep, you don't have to gloat," he said, passing me the ball. I went for an easy shot this time, a lay-up. He followed, easily making it as well. The next shot I took from the foul line.

*Swish.*

"Can I ask you something?"

"Sure," I said, passing him the ball.

"Why aren't you trying for a D-One school?" he asked.

"Is talking helping you concentrate?" I asked.

"Well, no, but I mean, you're good. Just wondering," he said, dribbling a bit before lining up his shot. He aimed, tossed the ball toward the basket. It hit the backboard and went in.

"Nice," I said.

"Seriously though, Hobbs. Why aren't you going for it like Taj or Pat? Or me, I guess."

I sighed, went to make the basket but missed. "I'm good for high school. This has been fun and all, but I want something different. I don't want to eat, sleep, hoop the rest of my life."

"That must be nice, having the freedom to think like that," he said, holding out the ball to me.

"Well, it seems pretty cool to have your own Bash Is Beast cheering section," I said.

He shook his head. "God, I hate that."

"You shouldn't, it's pretty dope your family supports you the way they do."

"I know I'm lucky. They make me crazy sometimes. My dad is intense, like I have no time to do anything but hoop and school. When I'm not here, I'm watching highlight reels or in the gym working on my fast-twitch muscles for speed. Just once, I'd like to sneak off and spend the day with my girl, grab Taco Bell, see a movie or something," he said.

Sneaking off and spending the day with my girl sounded amazing. Something I hoped to do with Sarah in the very near future.

"You should do it, just disappear for a day," I said, envying his ability to even think of it as a possibility.

"I can't imagine what would happen though. I'd probably be grounded the rest of the season, working out double-time."

"Is she worth it?"

He lined up the shot, missed, but grinned. "Yeah."

On the next basket, I won. We headed toward the locker room.

"Hobbs, I'm sorry for being an asshole in the fall. What I said about your friend. I didn't know him, but from what I've heard he was a great guy. I don't know why I said that."

I shrugged. "People say stupid shit when they're angry. I was kind of an asshole to you too, so let's say we call it even."

After dinner, I went online to complete my mission from Holly to find the best prices and colors for balloons for the dance. When I agreed to cochair, I had no clue how many details went into planning this thing, and I could have lived without ever knowing. There were way too many shades of purple to choose from: lilac, spring lavender, amethyst, grape. Who knew?

I was busy noting the best prices when there was a knock at my door. Joe wandered in—he was still on winter break from Rutgers. I'd forgotten how much he needed to be entertained. He came in and flopped on my bed, flicked on the galaxy light.

"You really need this to sleep?" he asked.

"*Need* is a strong word," I said, closing the Balloon Warehouse website down before Joe had any chance of ribbing me about it.

"It's cool, maybe I could borrow it for the apartment," he said.

"Maybe you could get one of your own," I said.

"Feel like taking a ride up there sometime this week?"

"Why?"

"Newt's got tickets for the Devils game next week. He can't make it; said he'd leave them at the apartment if I wanted to pick them up."

"Is it really a two-person job?"

"Nah, but we could hit that pizza place, hang out."

"Did Mom put you up to this?"

Mom was not into me going to Colorado either and kept putting brochures of in-state schools on my desk.

"Are there even Devils tickets?"

"No. And yes. Just trying to see if you wanted to do something. A little bro-bonding time."

"So, is anyone else at the apartment right now?" I asked.

"In and out. Most everyone wants home-cooked meals for a month. Why?"

I shrugged but thought maybe this was the perfect place for sneaking off and spending the day with Sarah. It was out of the way, a place no one would know about. We could be alone.

"Hmmm, are you thinking you'd rather bond with Sarah?"

"It's not like that," I lied, but he saw through it.

He grinned. "Don't forget to pick up the tickets."

# sarah

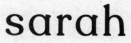

I WOKE UP ON SATURDAY MORNING, AN HOUR EARLIER than I needed to. In exchange for asking her to cover for me over winter break, I'd promised Trinity a crew morning. I got up, showered, and dressed. Mom was sitting at the breakfast bar, her laptop in front of her. She smiled when she saw me.

"Water's still warm if you want some tea," she said.

"Oh, no, thanks. My friends should be here soon," I said.

She took off her reading glasses and rubbed her eyes. "How long do you think you'll be? Maybe we can get a late lunch at Sophie's."

"We might run lines after we go thrifting, so I don't know, I'll probably be home by dinner," I said, the lie spilling out easily. I hadn't told my mother about my plans with Jake, didn't think she'd approve of me heading off to a college apartment to pick up some Devils tickets.

"Well, maybe dinner, then. Text me if anything changes," she said.

My phone buzzed with a text from Trinity, letting me know they were downstairs.

"See you later, Mom," I said, grabbing my coat and scarf and pulling them on as I trotted down the stairwell.

After a hearty breakfast of pancakes and bacon, and belting out the first twenty minutes of *Hamilton* as Dylan, Trinity, Cullyn, and I waited, we were off to Goodwill. Once inside, Trinity grabbed me by the elbow and directed us down an aisle. The clothing was separated by color.

"Okay, spill. Why did you need me to cover for you?"

"There's really nothing to it," I said, smiling, perusing the racks of secondhand clothes. "Do you think my character would wear this?" I asked holding up a chartreuse sweater with a faux fur collar.

Trini clucked her tongue. "You already have your costume *and* you're avoiding my question."

"Just doing some character building," I teased, moving onto the next rack.

"C'mon, I have to know what's going on in the lives of my cast. Especially if they enlist me to lie for them." She raised her eyebrows. I gave in.

"I went to a party in Brooklyn over break," I said.

"Ooh, like to Pratt?" she asked.

"What? No, a place called Carmine's. A family party," I said. We moved on to another aisle. Trini and I walked shoulder to shoulder, she turned her face toward me.

"All right, I suspect it's not the *where* but the *who* that made this such a secret," she said, lowering her voice.

"You make it sound dirty," I joked.

"It wasn't? Crap, I was hoping that I covered for something semi-scandalous."

"Okay, fine. I was with—"

"Jake Hobbs," she finished. I stopped cold in my tracks. She blinked a few times, self-satisfied grin on her face.

"How did you know that?"

"Well, it was obvious you were into him that time he walked into Adele's. But also . . . I may have had some help deducing. Perhaps you're not the only one with a secret," she said, speeding up. I caught up to her in the houseware section.

"Now it's your turn to spill," I said.

"Who, me? I don't kiss and tell," she said, picking up a small blue milk pitcher and putting it down again.

"Cullyn?" I asked.

She shook her head. "Please, he's like a sibling."

"Dylan?!"

"Shhh," she said, widening her eyes.

"Omigod, that's bigger news than me and Jake. Explain," I said.

Trini walked back toward the clothing department, motioned for me to follow her. We went down an aisle with high racks of winter coats. She bit her lip before speaking.

"Over break, Dylan wanted to run some lines—"

"Are you kidding me? What a line!"

She grinned. "I know, right, we did run lines, but then I don't know, one thing sort of led to another . . . I mean, he's Dylan."

"Wow, how very Broadway of you, director and actor falling for each other. All those hours together under the hot lights," I teased. She grabbed my elbow.

"Okay, but this is between you and me."

"Cullyn doesn't even know?"

She shook her head. "Back to you. Why are you keeping Jake Hobbs a secret?"

"It's complicated," I said.

"You did not just say that."

I sighed. "Ash McKenna thinks he's like a constant reminder of what happened. And it would be totally shitty of me to date Alex's best friend, right?"

Trinity puzzled. "Um, no?"

"Really?" I asked. "You think that's okay?"

"It doesn't matter what I think or what anyone else thinks. It's actually no one's business but yours and Jake's. But for the record, I think it's more than okay."

Hearing Trinity's take on it made me hopeful.

When we were finished, Trinity, Dylan, and Cullyn dropped me off at school. I'd told Jake to pick me up there. Ten minutes passed before I saw his car turn through the gates and come down the drive. I pressed my lips together to keep from grinning as I hopped off the bench. The tip of my nose was frozen, but I was instantly warm thinking about spending the rest of the afternoon with him.

"Hey, you," he said, smiling as I slid into the passenger seat. He leaned over to kiss me. Just a quick brush across my cheek, but it warmed me all the same.

"How was rehearsal?" he asked as we drove off campus and toward the turnpike. There was always a little thrill driving out of town, leaving the sleepiness of tree-lined streets and familiarity for uncertainty. Even though we were only going to his brother's apartment to pick up some tickets, it was an adventure to me.

"It was more of a prop-finding mission. We went to a few thrift stores, found some stuff for the show."

276

"Sounds fun," he said.

I laughed. "It was."

Once we went through the tollbooth and out onto the open highway, I began to relax a little. The odds of seeing anyone I knew diminished the farther we got out of town. Jake checked the rear-view, flicked the blinker, and changed lanes to pass a pickup truck with a ladder hanging out of the flatbed, a red flag tied on the top rung and whipping in the wind.

I shifted in my seat so I could inconspicuously steal a glance at him. I didn't want to stare at him outright. Okay, maybe I did. I did that sometimes when I found a person interesting-looking—not because I was crushing on them or anything, anyone was fair game. I liked to imagine people's stories, what went on behind their eyes, what made them tick. On the bus. In a restaurant. In this car.

Jake was relaxed behind the wheel, forefinger drumming to his own beat as he surveyed the traffic. The midday winter sun brought out coppery highlights in his dark hair. I'd never noticed that before. His insanely perfect lashes. Or the way his upper lip and lower lip were the same size, his upper lip nicely defined and curved. I couldn't wait kiss him again. He caught me staring. I blushed and looked straight ahead.

"You're awfully quiet," he said.

For the first time, I was nervous. Thinking about where we were going, what might happen. How we were going to be *alone*, alone, no interruptions. I smiled.

"How much longer till we get there?"

# jake

"ABOUT HALF AN HOUR, DEPENDING ON TRAFFIC," I said, checking the directions on my phone. I'd been to Joe's apartment before, I knew the way, but I couldn't shake my nervous energy. Maybe this wasn't a good idea, I had no idea what condition the place would be in. What if I was walking her into a train wreck—not exactly the seductive scene I hoped would be set. Not that I thought anything would happen, it was a place to be alone for a bit.

Simple as that. No distractions, no worries of anyone seeing us.

*"Who are you kidding, Hobbs? You know exactly what you want."*

*Not true, Alex.*

"Cool," she said.

I reached over and put my hand over hers, gave it a squeeze.

Once we got closer to campus, I pointed out landmarks. I'd been up to see Joe only a few times over the two years he'd been there, but I liked making it sound like I knew my way around.

"My brother works at that club; he'll be bartending next year."

"If you keep going straight, there's a kick-ass pizza place with slices the size of your head."

"Look between those trees, you can see some of the dorms on campus."

Sarah took it all in, wide-eyed, with that small secretive smile on her face that made me curious about what was going on in her mind.

Five minutes later we pulled up in front of Joe's apartment complex. I walked over to the passenger side to open the door for Sarah, but she'd already stepped out. I reached for her hand. She smiled as our fingers entwined. It was incredible to be able to do that, just walk hand in hand, no worries who would see us.

"C'mon," I said, leading her to the walkway toward Joe's building.

It wasn't exactly luxurious or anything. Okay, *dump* might have been the best description, but it was a transient place. Somewhere to study, rest your head, and party, while you prepped for the rest of your life. There was a couch on the curb with a few empty beer bottles next to an overflowing trash can. Maybe it wasn't the best idea to bring her here.

"It's so quiet," Sarah said.

"Winter break, a lot of people go home," I said.

We walked a little farther until we came upon 111. Joe's place. I pulled out the set of keys he'd given me and opened the door. The first door led to a shared corridor. Sarah put her hand up to her face when we were hit by a wall of sharp smell that reminded me of a zoo. I tried to ignore it, but *holy shit*. I opened the door to Joe's apartment quickly and we went in. Thankfully it was better inside. We both laughed, I turned on the light.

It wasn't that bad. At least no visible garbage, it looked orderly. A boxy-looking couch covered with a fleece New Jersey Devils blanket was the only place to sit in the living room area—if that's what you could even call it. The common area of the apartment was one big room. Stark, white walls covered here and there with posters. A basic table and chairs in the kitchen. There was a large cardboard cutout of Keanu Reeves from *John Wick* mounted on the one wall and a *Rick and Morty* banner on the other. A flat-screen TV and makeshift coffee table of milk crates holding up an old door completed the look.

We both stood there gawking for a long second.

"So, this is what college is like," she said.

"We don't have to stay," I said. "I'll, um, just go grab the tickets."

I walked down the hall to Joe's room and looked on his desk to see if there was an envelope or something that looked like tickets. Nothing. I texted him.

Thought you said tix on desk?

No. Fridge. Don't forget tix.

K

Or a condom. Top right drawer. Desk.

I left that unanswered and returned to the kitchen. Sarah had taken off her coat. She stood in front of the refrigerator; arms crossed.

"I think the tickets are here," she said, pointing to the fridge.

They were there, held by a magnetic clip. There was a small poster of a condom and beer bottle fighting each other in a boxing ring underneath the envelope. A campaign that sex and booze didn't mix.

"See what I have to look forward to next year," I said.

She laughed, leaned against the counter. She seemed unsure. Or maybe that was me. I moved closer, put my hands on her waist.

"Hey," I said.

280

"Hey."

"Sorry I couldn't do better for us. I know this place sucks."

"It doesn't suck," she said, putting her arms around my shoulders. "Confession? When we listen to ocean waves at night, the virtual beach date, I usually imagined more than just . . . you know, sitting there."

I grinned. "Oh, really, like what?"

"Like this," she said, brushing her lips against mine.

"Nice," I said between kisses. "What else?"

"And this," she said, kissing me again.

The place with its shabby walls and dude-bro style disappeared as I got caught up in the warmth of Sarah's arms around me, our mouths touching. I thought about being alone with her for weeks, but nothing prepared me for the reality. I couldn't kiss her enough. The feel of her body against mine was so overwhelming. I didn't want to move, I wanted to stay there in that moment all night. Although in the back of my mind I knew we'd be more comfortable on the couch.

With my hands still around her waist and our lips together, I began moving back, pulling her with me. She laughed, caught on. We finally gave up kissing halfway over and sort of spun, falling back together on the couch.

"Ow," she said, smiling. She slid her phone out of her back pocket. Her brow furrowed when she looked at the screen.

"What?" I asked, eager to resume where we'd left off.

She shook her head and placed the phone down on the table in front of us. It buzzed again, but she threw her arms around me and we dropped back, me on top. She bent her knee, hooked her leg around mine. I ran my hand along the length of her body, buried my face in her neck, nibbled her earlobe.

"Jake," she whispered. My mouth found hers again.

Her phone rang, but we kept kissing. It no sooner stopped, then rang again.

She stiffened, pulled away. "Sorry, let me check that."

I moved back, helped her sit up. She ran a hand through her hair, kissed me quick, and picked up her phone, checking the number.

"Hmm."

"Everything okay?"

"Um, yeah I think so. It's Trinity, but she called me like three times. Do you mind if I call her back?"

"No, sure, I'll be over here, waiting," I teased. She walked over to the kitchen and made the call.

"Hey, what . . . Wait, what? Slow down," she said.

Sarah's eyes widened, she put her hand over her mouth. She didn't say anything, just listened for a long minute. I stood up and walked over to her. She turned her back to me.

"Oh, shit, well, what did she say? Okay, okay. It's not your fault, Trini. Thanks for letting me know, I guess. Sure. I'll, um, let you know how it goes."

She hung up the call and whispered, "Fuck." Her eyes wild when she looked at me.

"Is everything okay?" I asked knowing full well it wasn't, but what the hell could it be? A prop emergency?

"No. They ran into my mom. At Adele's."

"And—"

"I told my mom I'd be with drama group all day and I wasn't

there, and Cullyn might have unknowingly spilled a little bit too much info about dropping me back off at school, and, well . . . I kind of need to leave, like, now."

I reached for my jacket, but then I let her words sink in.

Wait.

"You lied to your mother about me? Again?"

She flustered. "Well, I guess, I mean . . . yes."

"Why?"

"Jake, you know why," she said.

"What does your mother have to do with Ash?"

"She sees her on occasion. The less people who know the better, right?"

She wasn't wrong, I knew that, but it still bothered me.

"You feel like you have to make a choice, don't you? Between me or your friendship with Ash."

"Don't put it that way," she said.

"What way do you want me to put it? It's the truth. Do you ever have any intention of telling her about us?"

"Yes," she said.

"Well, when?"

Her eyes welled with tears, and I felt like a colossal prick, but I was pissed too. We liked each other, we wanted to be with each other, why did it have to be so difficult?

"I don't know," she said.

"What about right now? Just call her up and tell her, or is it not worth it?"

"Stop."

"So, you don't want to be with me, then?"

"Stop pressuring me, okay? I'm in so much trouble—I have about ten texts from my mom. I can't deal with this right now."

"You didn't answer my question."

Her arms went up in exasperation. "Of course I want to be with you!"

"Then call her."

She put her hands up to her face. "I can't."

We were silent for a long moment. She swiped a tear away from her cheek with her sweater sleeve. Every impulse made me want to go over and hug her, forget the fight I'd picked, go back to groping each other on the couch, but I was too stubborn.

"There's my answer."

"Why are you doing this? You said you understood why we need to keep us a secret. That people wouldn't understand," she said.

Again, she wasn't wrong, but that was separate from this. The way I felt about her, I didn't give a flying fuck what people thought of us. But if she couldn't even imagine talking to Ash about us now, what were the odds she ever would? And then, there was Alex.

"He's always going to be between us, isn't he?"

"What?"

"Alex. In one way or another, he's always going to be here," I said, looking at her. The realization gutted me. Alex may have brought us together, but he was indirectly keeping us apart too.

*"Hey, that's not fair, Hobbs."*

*Fuck off, Alex.*

"That's not true," she said.

"But it already is, isn't it? You can't tell Ash because she looks at me as a constant reminder of the worst night of our lives. It was a stupid fucking accident, Sarah. I hate that it happened, but it was random and unfair, and I'm sick of being reminded of it every day of my life. And right now when I look at you? I'm still just a fuckup. I still feel guilty for being alive."

She moved closer to me, reached out, but I stepped back.

"Let's go," I said.

# sarah

I KEPT WIPING TEARS AWAY WITH THE SLEEVE OF MY jacket as we walked back to Jake's car, the mood decidedly different. He walked so fast I had to take two steps to his one just to keep up with him. Why had I lied to my mother? I wasn't embarrassed of Jake, I didn't want to keep him a secret, but any time I thought of breaking it to Ash . . . The truth was I was scared—what if it *wasn't* worth it?

Jake would be gone next year, whether he went to Colorado or not. If I blew up my friendship with Ash, where would that leave me? I didn't want to say that to him; I didn't want to add any more fuel to the fight.

Even in his anger, Jake opened the passenger door for me. Closed it gently. He did have a heavy foot on the gas pedal though, revved up the car before pulling out of the spot. The tires made a screeching noise as we turned out of the parking lot. He took a deep breath when we drove through town.

"Jake," I said.

"I don't feel like talking right now," he answered.

We drove home in a tense, charged silence. I sat immobile, stared straight ahead at the sea of red taillights in front of us. I was afraid to look at my phone, to read the texts from my mother. I had no clue what to expect when I got home.

What the hell was I going to tell her? *I'm seeing Jake on the sly, so we went to his brother's apartment to fool around, and if Ash finds out there's a chance she'll never speak to me again. I'll just send myself to my room indefinitely. Bye.*

There was traffic when we got back to town. I couldn't believe that we hadn't said a word to each other the entire ride home, and now I didn't even know what to say. I played with the lock on the car door as we inched toward the traffic light. Home was within walking distance. I certainly wasn't in a rush to get there. The walk would help me calm my nerves, clear my head before dealing with my mother.

"I'm, um, I'm gonna go," I said, opening the door.

Jake looked over at me, his voice urgent. "Sarah, don't. I can drive you home."

"I'll text you when I get in," I said, not looking back.

I closed the door behind me and trotted toward the sidewalk. Halfway up the street I pulled out my phone to check the texts. The first was a simple *Where are you?* Each text got more and more frantic in tone, unless that's just how I was hearing them in my head. Then I noticed my aunt had texted me.

Your mother is in a frenzy. Call her!

Oh shit. *Frenzy* was never a word you would use to describe my mom.

For a moment, I thought about going to Adele's, claiming sanctuary, begging my aunt to be mediator.

It was too far. I was too tired.

The sooner I got this off my chest, the better.

I texted Jake when I got to my building.

Home.

Sorry.

And walked up the stairs to face my fate.

# jake

"GOT MY TICKETS?" JOE ASKED AS I BARRELED THROUGH the front door.

"Oh, fuuuuuuck," I said, slamming the door behind me. I shook my fists at the ceiling and growled. Joe looked at me as if I were holding a live grenade and was about to toss it at him. He held his hands up.

"Okay, no need to be dramatic. They're just tickets. Jake, I ca get 'em tomorrow."

I sighed. Reset.

"I'm sorry. I had them in my hand. I think I left them *n* t table in the kitchen."

"Things go that well, huh?"

"I don't want to talk about it," I said, climbing the stairs *at* a time.

I slammed my door closed and collapsed onto my *felt* good to take out my aggression on an inanimate obje *cked* my phone and saw Sarah's text.

She was home.

She was sorry.

I didn't have the mental energy to text he

Why had I blown up like that? It had been so nice, spending time with her, being alone. Of course I understood why we needed to be a secret, but on the other hand—she seemed so okay with it. Too comfortable. And what would her mother think of me? Would she tell her where she'd been? I was just the deviant asshole who took her to a college guy's apartment.

And I was that guy who'd been with Alex McKenna the night he fell.

I hated letting Sarah go, hated the way I'd left things. I didn't want to think of my life without her in it, but I also wondered if being with her *would* keep me stuck. Would I always feel the shadow of Alex lurking when I least expected it?

time, Buzz. That's why when you said that before, I had to think about who you meant. We're not together anymore. We never really were, mostly because"—I paused, admitting my feelings for Jake was freeing—"I think because I knew I liked Jake. We've been talking for months, Mom. At first it was because we were both sad about Alex, but it grew into something more, and now, I'm in it pretty deep."

Her eyes grew round; she took in a deep breath and let it out. "And why does Ash not like him again?"

"She said he's like a reminder of the night Alex died. That she'd just as soon never see him again."

She nodded. "And you think lying to her and seeing him behind her back will make her change her mind?"

The situation sounded so ridiculous the way she said it, but it was the truth, wasn't it? What had I been doing?

I shook my head.

"There were times I wanted to tell her, but I don't want to say the wrong thing and upset her. She's been doing so much better these days."

"Honey, I think if she knows how much you care about Jake, she might feel differently, but you're not going to know unless you come clean to her."

"You make it sound so easy."

"The truth usually is," she said. "Or at least maybe it's less complicated."

My head hurt from crying and fighting. All I wanted to do was curl up in a ball. I looked at Mom. "Do you think I could have some hot chocolate?"

She nodded, caught me looking over wistfully toward my phone.

"Don't even think you're touching that for at least twenty-four hours."

After a brief panicked thought of *holyshitareyoukidding?* relief crept in. I could shut the world out for a while, check out of life.

At least for twenty-four hours.

# jake

I DIDN'T TEXT SARAH UNTIL SUNDAY NIGHT, JUST A general *Heyy*, to put the ball in her court. When she didn't text or call, I wondered if she was intentionally ghosting me. I stared up at my galaxy light ceiling, wishing I could go back in time and fix things, even if it was just a fantasy.

On Monday, I waited at the top of the stairwell before first period, hoping at least to see how she was doing, how things worked out with her mom. I waited until the second warning bell rang, but she never showed. She was scarce at lunch as well. Out sick? I finally saw her after school, at rehearsal. She didn't look over as she climbed up to the stage. My heart lifted at the sight of her, but then I felt shitty all over again because that meant she was ghosting me after all.

I decided to give it one more try. After practice I texted her.

**Need a ride home?**

If she didn't reply to that, I'd chill. Assume that was it. At least I'd have something to talk about that week with Dr. Hipster.

"Hey, Hobbs, do you have a minute?" Coach asked as I walked past his office. I kept my phone in my hand in case Sarah texted.

"Yeah, sure."

He finished typing something on his keyboard and gestured for me to sit down.

"You did a great job at the clinic over winter break," he said.

"Thanks, it was pretty cool helping the little ones," I said, and meant it. I glanced down at my phone—nothing from Sarah.

"How would you like to help out over the summer?"

The summer seemed so far away, another time, another place.

"What do you mean?"

"We hold clinics here for six weeks, two in June, two in July, and two in August. It's a little more involved than the one during winter break. And it's a longer day, but it's paid. There's a field trip or two. It's more like a summer camp with a concentration on basketball skills. You seemed like a natural with the kids."

"Alex used to do this, didn't he?"

"He did. The kids loved him. I see the same thing in you."

"You do?"

Coach nodded. "What do you think?"

My phone went off. I looked down—Sarah calling. I wanted to tell him to hold on a minute, but I couldn't. I'd have to call her back.

"Not sure if I'll be available for the August dates, Coach, with college and all."

"That's fine, you don't have to commit to all six weeks if you don't want to. Have you made any decisions about school?"

"Have you been talking to my parents?"

He smiled. "I heard Colorado is a possible choice. I know you said you didn't want to play ball, but if you change your mind, I can always make some calls. Plenty of small schools around here that would be happy to consider a kid with your game."

"I'll keep that in mind, sir. Thanks," I said.

I was barely out of his office when I called Sarah.

The call went straight to voice mail.

Damn. I ended the call, not knowing what to say.

*"You should have begged her to stay in the car last Saturday."*

*Great advice now, Alex.*

I noticed I had a voice mail. I listened while walking to my car.

"Hey, Jake, it's Sarah. In about five minutes I won't be able to talk to you because my mom will have custody of my phone again." She laughed. "So, I guess you can figure out how that all went on Saturday. I shouldn't have lied, Jake. I'm sorry about that, but it's probably better—" She hesitated. "I guess it would be better if we stop this. Now. Before it gets out of hand. Give each other some space. Um, okay, I have to go. Bye."

I listened to it again.

And again.

*Out of hand?* I think we'd passed that already.

After everything we'd been through, our late-night calls, that night in Brooklyn, was this really how she wanted it to end?

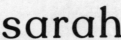

# sarah

"HAS IT EVER BEEN THIS SLOW?" I ASKED MARNIE. FOR as long as I'd worked at Adele's, there'd never been such a lull. I rearranged the rows of macarons in the pastry case, swept the floor, wiped down the tables. I needed something to keep me busy.

"It's a frozen-ass Thursday in January. Maybe people don't want to brave the cold for pastries," Marnie said, flipping a page of her book.

I envied her carefree attitude. I kept checking the door, hoping against hope that Jake would surprise me with an ambush visit. But why would he? I'd made it clear that I thought the best thing was to ~~g~~ive each other some space. And he'd given it to me. I hadn't even ~~cau~~ght a glimpse of him in the usual places in school.

~~"I'~~m going to wipe down the tables again."

~~"Suit~~ yourself," Marnie said.

~~I grabb~~ed a clean rag and the spray bottle. After I wiped down ~~the last ta~~ble, the bell on the front door jingled. I looked up.

~~"What~~ a great surprise!" I said, smiling. She had her guitar ~~over he~~r shoulder.

~~"I finis~~hed early, thought I'd drop in and wait for my ~~ride to pick me~~ up. Think you could hang for like ten min-

I looked at Marnie; she was still reading but gestured to me that it was okay with a wave of her hand. I made some hot chocolates and headed over to where Ash was sitting. She loosened her scarf and undid the top buttons on her jacket as I placed the steaming mug in front of her and sat down.

She put her hands around the mug to warm them. "I hate being frozen."

"I remember someone saying this winter was going to be epic," I said.

"Well, it is epic, just wish it wasn't sixteen degrees epic," she said, taking a quick sip and letting the drink work its magic.

"How's the band going?" I asked.

She grinned. "It's perfect. Bran just told me we have a new gig," she said. "It probably sounds corny as hell, but I love saying that word. I'm in a band, Sar!" She lifted up her hand and pushed back the sleeve of her jacket to reveal the braided bracelet with the music notes. I lifted my hand to show her my drama mask bracelet. I hadn't taken it off since Ash had given it to me, even to shower.

"East Village, here we come," I said.

"Right? I mean, that's a big leap, but it feels like a baby step in that direction," she said. "Aren't you going to ask me where we're playing?"

"Well, naturally I assumed the Beacon Theatre," I joked.

"Ha. We're doing that scholarship dance, the one for Alex."

"Really? Wait, I thought we were having a deejay? How do you know this before me?"

"The deejay fell through. Holly was frantic; Bran just happened to be there when she got the news and offered up Crush. You know, I wasn't even sure I was going to that dance, but . . . this sounds ridiculous . . . I feel like it's Alex's way of saying he wants me there. It feels right, you know?"

I sucked in a breath. "Yes, wow."

"So, will you be out of your exile by then?"

I'd told Ash that I'd been grounded because of an awful fight with my mother. She hadn't pressed me further, but only said, "It must have been some fight."

"Yes," I said, laughing.

"So, are you thinking of asking anyone to go?"

I stared into my mug. What if I told her about Jake? Just blurted out the whole story. The drama mask charm glinted in the light, a symbol of our dreams as friends. What purpose would that serve to tell her about him now? We weren't together. She'd been so happy a moment ago as she spoke about the band. I didn't want to screw with that.

"Me?" I asked, laughing. "No, I'll be working it, probably no time to dance anyway."

"I think you need to get out there again, Sarah. I think Alex would want that for you."

My cheeks warmed. I didn't know what to say.

"Look, if you're open to something, the bass player in Crush is hot and very single. His name is Wyatt, and he goes to Cedar Hills High."

"Ash!"

"I'm just saying, I could introduce you at the dance, see what happens," she said, playfully arching her eyebrows.

"We know what happened the last time you nudged me in someone's direction," I said.

300

"Yeah, but that was different. Wyatt is totally magnet-pull material," she said, laughing. Her phone chirped. "Oh, hey, my dad's out front."

She pushed back from the table, buttoned her coat. I stood up, collected the mugs.

"It's great to see you excited about music again, Ash," I said.

She grabbed her guitar case, smiled.

"Feels good too. Thanks, Sar. Later," she said, heading out to catch her ride.

I stood there watching as she trotted over to the car. The café felt so empty again. But it was more than Ash leaving. Something felt off. That's when I realized, still no Kermit chair.

I walked back to the counter with the mugs. Aunt Sophie had come out from the back and was chatting with Marnie. I placed the dirty mugs in the dish bin.

"Hey, when are you getting the Kermit chair back?" I asked.

"The what?" my aunt asked.

"You know, the big green chair that you sent out to get cleaned?"

She and Marnie shared a look.

"What?" I said.

"It wasn't sent out to be cleaned," Marnie said, looking sheepish. "I told you that because I knew how much it meant to you."

"Sarah, I gave that chair away," Aunt Sophie said. "The Salvation Army came and picked up some of the older furniture. I have some new pieces on order, to freshen the place up. I had no idea you were so attached to that lumpy green chair. Marnie filled me in, but by the time I realized that it was—"

"The chair Alex used to sit in," I said, finishing her sentence.

She winced. "It was gone. It only lasted a day or so in the store. I tried to get it back, if I'd known I never would have donated it."

"So it's *gone*, gone," I said.

She nodded. "I'm afraid so."

I kept waiting for a wave of sadness, but I felt nothing. I knew in the coming days it would probably hit me, that I'd never see this special reminder of Alex again, but at the moment, it just seemed like one more thing that was beyond my control.

# february

# jake

I CLIMBED UP HOLLY'S IMPRESSIVE SET OF DOUBLE stairs to her front porch and rang the doorbell, heard the formal high-pitched chimes followed by a racket of yips and barks and scampering of claws. I stood there, chai in one hand, mochaccino in the other, unsure of what it was that she liked, hoping I'd chosen wisely.

The last time I'd been in Holly's house was after Alex's wake, when we were all too stunned to be alone with our thoughts. Now, I was here to go over final details for the scholarship dance in his name. It still felt unreal, Alex was a strong presence in our lives but not physically here. Holly opened the door, gesturing for me to come in while shooing away her pups, Coco and Winston.

"Sorry about the mess," she said, leading me over to her dining room table, the dogs dancing around our feet. I laughed, put the cups on the table, and reached down to give both of them equal shares of ear scratches. She moved some papers aside, gestured for me to take a seat. "I've been working on some of our second-semester senior-year stuff too. And finishing up some scholarship essays. I swear it's more organized than it looks."

"All this and the dance too. Geez, Holls, you ever take a break?"

She sighed. "Being busy is my therapy. If I slow down, I don't know, I get anxious. Alex was always good at getting me to slow down though."

It was nice to hear her talk about Alex in a positive way.

"Does Pat help slow things down?"

She laughed, glanced away. "He's pretty good at it too, I guess. Hey, is one of those mine?" she asked, pointing at the to-go cups.

"Oh, yeah, chai or mocha?"

"Chai, please."

She sat across from me, folding one of her legs underneath her and grabbing the chai with both hands. She blew on the lid before taking a sip.

"So, we're all set with balloons, hell, never realized there were so many choices. And the party place has tablecloths too. And my mom took me to Costco, I think I got all the paper products we needed. I can get to school early, to be there for the deliveries. Do you think you could pick up the stuff from Adele's?"

She nodded. "Jake, I'm not worried about the dance. At this point, these things run their course. Maybe a hiccup here or there, but we've got this. I can't believe I'm going to say this, but I'm glad you brought Sarah on to help with refreshments. Adele's is amazing."

"Yeah, it is."

"I'd be happy to do the pickup, but I thought you were doing that."

"You should be there to make sure we get the right colors."

"I've been checking in with Sarah's aunt weekly. I trust everything will be perfect. What's up with that?" she asked, as she took a sip of her chai.

"What's up with what?"

She arched an eyebrow, stared at me until I laughed.

"No, really, what?"

"You and Sarah?"

"Why would you ask that?"

"I have eyes. Also, Court came to me after your split and said she suspected as much."

"There was nothing going on when I ended things with Court."

"But there is now?"

I wanted to trust Holly, but I still wasn't sure if this was a ploy to get me to spill my guts.

"No, we decided to cool it."

"That's too bad."

Her response surprised me. "Really? Don't you think it would be weird for her to hook up with me, since, you know, Alex?"

She shook her head. "I mean, maybe at one time, but honest? You have to live in the moment, because who knows how many you're going to have."

If only I could get Sarah to see it that way.

# sarah

"IS THAT WHAT YOU'RE WEARING TO THE DANCE?"
Aunt Sophie asked when I walked into Adele's. I glanced down
at my knee-high boots, black leggings, and fuzzy green sweater. I
mean, I thought I looked pretty dope for a school event.

"Um, yeah?"

"You dress like that for the movies, you really had nothing else?"

"Omigod, did you and Mom work on this coordinated attack?"
I tossed my coat on the back of a chair. I didn't think I could take
another wistful lecture about how dances were different back in the
day. "It's not that kind of a dance; it's in the cafeteria. It's more like
a 'hang out awkwardly and eat snacks while the band plays' sort of
a thing."

She frowned.

"And now you're calling my beautiful lavender and silver macarons *snacks*? Will it never end?" she asked, clutching her chest and
laughing. "C'mon, Holly is in the back helping us pack things up."

*Holly?*

My mood fell a bit, I'd been hoping, even after everything, Jake
was still going to pick me up. After all, I was supposed to be working with him. I'd said I needed space, and he was giving it to me,

I couldn't be upset about that. Holly smiled when she saw me. She was in a minidress and heels, which made me want to go home and change into something less casual. Our versions of low-key were vastly different.

"Hey, you look great," she said.

"Thanks, same," I said, heading over to help finish box up the various cookies. Her being nice to me was unsettling. Along with Marnie and Aunt Sophie, we made quick work of packing up the cookies, then took the boxes out to Holly's SUV.

"Enjoy yourself! Take pics for our social media," Aunt Sophie said as we drove off. We both laughed at her enthusiasm, but then silence fell over the car as we traveled toward school. I never would have anticipated being in this situation with Holly Matthews. As if she sensed that, she spoke.

"Jake wanted to be there for the delivery of the balloons, since he was the one who ordered them," she said. "But, really, I think he thought you might feel more comfortable arriving with me."

I couldn't help but snicker. Was this a joke?

"What?" she asked.

"I don't know what's going on, but I doubt Jake thought I'd be more comfortable with you. I mean, it's okay, we're whatever. It's fine," I said. I didn't trust her being so nice.

She sighed, kept her eyes on the road.

"I get it. We shouldn't get along, because of Alex."

"Um, yeah? You didn't exactly welcome me at that first meeting."

"I know that; I'm sorry. I was in a different place then," she said. "When Jake brought you on board, I was hurt, it's like it brought up all these bad memories from last year."

"Gee, thanks," I said.

"Sorry, I'm not trying to make you feel bad. I don't feel that way anymore. Sarah, I've adored Alex for as long as I can remember, always waiting for him to wake up and see how great we'd be together. When we broke up, I lashed out, acted stupid. Threw myself into proving that our relationship meant more than yours."

Being validated that I hadn't imagined it didn't make me feel as good as I once thought it would. We both lost Alex. It wasn't a contest of whose grief meant more. Still, her admission made me unexpectedly tear up.

"I was jealous of the time you had with him," I admitted, swiping the tear away.

"I think that's how I wanted you to feel. It sounds so stupid now. And mean. I'm sorry I acted that way. I'm happy you're working on this. I think if Alex really is somewhere, he's enjoying us getting along, putting this together to honor him. Sometimes I swear I feel him around, don't you?"

The question felt like another test to prove yet again that Holly's relationship with Alex meant more because no, as hard as I tried, I didn't *feel* Alex anywhere. I wanted to believe, wanted a sign, but all I had were the photos on my phone. The one Snapchat where he called me babe. Even when I'd been in his room, I didn't feel him. I remembered him. There was a difference.

"Yeah," I lied.

We pulled onto campus and into her "Spot Reserved for Student Council President" parking space.

"Wow, your own spot," I said, laughing.

310

"Guess being president has its perks," she said. She texted a few people to come help us, and we brought the boxes to the cafeteria. I had to stop a moment, while yes, it was the cafeteria—it had been transformed into a purple-and-silver wonderland with fairy lights, sparkly netting, and bouquets of balloons everywhere.

I smiled. "Wow."

"I know. We do good work," Holly said.

Crush made an entrance forty minutes before the door was set to open. Bran sauntered in, followed by a taller guy with shaggy hair and sunglasses. Ash had told me they'd been in the caf earlier for sound check but left to get ready. She and Mike arrived, holding hands, followed by a petite girl with short dark hair who was arm in arm with . . . Buzz? For a moment my feet felt unsteady. Ash hadn't said anything to me about that. Had they all been hanging out?

"Hey," I said, waving, thankful to see a friendly face. I'd been there for half an hour setting up the refreshments table and still hadn't seen Jake. Ash smiled as I walked up to her, she let go of Mike's hand and discreetly motioned to the dude with the sunglasses, who was busy plunking the strings of his bass. Ah, Wyatt.

I shook my head and smiled.

"C'mon, he's cute, no?"

"I don't get the sunglasses."

"It's part of his laid-back bass player persona," she said, laughing, then squeezed my forearm. "Why am I so nervous? It's just the school cafeteria."

"Well, it's *your* school cafeteria. No hiding if you suck," I joked.

"Sarah!"

"I'm kidding, Ash. You know you guys are going to *crush* it. See what I did there?"

"Ha, ha," she said, then stepped aside, pulling the dark-haired girl with Buzz into our conversation. "Oh, hey, this is Bailey, our drummer."

Bailey's hair was short and choppy with a dramatic swoop of bangs completely covering one eye.

"Hi, I'm Sarah," I said.

"Ah, Sarah. Have heard sooo much about you," she said, flicking her head to the side to swish her bangs out of her eyes. She shared a look with Buzz that made me realize she'd probably heard some things about me from him, not Ash. Yeesh.

"Hey, Ash? Bay? We need you up here," a voice called from behind me.

"Later, Sar," Ash said.

Mike followed her to the band setup.

"Gotta run, sugar," Bailey said, kissing Buzz.

He grinned as she walked away.

"That happened fast, *sugar*," I said, ribbing him. "I'm happy for you."

"When someone is into you, it's not that complicated," he replied.

There was a beat, where I let his words sink in, and then we both cracked up.

"True," I said.

The caf started filling up, and pretty soon it actually looked like we were having a dance. I found my place behind the refreshment table, scanned the room for familiar faces. I saw some people from drama club—Trinity and Dylan caught my eye and waved. Pat Boyle and the guys from the basketball team were in the back, commandeering at least two tables. Courtney was there with the cheer squad. The night was already a success with such a great turnout.

"Sarah."

Jake was suddenly standing next to me, I wasn't sure where he'd come from, I hadn't even seen him walk over. What had I expected to accomplish by avoiding him all this time?

The adrenaline rush from seeing him, from hearing him say my name, was dizzying. It was an effort not to throw my arms around him, plant my mouth on his. So, this was the magnet-pull thing? No wonder Ash and Mike were so damn crazy. I stood there mute, realizing it was my turn to say something.

"Hi, Jake," I said.

"You good here?" he asked, all business.

"I think so."

"Cool. I have someone else lined up for the next shift, so you know, you don't have to stay behind the table all night, you're allowed to have fun at this thing," he said.

"Okay."

"Hey, Jake, c'mon," Holly called over to him.

He paused a moment, looking as though he wanted to say something more.

"Gotta run, I'll check back in a bit," he said, and walked over toward Holly.

All at once I felt like crying, but at least it was over with now. We saw each other, it was awkward, and now I could move on.

Holly and Jake walked through the center of the room. The crowd parted as she arrived up front. She waved to a few people before tapping the mic. Bran didn't look thrilled and whispered something in her ear as he adjusted it.

"Hey, everyone, just wanted to welcome you to the festivities. I'm completely overwhelmed with the response, but I guess when you ask Crusaders to do something, they rise to the occasion! C'mon, Jake, get your butt over here."

The guys from the basketball team clapped and chanted his name. He stepped into the spotlight and raised his hands to quiet down the cheers. Holly put her hand over the mic and said something to him. He shook his head.

"Jake wants to say a few words. C'mon," Holly said.

He leaned toward the mic. "Thanks for being here!" Then leaned away from it and laughed. Holly rolled her eyes at him, but in a good-natured *gosh, darn* kind of way and resumed her emcee duties.

"With your help we've raised over five hundred dollars for the Alex McKenna basketball scholarship. It's going to help send kids to basketball clinics over the summer. And without further ado, here's . . ."

She pulled Jake down toward the mic so they could introduce the band together.

"Crush." They said together and made their way to the dance floor as Crush launched into an up-tempo song that immediately sent the crowd into a frenzy. I tried to keep my eyes on Jake, but he got swallowed up in the crowd.

Crush killed it. Ash looked like she'd been part of the band forever. She and Bran kept sharing looks now and then, as if they had their own private language through music. At one point, they even leaned into each other, back-to-back. Maybe I understood why Mike was suspicious of Bran, but it was all for show, wasn't it? Mike was standing toward the back of the crowd, arms crossed, looking as serious as a bouncer. When Ash and Bran leaned into each other again, he came over to me.

"Hey, want something to drink?" I asked, trying to feel out his mood.

"You have vodka?"

Oh, shit.

"Um, no," I said, laughing.

"Then I'm good."

"What's wrong?" I asked, even though I had a pretty good idea.

He motioned for me to lean closer.

"That dude is totally into her, go ahead, tell me I'm paranoid," he said.

I looked toward the band, and sure enough, Ash and Bran were singing, heads tilted toward each other, only inches apart. Oof. He wasn't being paranoid, but if there was anything going on, I didn't think Ash would be that deliberate about it in front of Mike.

"She wouldn't do anything like that to hurt you, you have to know that. They're just caught up in the music."

"Why doesn't that make me feel better?" he asked. He turned away and resumed his serious-bouncer stance at the back of the room. I kept an eye on him while I helped some people with a few drinks.

"Hey, I'm here," Jake sidled up to me, a little breathless and sweaty. He grabbed a bottle of water and just about chugged the entire thing. I couldn't help but laugh.

"You were going pretty hard out there," I said.

He smiled, ran a hand through his hair. "Yeah, Holly wouldn't let that go. She wanted us to set an example, then they wouldn't let me leave."

"Looked fun," I said.

"Well, you can take a break if you want. Go hit the dance floor," he said.

I imagined confessing that I'd rather stand behind the refreshments table with him than hit the dance floor but decided against it. "Maybe in a bit."

More people came up for drinks. Jake and I made quick work of it. I scooped ice into cups, and he poured. I handed out napkins for the cookies. When the line died down, I refilled the steadily dwindling plate of cookies. Jake helped. At one point, we reached into the box together, and our fingers brushed. We both stopped, lingered. Jake took my hand in his.

I gathered the nerve to look up at him.

"Hey," he said.

"Jake!"

We startled, and I pulled away. If Holly had seen us holding hands she didn't let on. I grabbed the empty box and tossed it in the garbage while Jake poured her a soda. I kept myself busy, straightening up the table as they spoke, trying to let my heartrate get back to normal.

Onstage, Ash and Bran changed over to acoustic guitars. Tuned up a bit.

"Time to slow it down," Bran said.

The crowd that had been gathered in front of them dispersed, a few groans here and there. Someone shouted *buzzkill*. Bran laughed, low and sexy into the microphone before launching into the number. An Ed Sheeran song, a duet with him and Ash and their guitars. I saw Mike move quickly through the crowd, he had his jacket in hand and left the cafeteria.

"Shit," I said.

"What's wrong?" Jake asked.

"Can I take that break now?" I asked, looking between him and Holly.

"Ah, sure, everything okay?"

"Yeah, I just need to stop Mike from making a huge mistake," I said, rushing out from behind the table. I walked out of the caf and up the stairs, sure I'd be able to catch up to him. He must have moved fast because he wasn't in the stairwell, or the hallway, and when I finally reached the front of the building there was still no sign of him. I pushed open the front door and went outside. It was cold, but bearable, at least for the moment.

"Mike?" I called, walking down the steps.

Crickets. I scanned the parking lot to see any telltale headlights or movement. I was about to walk around to the side parking lot, when the front door opened.

"Sarah."

I turned to see Jake, the door closing behind him as he stepped toward me.

"Thought you might need some help," he said.

"Oh, sure," I said. "I was just going to check the other parking lot."

He nodded and followed me to the side of the building. We

walked in silence, peering over the rows of cars. There was no movement there either. We walked back toward school. Jake stopped.

"Okay, this is bullshit. I didn't come out here to help, Sarah. I came out to see you."

"Jake."

"Wait, what I really mean is," he said, holding my gaze. "It's great to see you."

He was so sincere, and the feeling was completely mutual. I choked up. A million thoughts ready to spill out.

"I screwed everything up. I'm sorry. I shouldn't have lied. Shouldn't have left you a voice mail. I knew if I saw you, I'd never be able to—"

"I'm sorry too. You said you needed time, and I pushed you. My stupid pride got the best of me. I acted like a jackass."

"Only because I acted like a jackass first," I said. And suddenly we weren't in the parking lot anymore. We were right back to that day at his brother's apartment, our argument fresh and unresolved. He reached for my hand. I didn't resist. Our fingers entwined, we walked over to the bench where I first gave him my phone number and sat down.

"What you said that day . . . about feeling guilty for being alive . . . is that true?" I asked.

He let out a slow breath, then looked at me.

"In that moment? Yes. Not all the time, but I mean, look at me. I'm captain of the basketball team, making the moves on his girl, hell, Coach even offered me Alex's old summer job, so yeah, sometimes I feel like I'm living his life. I wonder why the bad stuff happened to him. Why not me?"

"Don't say that," I said.

"I'm not saying I wish it happened to me, I don't. Then I feel guilty about that too. If I was in Ash's place, I probably wouldn't want to see me either. There's times I even question why you wanted to be with me."

"What? Why?"

He sighed. "Maybe I don't have a right to ask this, but sometimes I wonder if I'm just a replacement for Alex. Not quite him, but almost. Maybe that's why you didn't want to tell Ash. Or introduce me to your mom."

I shifted so I was facing him, took both his hands in mine.

"Replacement? What we have is so much different from my relationship with Alex. And it's more than just the time we've spent together, it's the way I feel about you. I'm not afraid to be myself with you. I never talked with him the way we talk. Never opened up to anyone like you. There's no comparison, really. I love you, Jake."

I hadn't intended to say it, but there it was.

The words slipped out without effort or thought. Three words that named this quiet emotion that had begun during our late-night conversations. A feeling that had evolved and grown stronger when I wasn't looking or thinking. It just was, and in a year full of grief and doubt, *I love you* was a surprising and solid truth.

He laughed, low, touched his forehead to mine. "I love *you*, Sarah."

I wrapped my arms around him.

"God, I missed you so much," he said, hugging me back.

"I missed you too," I whispered, then my lips found his, and we made up a month's worth of kisses in five minutes.

I never wanted it to stop. He was worth it. We were worth it. And whatever courage I had to conjure up to tell Ash, I would do it. I never wanted to lose this feeling again. I pulled away from him.

"I'll tell her tonight. After the dance."

He smiled, gave my hand a squeeze. "We'll tell her."

We walked back into school hand in hand. I knew we'd have to cool it once we hit the cafeteria again, at least for a bit, but I couldn't stop smiling. We turned down the hallway and walked right smack into . . . Ash.

Or more accurately, Ash, Buzz, and Bailey. For a second we were all laughing and *Oops* and *Excuse me* until we recognized one another, and reality set in. Ash's eyes took in our clasped hands. Buzz's eyes widened, and he whispered the word *wow*. Bailey . . . well, I didn't know what was going on with her because her hair covered half her face.

"Hey," I said. My resolve to tell Ash was still there, but the words escaped me. "What are you guys doing here?"

Ash looked between me and Jake. "Looking for Mike."

"Same," I said, my voice high-pitched. "I saw him leave and wanted to make sure everything was okay, and then Jake came out to help me."

"Yes, I did," Jake added.

"And now you're holding hands?" Ash asked. "What the fuck is going on?"

Her f-bomb made me flinch. Jake and I looked at each other.

"Ash," he began.

"I'm not talking to you, I'm talking to Sarah," she said. There was a noise, and we all turned to look.

Mike walked in, the front door clattering behind him. He stopped and took in the scene, his face registering confusion.

"What's up?" he asked, walking over.

Ash resumed glaring at me. "Well?"

I took a breath. "We're together. Me and Jake. Like, *together*, together." Not exactly the eloquent speech I imagined making, but it was the truth. I squeezed his hand.

"Holy shit," Mike said.

"I can see that, Sarah," Ash said. "Did this just happen tonight?"

"Can we talk about this privately?" I pleaded. I didn't feel like divulging the entirety of our relationship in front of everyone.

"Just answer my question."

"We've been together for a bit," I said.

"A bit?" She huffed, shook her head. "So, have you been laughing behind our backs?"

"No, Ash it's not like that," I said.

"Then what's it like? You're at a scholarship dance for Alex, and you honor him by hooking up with his best friend?"

Her voice kept rising.

Mike intervened. "Hey, Ash, calm down."

"Don't tell me what to do, Michael," she said. "Especially the way you've been acting."

"What's that supposed to mean?" he asked.

"Nothing. I don't have time for this," she said, waving her hands in exasperation. "I have to get back for the next set."

"Ash, can we talk after?" I asked.

"Have a nice life," she said, and stormed off.

Bailey caught up to Ash. Buzz and Mike followed.

"That didn't go well," I said.

"She didn't mean that," Jake said, putting his arm around me. I turned into him, burying my face in his sweater. He kissed the top of my head.

"It's gonna be okay," he said.

I wanted desperately to believe him.

# jake

MONDAY WAS JUST ANOTHER DAY. THE SUN ROSE, THE alarm went off, the first floor of my house smelled like coffee and toast. Mom came in from her night shift at the hospital. Dad left to drive Annie to school. I grabbed a granola bar and my backpack and passed Mom, who was already on her second cup of coffee and watching the *Today* show. She called, "Have a good day," to me as I walked out into the cold. I mumbled a goodbye in return, and even though I would never admit it, I liked to hear her telling me to have a good day. It always felt like a verbal good luck charm. At least someone on the planet cared how my day went. I warmed up the car and scrolled through my phone as the windshield defrosted. Yep, just another day in the life of Jake Hobbs.

And yet, it was completely different.

Sarah Walsh loved me.

We were together.

Anything was possible.

We hadn't dealt with the fallout from Saturday, which had been a choice. Even after the dance, Ash didn't want to talk, and Sarah decided to let her be for a while. Maybe not the most mature way to deal with a problem, but after months of ignoring our feelings and being secretive, we just wanted to hang out. We went for a walk, held hands, ended up at her place. I met her mom. We watched some Netflix. Then, later, talked on the phone until we fell asleep on our virtual beach date.

And any time I had the chance to kiss her, I did.

So even though it was Monday and it sucked, we were together. And that's what made it bearable.

Sarah was on her corner when I pulled up. Another change that I could get used to. Daily rides with her. She smiled when she saw me.

"Hey," she said as she got in. She leaned in, and we kissed.

"Anything?" I asked.

She shook her head as I took off for school.

"I texted Ash, told her I wanted to talk. She hasn't replied. I might try to talk to Mike before school starts, see if he knows what's up. Although she didn't seem too happy with him on Saturday either."

"Well, I'm going over to the McKennas' today with Holly. I'll see what I can find out."

"Nervous?"

"A little, but it's something I need to do."

The last time I'd been to the McKennas' was the night Alex died. I'd picked him up on our way to the cliffs. It was one of what had felt like a thousand times, times I took for granted. Why wouldn't I? We had everything ahead of us. And when Holly and I approached the front of the house, I half expected to see Alex open the front door.

My heart raced as we climbed up to the porch. The McKennas were waiting for us, we had to go in, but it took everything in me not to turn and run. We stood in front of the door for a moment before Holly leaned over and rang the bell.

"Jake, breathe," she said.

Mr. McKenna greeted us with a tired smile and took our coats. Mrs. McKenna—Deb, as we always called her—and Ash stood there too. Holly went over and embraced both of them. She was so good at this stuff, saying the right thing, really looking into people's eyes. I knew sometimes it came across as over-the-top, but it was better than just standing there with a blank stare like I was doing. I gave Mr. McKenna a hearty handshake, bantered about the basketball team. Then I moved to Ash.

I wanted to blurt out, *Don't hate me*, and hoped to convey that with a hug, but it was awkward. I went for a hug, she went for a handshake, then we switched. Laughed nervously. She crossed her arms. Then I ended up sort of patting the side of her shoulder.

"Jake," Deb McKenna said, her arms outstretched.

I wasn't prepared for the rush of sadness that came out of nowhere when my eyes met hers. Or maybe it was the tone of her voice. The friendliness, the history behind it. She sounded pleased to see me. I practically folded myself into her as she embraced me, stronger than I anticipated.

"I'm sorry," I whispered into her hair.

"I know, Jake, I know. It's so good to see you."

We stayed like that for a bit, until we both let go. I stepped back.

"I should have stopped by sooner," I said.

"You're here now, c'mon, let's sit. What have you got for us?"

We sat around the dining room table, a plate of cookies and iced tea, as if we were discussing something fun. Once again, Holly took the lead and walked the McKennas through what we'd done for the scholarship fund. What our plans were. How successful the dance was, how brilliant Ashley and Crush had been. Ash smiled at that.

"Jake was the one who suggested the summer clinic for the scholarship funds," she said.

"I think that amount will go a long way there," I said.

"Thank you, both," Mrs. McKenna said. "It's a comfort knowing you wanted to honor Alex this way. He really loved working with his summer kids."

"They loved him too," I said.

Holly reached over and gave my shoulder a squeeze. The weight of the situation clouded the room, made us silent. There was one more thing I had to get off my chest.

"I'm sorry I didn't sign the pledge. I didn't mean to be disrespectful or anything. I was angry at the time, it seemed like such an empty gesture," I said.

Mrs. McKenna spoke. "Jake, we weren't angry at you for not signing it, we were worried that you didn't. It's good to know you're doing okay."

"If I could change even one thing from that night, I would."

Mr. McKenna reached over and covered my hand with his. "Hey, Jake, we know."

"There's a box of basketball sneakers upstairs, probably about ten pairs, some of them hardly worn. I've been wanting to give them to Coach Callard. I'd rather send them somewhere I know they'll be used than drop them off to a thrift store. Do you think you could take them to him?" Mrs. McKenna asked.

"Yeah, sure," I said.

Ash stood up. "I'll get them."

"We better get going," Holly said, standing up. We said our goodbyes and let them know we'd keep them informed about the scholarship. Ash came down the stairs with a large box in her arms. She placed it down on the bottom landing and put on her coat.

"I'll walk them out," she said. We stepped onto the porch.

"I'll meet you at the car, Jake," Holly said. "Nice seeing you, Ash. Take care."

Ash and I looked at each other, she shifted the box toward me. Maybe a little harder than necessary.

"I'm sorry about the other night, the way things happened. Sarah didn't know how to tell you."

Ash sighed. "Well, from the previews, I think I know what the movie is about."

I laughed. I wasn't sure if it was okay, but then Ash laughed too.

"We're together. We've been talking for a while. At first it was about Alex, but then it turned into something more. We weren't laughing behind your back."

Ash held up her hand. "I know that, Jake. I was caught in the moment. I think I just wanted to say something I knew would hurt the both of you. I'm sorry."

"It was a shit way to find out about us, so I'm sorry for that. We should have talked to you before. I know it's hard to separate me from that night at the cliffs, but I wish you would."

"It's getting easier," she said, and smiled.

\* \* \*

As dramatic as it sounded, I felt like I could take flight. I couldn't get to Adele's fast enough. I wanted to tell Sarah how it went. I found a parking spot and hurried along the sidewalk. My phone rang. Mom. I answered it.

"Hey," I said, slowing my pace to catch my breath.

"Jake, where are you?"

"Uh, just left the McKennas'. I was stopping by to see Sarah before heading home. Is everything okay?"

"Yes, everything's fine. Greg called."

"Who?"

She laughed. "Oh, wait, I forgot you call him Dr. Hipster. You missed your appointment today."

I stopped.

"Wow, sorry, Mom. I, um . . . can't believe I forgot."

"I rescheduled for Thursday, why don't you put it in the calendar on your phone?"

"Okay, I'll do that."

"Not too late," she said.

"I know," I said.

I slid my phone in my back pocket and walked into Adele's. Sarah was behind the counter, helping a customer pick out which macaron flavors they wanted. Her hair was up, and she had on her bright pink apron over a plain gray tee, she laughed when she spoke, taking her time with the woman. Marnie tapped her on the shoulder and gestured toward me. Sarah looked over; her eyes lit up when she saw me. I'd never seen someone more beautiful.

*"Starting to feel like a bit of a third wheel here, Hobbs."*

*It's okay, I'm good now, Al. There's got to be something more exciting for you to do in the afterlife than hang out in my head.*

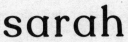

# sarah

ASH FINALLY ANSWERED MY TEXTS ON THURSDAY.

**Come over tonight?**

**K**

I reached the McKennas' at seven. Ash greeted me with a quick hello, and we went up to Alex's room. The room looked similar to when I saw it in December, except the Gatorade bottle and the roll of Mentos were gone. Less lived in, more like Alex was maybe at college for the semester. I liked thinking about him like that, like he was just away somewhere. Ash pulled open a draw full of neatly folded tees and took out a stack.

"Here are the shirts I told you about; you can look through them and see if there's anything you want," she said. "Unless of course, you don't want one now."

"I'd like one, if that's okay," I said.

"I wouldn't have offered if it wasn't okay," she said, handing me the pile. There was an edge to her voice, I thought I was there so we could make up.

I thumbed through the shirts with care, found an old CBGB shirt that Alex used to wear when he came into Adele's. "Can I have this one?"

She nodded.

"Ash, I know I'm not here to talk about T-shirts, I just don't know where to begin," I said.

"How about that was an awful way for me to find out about you and Jake," she said.

"I know, I'm sorry. We were going to tell you that night, after the dance, but then you saw us, and well, here we are."

She took the rest of the shirts from me and put them back into the drawer, then turned around and leaned against the dresser.

"Why couldn't you tell me before then? Especially since it's obvious you've been together for a while."

I sighed. "I thought it would upset you, and my job for the last few months was to make sure you were okay."

"I never asked you to do that," she said.

"I know, but when you said Jake was a reminder of what happened, and you'd just as soon never see him again, I thought it would upset you too much to bring it up," I said.

"Okay, then, tell me, from the beginning—how long has this been going on?" she said.

I told her about Jake coming to see me about the bench in the summer. Then asking me to be a part of the scholarship committee, how we talked on the phone at night. Sometimes even fell asleep on the phone. I left out the virtual beach date. I wanted to keep that for myself. I told her about hooking up with him over winter break.

She sat there, listened. Taking it all in.

"I thought you were different after break," she said.

"Really? How?"

"You were happier than you'd been, but it didn't really add up. You'd broken up with Buzz right before Christmas and, I mean, I know you guys weren't that serious, but it was still a breakup. And then you showed zero interest in Wyatt. I knew there had to be a reason."

I laughed. "I'm sorry, Ash. I should have told you sooner. I wish I could—"

"Don't do that," she said, pointing at me for emphasis. "We can't go back, can we? Or there'd be a lot of stuff we'd change. You can really separate Jake from Alex? From what happened?"

I nodded.

"Well, then I guess maybe I can too."

"How are things with Mike? You didn't seem too happy with him on Saturday."

"We're good. Working through some stuff. He was better about me being in the band but still suspicious about Bran. I was angry that he left like that, but when he explained why—I couldn't really fault him. Bran and I were getting pretty close on Saturday."

"But it was all a part of the act, right?"

She smiled. "Mike told me you said that. Thanks for having my back. I mean, yes, it was part of the act, but some of it—maybe not."

"Wait, what are you telling me?"

"You want to know what the worst thing is?"

"What?"

"Mike was right about Bran."

"Holy shit, shut up," I said.

"Bran's been flirting with me since day one. I loved the attention. At practice I could be this totally different person, separate from everything going on in my life. Separate from my family, from Mike, even you. I got carried away, I guess. I mean standing up there looking into Bran's eyes, singing about love and kissing and believing it wasn't that difficult. I never acted on that feeling or anything, but our mouths were pretty close. I quit Crush after the dance."

"You did?"

"Yep, me and Bailey are going to start up our own band. I wish you played something, maybe we can set you up with a tambourine," she joked.

"Or cowbell," I said, smiling.

"So, I guess we both had some secrets."

"How about we start fresh, right now."

She nodded.

"Maybe one more," she said.

"What?"

"I may have acted upset when you and Alex told me you were dating, but part of me was secretly thrilled that you two were together."

"Wow, really?"

"I know it's crazy, but I thought, what if you were one of those high school couples who stayed together forever. We would really be sisters, then. In each other's lives forever."

"Ash," I said. "We'll still be in each other's lives forever."

"You think?"

"I know."

# opening night

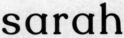

# sarah

"YOU'VE WORKED SO HARD, I KNOW YOU'RE GOING TO be brilliant," Trinity said. "Let's do this!"

The cast and crew stood around the stage; hands clasped. Trinity called this circle time, our moment to get prepped and hyped before the performance. The drama-kid version of a huddle. After a few inspirational words, everyone took their places. Dylan and I had at least ten minutes before we had to be onstage, so I waited in the wings, listened as the audience hushed.

My heart raced. The adrenaline rush of opening night always made me jittery. I tried not to think of my friends and family in the audience. Mom. Aunt Sophie. Marnie. Ash and Mike. Jake. Jake, who would see me kissing Dylan Jacobs for the first time onstage! After months of rehearsal and dreaming of what opening night would be like, it was hard to believe it arrived.

I said a silent prayer of my own and touched the drama mask charm for good luck, then tucked the bracelet back under my sleeve. I took a breath and centered myself. That's when I saw it.

I blinked a few times, hard, just to make sure I wasn't seeing things—stress could make you hallucinate, right?

But it wasn't a hallucination.

It was the Kermit chair.

Against the back wall near a small control panel, visible in the dim running lights.

It was so unexpected that I gasped. Dylan noticed.

"Everything okay?" he whispered. I nodded, moved as silently as possible toward the chair. How could this be real?

And yet, there it was.

I reached out, ran my hand along the arm of the chair, smiled. Cullyn must have found it on a thrifting trip. And the chair found its way back to me.

"Alex," I whispered.

And before my logical mind could explain it away:

I felt Alex.

I mean, not like a ghost, but seeing the chair was like a message.

A personal sign for me.

Everything's going to work out.

I'm okay.

You go do your thing now.

For months, I'd wanted to feel something, see something, have a moment with Alex. I didn't think it was a coincidence that it happened at just the right time.

I went back to Dylan, we watched the show unfold, until it was finally our scene.

The jittery feeling I'd had was replaced by a calm that I hadn't felt before. I knew my character, my lines, and now it was my job to take the audience on that journey too. I wasn't on a stage, I was in a backyard in Maine, holding a paper bag with the pieces of my broken heart. It wasn't Dylan and me kissing, it was East and

Glory, and when Glory saw the northern lights to say goodbye to her husband . . .

Well, maybe that was me, thinking of Alex.

Saying a private goodbye.

And for the first time, I knew he heard me.

# a random
# tuesday in june

# sarah

THERE WASN'T A CLOUD IN THE SKY, AND THE MID-morning sun was relentless. My back felt like it was beginning to burn through the thin bathing suit cover-up. A breeze came off the ocean. I closed my eyes for a second and let my senses take over.

The sound of gulls. Pounding waves. Salty air.

A perfect beach day.

Jake was busy at the beach-tag booth, getting our wristbands. I had the day off from Adele's, and Jake didn't start at the basketball clinic until the following week, so we decided to steal away and turn our virtual beach date into a real one.

"Hold out your wrist, Walsh."

I opened my eyes to Jake peering down at me over his aviator shades. He still called me Walsh at playful moments. I loved it. I held out my wrist, and he snapped the bright green band on.

"Let's do this," I said.

We showed our bands to the attendant, kicked off our shoes, and walked onto the sand. After about five minutes, we found a great spot midway between the ocean and the boardwalk. It was still early in the summer, and the beach wasn't that crowded yet. There were families and groups of kids our age. Farther down, some people had gathered to play volleyball. I took the blanket out of my beach tote, and Jake helped me lay it down on the sand. We put our shoes on opposite corners to weigh it down, then stood there, maybe not sure what to do next.

I'd never been to the beach on a date. Not in reality anyway. I'd been with my mom, and on camp trips, and with Ash and her parents. Never alone, with a boy, and suddenly I was self-conscious about taking off my cover-up. Maybe Jake was feeling it too, because he laughed before finally taking off his tee. I shimmied out of my cutoffs and let my cover-up slide off my shoulders. I made a fuss of folding it up and stuffing it into my bag. I grabbed my sunscreen.

"Help me?" I asked, handing him the bottle.

He grinned. "Of course."

He sprayed on the sunscreen, and I let out a yelp. The blast was freezing, I clamped my hand over my mouth.

"It can't be that bad," he joked, taking a moment to rub it into my skin. The momentary discomfort was worth having his hands on me. When the tables were turned, and I applied it to his back, he let out the same yelp.

"HolyshitIthoughtyouwerekidding," he said, recoiling.

I laughed.

Slick with sunscreen we sat down on the blanket. He leaned back on his elbows. I sat up, my arms behind me, hands supporting my weight. We were silent, taking in the scene.

"You want a smoothie bowl?" he asked.

"Nah, how about pizza?" I asked.

"Too early. Maybe later," he said. "Hey, come down here."

I laughed, turned on my side to face him. My reflection visible in his sunglasses. I reached over and slid them off.

"That's better," I said, handing them to him.

He leaned over and tucked them beside his shoe.

"Hi," he said, when he turned back to face me.

"So, this is where we usually fall asleep," I joked.

"Maybe you fell asleep. I imagined us doing all sorts of things," he said suggestively.

"Jake!" I covered my eyes.

"I'm talking about looking up at the stars, Sar, I don't want to know what dirty thoughts you're having," he said, taking my hand and smiling. "Or maybe I do."

"Did you hear any more about your orientation?" I asked. Jake was going to Rutgers in the fall. He would be away, but at least not that far.

"Way to kill the mood," he scoffed. "We made a pact, remember? Live in the moment this summer."

"Fine, then," I said, standing. "Get up."

He groaned a little but acquiesced. We walked hand in hand, toward the water.

"You know, I really don't like the ocean," he said.

"Are you serious?"

He nodded. "I mean I like it in theory, like the sound of it, like looking at it. But the whole sharp shells, seaweed, oh, and sharks—sort of kills it for me."

"We can just walk along the shoreline, then," I said, a little surprised, but that's what it was like getting to know someone, wasn't it? New things every moment.

We walked parallel to the surf. Every so often a wave lapping across our feet. Maybe it was better that Jake didn't like the ocean. The water was freezing. A large wave crashed, and the surf came rushing up. We were knee-deep. I sucked in a breath at the cold. I looked at Jake, he grinned.

"Guess what?" he asked.

"What?"

"I'm just messing with you," he said, taking both hands and pulling me toward the water.

"Jake."

"I love the ocean, c'mon."

"It's freezing!"

"Look at all the little kids here, it's not bothering them. You'll get used to it."

My feet sunk in the sand as I momentarily stood my ground.

"What about the shells, the seaweed, the sharks?" I joked.

"Live in the moment, Walsh."

I fell a little bit deeper in love with him. This fun, lighthearted side that came out more and more. His laugh. His smile. It was a bit of a miracle getting to know someone, for a stranger to become a friend, and then more. The reality of being at the beach with Jake was so much better than any fantasy.

He pulled me in closer for a quick kiss, and when the next wave rose, we dove right in.

# ACKNOWLEDGMENTS

My first drafts are usually uneven and angry, with my characters treating each other carelessly and doing horrible things. This story was no exception. It was quite the journey to shape so much unwieldiness into the novel you have in your hands. I don't like picking favorites, but having this story to turn to during an incredibly tumultuous time was life-affirming. I hope you find as much joy in Sarah and Jake's story as I have.

Much gratitude to Tamar Rydzinski and the team at Context Lit. Thank you for being my champion, especially during the times I wasn't sure I still needed one. Your guidance and support over the years have kept me afloat.

Donna Bray, thank you for seeing what this novel could become and for challenging me to take it there. Your patience, humor, and intelligence make you such a dream to work with.

A million thanks to Tiara Kitrell: your ability to pinpoint what was needed to make a scene pop, or a paragraph smoother, or a kiss more swoon-worthy, was invaluable.

Humble thanks to everyone at Balzer + Bray/HarperCollins who worked behind the scenes on my behalf, especially Dominic Bugatto for the beautiful cover art; Catherine Lee, Sarah Kaufman, and Alison Donalty for the cover design; production editor Erin DeSalvatore; copyeditor Erica Ferguson; publicist Katie Boni; and marketing director Audrey Diestelkamp.

Thank you to Yael Gold, PhD, and Jennifer Upchurch, LCSW, for your expertise and sage advice while I was writing and revising Jake's therapy scenes.

To my Nebo & Folly fam: Jaye Robin Brown, Rebecca Petruck, Amber Gellar-Smith, Amy Reed, Joy Neaves, Frankie Bolt, Jocelyn Rish, and Samantha Gellar-Smith. Thank you for listening, reading, keeping the coffeepot full, chatting endlessly about the creative process, and for simply being your amazing selves.

Big love for my mom, thank you for always asking, "How's the book going?" and meaning it.

Thank you to my family, the one I was born with and the one I've found along the way. Your support means everything to me.

And finally, to my core four, thank you for reminding me when I need a break.

Love you, always.